THE
GOLDEN
SPOON

THE
GOLDEN
SPOON

– A Novel –

JESSA MAXWELL

ATRIA BOOKS

New York London Toronto Sydney New Delhi

ATRIA
BOOKS

An Imprint of Simon & Schuster, Inc.
1230 Avenue of the Americas
New York, NY 10020

First Atria Books hardcover edition March 2023

ATRIA BOOKS and colophon are trademarks of Simon & Schuster, Inc.

For information about special discounts for bulk purchases, please contact Simon & Schuster Special Sales at 1-866-506-1949 or business@simonandschuster.com.

The Simon & Schuster Speakers Bureau can bring authors to your live event. For more information or to book an event, contact the Simon & Schuster Speakers Bureau at 1-866-248-3049 or visit our website at www.simonspeakers.com.

Interior design by Jill Putorti

Manufactured in the United States of America

1 3 5 7 9 10 8 6 4 2

Library of Congress Cataloging-in-Publication Data
Names: Maxwell, Jessa, author.
Title: The golden spoon / by Jessa Maxwell.
Description: New York : Atria Books, 2023.
Identifiers: LCCN 2022026279 | ISBN 9781668008003 (hardcover) | ISBN 9781668008010 (paperback) | ISBN 9781668008027 (ebook)
Subjects: LCGFT: Detective and mystery fiction. | Novels.
Classification: LCC PS3613.A8997 G65 2023 | DDC 813/.6—dc23/eng/20220629
LC record available at https://lccn.loc.gov/2022026279

ISBN 978-1-6680-0800-3
ISBN 978-1-6680-0802-7 (ebook)

To Tim, the icing and the cake

THE
GOLDEN
SPOON

Prologue

BETSY

Betsy presses her cell phone to her ear, trying to hear. The wind and rain howl at the windows, rattling the glass. "We're stuck out here. We won't be able to come back for a while," Melanie's voice crackles with static. "This weather has taken down a bunch of trees. We're waiting for emergency services to get them out of the road, but there's no sign of them yet. We won't be—"

"You're cut off from Grafton?" Betsy can feel the panic rising in her chest. The whole crew has already left for the day, packing up quickly and going into town to avoid driving in the storm, and now it's just her and Archie and the contestants alone in the manor. The thought fills her with dread. She shudders and pulls her thin cashmere sweater closer around her.

"What? The line keeps cutting out. Someone is going to have to go check on the tent. There's a ton of camera equipment out there. I know the tech stuff isn't your domain, but could you just go outside and make sure the flaps are sealed? I am just praying that tent is sturdy enough to make it through the storm. They're saying it's going to get worse tonight before it gets better. I'm sorry to ask you but there's no one else. I tried calling Archie, but he didn't pick up. Maybe you could—"

"I'll do it," Betsy snaps. There is no way she is going to ask anything of that man after what he's done. "But this is really . . . unacceptable." She feels a surge of anger as she hangs up. In the ten years she has been the host of *Bake Week*, she has never had to do any of the grunt work. Checking on the tent in the dark in the middle of a torrential downpour is not in her job description. She takes a deep breath. It was partly her fault, she realizes, for making the crew stay in town. She could never bear the thought of them traipsing through Grafton Manor with all their equipment and dirty shoes.

There's a flash of lightning at the window followed by a violent bang of thunder. Betsy goes into her walk-in closet and reaches for her father's heavy yellow rain jacket. As she slides her arms into it, she is disappointed to find it no longer smells of his cigars, only of the slightly mildewy musk that comes with neglect. It's a smell and a state she is constantly battling at Grafton Manor. She feels a pang of guilt. Richard Grafton would be devastated to see this place so down at the heels. He was always devoted to the manor. He'd have found a way to keep it going, no matter the cost. She sighs, stretching to get an old metal flashlight off the shelf.

Betsy makes her way through the corridor and out into the main stairwell. Rain taps frantically on the two floor to ceiling windows in the foyer. She hurries down the steps to the front door, already feeling vulnerable. She pulls her hood up and forces the heavy wood door open, struggling against the wind. The tent is only ten feet away at most, but the rain is so heavy it appears as a white blur. She steels herself and steps outside. The wind drives the rain sideways, nearly blinding her as she descends the front steps, flanked by two stone lions. Their heads rest wearily in their crossed paws, as if they've given in to the storm. She crosses the short patch of gravel drive to the lawn, the rain pelting her in sheets. As soon as her feet hit the lawn, the heel of her right shoe descends into the fresh sod. It sticks there, making her nearly lose her balance. She hops on one foot, pulling the shoe up from the mud with a sucking sound and shoving her wet foot back inside. She is already drenched. She angrily anticipates the cleanup they'll have to do before filming resumes. It will delay everything. It will cost money, lots of it. This season is turning into a horrible mess.

"Their chemistry is lacking," that's what *The Post* wrote recently after the footage from the first day was leaked. It was under the headline "What Will Happen to *Bake Week*?" As if somehow the press believes that the problem is both of them. No one ever complained about her chemistry before *he* got here. There was no problem with *anything* until he got here.

Angrily, she pulls open the flap at the back of the tent, switching on her flashlight. The rain hits the tent in noisy bursts drumming at the peaked canvas ceiling. She sweeps the flashlight around the open space. Each table is immaculately arranged, as is usual after the crew cleans them at the end of the day, before the bakers will return in the early morning to dirty every surface imaginable with dustings of flour and gobs of dough. Now every stand mixer is perfectly aligned with the next, each carefully arranged colander of baking utensils on display. It's an optimistic scene of pastel colors and light woods. One that lends itself well to the show's folksy niceness. And generally it's true that the bakers, chosen and vetted to within an inch of their lives, are also nice. Betsy makes sure of it. Some of them can be a bit curmudgeonly. But they try so hard, they want so desperately to be perfect, to win, so you have to give them that. Betsy knows she hasn't ever had to work so hard as some of them. This group is no different. Sure, there have been . . . challenges. It certainly hasn't been easy this time around.

There's another crack of lightning, a violent bang as it connects to something nearby. Betsy shudders and makes her way up to the bank of cameras on the right. They look secure enough. The ground around them is dry.

She swings the flashlight around the tent one last time, ready to go back inside and warm herself up with a glass of port. To try to forget today ever happened. But then she notices something at the front of the tent. There is on object sitting on the judging table. She trains the flashlight on it, approaching slowly. It looks like a cake. Someone must have left it there from today's baking challenge, which is odd. Usually everything is cleaned up after filming. As she moves forward, she can see that it's already baked, a slice cleaved neatly from it. Cherry red liquid dribbles from the stand, down the back of the table where it mingles with a deep puddle of water. The rain has found its way inside. She steps closer, her heart sinking. A mess this big will cause a delay in filming. It will be expensive and taxing.

A drop of water lands on her face and she jumps. She reaches her hand up to wipe it away. The liquid feels smooth and slippery. Reaching her fingers in the beam of the flashlight, she is shocked to find they are streaked with bright red. It feels like—

She turns her flashlight up. Its spotlight trails into the peaked roof of the tent until it stops on something. Before her eyes even make sense of the horror above her, she starts to scream.

TWO WEEKS AGO

For immediate release:

Grafton, Vermont [May 23, 2023]—Flixer streaming service announces they are beginning to film season ten of the hit show *Bake Week*. The beloved baking show, which captured the world's hearts a decade ago, has upped the ante this season for its tenth anniversary with a new cohost at the front of the tent. Veteran judge and show creator Betsy Martin is slated to return but this year she'll be joined by award-winning baker and *Cutting Board* host Archie Morris. This is the first time in the show's history that Betsy has shared the tent with another host. Filming will once again take place on the grounds of Betsy Martin's family estate in the mountains of northern Vermont.

Six home bakers will descend on Grafton Manor on June 5 to compete for the title of America's best baker. They will compete from Monday to Friday in a series of five intensive, daylong competitions, leading to a showdown between the final two bakers on Friday. The winner of *Bake Week* will receive a contract for their own baking-focused cookbook, published with Flying Fork Press, a division of Magnus

Books, the preeminent cookbook publisher in America. Most importantly, the winner will take home the coveted Golden Spoon trophy and the title of America's Best Home Baker.

We are ready to announce the identities of the six bakers who have been hand-selected from among over ten thousand eager applicants. They are all excellent bakers at home, but we are eager to see how they do in the tent.

STELLA VELASQUEZ

A former journalist for *The Republic*, Stella lives in Brooklyn, New York. After challenging herself to master the art of baking in just under a year, Stella is the competition's most inexperienced contestant, though her skill level is that of a much more seasoned baker. She prefers cakes above all other bakes and adores making and decorating them for friends in New York. Stella loves all things *Bake Week* and credits the show and Betsy Martin with helping her through many hard times in her life. "It's an honor of a lifetime to compete in *Bake Week* in spite of being such a newbie, but meeting my hero Betsy Martin will be an accomplishment all on its own."

HANNAH SEVERSON

Hannah hails from Eden Lake, Minnesota. She is the pride and joy of the local diner, Polly's, where she has worked as a baker and server since she was fifteen years old. Her innovative pie recipes have made her into a local legend. A bit of a prodigy at twenty-one, Hannah is the second-youngest contestant in the history of *Bake Week*, a testament to her dedication to baking. When she is not causing a stir with her pies at Polly's Diner, she likes to test out her recipes for breads and desserts on her family and neighbors, especially her boyfriend, Ben. "Baking is everything to me, I can't wait to show the world what I'm made of."

GERALD BAPTISTE

Gerald is a Bronx, New York, native whose day job is as a math teacher for advanced high school students. He spends his spare time sourcing new ingredients for his highly scientific bakes. As a result, Gerald has formed close ties with local grain farmers, whom he often visits upstate. When he can he likes to hand-grind his own flours as well as make his own essences and extracts from scratch. "Baking, very much like life, is about formulating the best possible outcome with the variables you are given."

PRADYUMNA DAS

Entrepreneur Pradyumna is the creator and former CEO of the company Spacer, an app that identifies free parking spaces across urban areas. After selling his company, Pradyumna took to the more relaxing pastime of baking, which he does for friends, often entertaining at his Boston penthouse. His approach to baking is laid-back, and he often improvises ingredients and techniques when whipping up his unique creations. "This competition isn't about winning for me, it's about experiencing something new and pushing my boundaries to see what kind of baker and person I can become."

LOTTIE BYRNE

Lottie is a retired registered nurse from Kingston, Rhode Island. In her spare time, Lottie loves to bake treats for her daughter, Molly. She has an impressive collection of mixing bowls decorating her cottage. Lottie was taught to bake by her mother, and she has been working on her recipes from a very young age. Her specialty is adapting traditional bakes with a contemporary edge. "It has been my life's mission to compete on *Bake Week*. I cannot wait to show Betsy Martin what kind of baker I am."

PETER GELLAR

Peter lives with his family in Woodsville, New Hampshire. He works in construction and specializes in the restoration of old buildings. When Peter isn't traveling the East Coast repairing molding and inlaid floors, he can be found in his favorite place—his family kitchen—baking delicious treats for his husband, Frederick, and their three-year-old daughter, Lulu. "Recipes are like architecture; a combination of tested methods with personal elements is what makes a bake memorable."

FOUR DAYS EARLIER

GERALD

I wasn't surprised when I got the call, though my heart rate did accelerate rapidly. I know this because my watch lit up and gave me one reward point for exercising. And I wasn't surprised at all when they told me I'd been accepted as a contestant on *Bake Week* because I am an excellent baker. Anyone can be an excellent baker if they're disciplined enough. It's just chemistry. To make a perfect cake, all you need are the right equations. Measurements must be precise to yield a crispy mille-feuille, a lacy Florentine, a perfectly chewy pie crust. Temperatures must be controlled and deliberate, if you want to make a soufflé rise or chocolate glaze shine like glass. You can find equations everywhere in life, if you look in the right places.

Say you want to take public transportation all the way from your apartment in the Bronx to a country estate in Vermont for a televised cooking show, as I am doing now. You just need to be fully acquainted with the timetables. You'll take the D subway line to 34th Street, exiting out of the northwest entrance and coming out onto 34th Street. Then you'll walk two avenues west to the northeast entrance of the Moynihan Train Hall, leaving you exactly eleven minutes to wait for the Vermonter train, which departs at 8:15. That will get you into Brattleboro at exactly 3:45. There, you'll have time for a coffee at a café across from the station before you hop on the shuttle you've scheduled to drive you out to the entrance of Grafton Manor.

I've mapped Grafton Manor out using blueprints I downloaded from the Vermont Historical Society's online database. It's an enormous house, but I feel like I know the place now, which brings me some comfort as I do not generally enjoy being in new places, particularly not with strangers and for an entire week. I've memorized routes from the guest rooms to the dining room, the dining room to the tent, and calculated the length of time it will take me to get to each.

I've gone over the variables of my journey so many times that I barely need to look at the schedule I've made up for myself as I get off the subway car with my bags and walk briskly down the platform. A man is playing the violin on the platform, Bach. I recognize it immediately as Violin Sonata No. 1 in G minor. As I was able to get an express train, I allow myself two minutes to listen. I close my eyes. The music carries me away from the filthy station back to my childhood kitchen table. I remember every detail, every nick in the wood, every tear in the vinyl-backed chairs my mother would make me sit at until I finished my homework. She would switch on the radio, filling the tiny kitchen with grand symphonies. Classical music was good for studying, she said. While I solved mathematical equations, she would bake, the air becoming thick with the fragrance of cakes in the oven, melted chocolate, sugary fruit reducing on the tiny stovetop.

My mother was an immigrant from Grenada. She'd been trained as a chemist, but when she came to the United States she was unable to use her degree, so she took a job cleaning for a rich family in Manhattan. When the wife got wind of her cooking ability, she was tasked with providing meals for them as well. It was her cakes that garnered her the most attention. Soon all the families in Tribeca were asking for my mother to make treats for their children's school birthdays or their evening cocktail parties. My mother took baking very seriously and practiced at home, and often in the middle of the night I would wander out and she'd give me a glass of warm milk and a taste of whatever she was cooking. Finally, the year I turned fifteen, after nearly two decades of patiently practicing and saving, she opened her own bakery. I begged to work there instead of going to school, but she never relented. My baking education was to be done after schoolwork if time allowed. I explained all this in the application video, plus my expertise in hand-ground flours.

Filming falls during my school's summer break, so I am not bound to my teaching job right now. Of course, I still have a routine I adhere to when school is not in session. I've broken down the benefit-to-detriment ratios, though, and the numbers always come out in favor of going. If I win, which I have at least a one in six if not higher chance given my expertise, I will have proven to myself that I am what I think I am, that my calculations are correct. If I lose, I will return to my normal schedule in just a week's time.

I give the violinist ten dollars and carry on to the exit, emerging into the bright New York morning. I make my way down 34th Street, jostling with tourists and pedestrians, dodging men on the sidewalk selling knockoff sunglasses and flavored ices. I've allotted time for them in my schedule. Finally, I arrive at the northeast entrance to the train station. I check my watch: 8:04.

I feel the warm assurance of being on time, of having gotten it right. I carry my bags into the central hall, scanning the timetable to be sure, though I know it by heart.

I look for the Vermonter, but it is not listed where it should be, right between the Northeast Regional and the Acela service to Washington. I instantly scan and find it farther down the list flashing in red: *Delayed, stand by for more info.*

A cold dread descends on me. Things never go well when they don't go according to plan.

HANNAH

Other than the wave of blue mountains in the distance, I'm disheartened to see that Vermont isn't much different from where I live in Eden Lake, Minnesota. The same small towns cling to the sides of the same state highways with the same abandoned gas stations and part-empty strip malls. The same lonely white churches sit in the same overgrown parking lots, their peeling paint visible from the road as I speed past in the back of a black SUV. The driver had been there to meet me at the airport in Burlington just like the *Bake Week* coordinators had said he would, holding a printed placard with my name, Hannah Severson. I had expected a bit more fanfare, to be honest, not that I'd thought that Betsy Martin would come fetch me herself, but maybe there'd be someone else there with the driver, a producer or an assistant, someone to welcome me and talk to me on the journey. The driver silently huffed my bags onto a trolly and walked out to the parking lot. I could only assume I was to follow him.

"Ride's just over two hours," he'd said, opening the back door and handing me a small bottle of water.

The soft hum of the air conditioner is the only sound as we drive through the rural landscape, each town we pass smaller and emptier than the last. I try to shake off this initial disappointment. *Bake Week* is merely a stepping-stone to my future, not the entire thing, I try to remind myself. I have far more glamour in store for me. After all, I'm only twenty-one. That's still very young. Only the second-youngest contestant ever to compete on *Bake Week*. And besides, there's nothing like Grafton Manor in Eden Lake. It will all be in my grasp in less than two hours.

"Just have fun," Ben had told me this morning when he dropped me off at the airport. As I'd leaned over to kiss him goodbye, his hound Frank poked his head in between our seats and licked my chin. I'd petted him and laughed, mentally reminding myself to touch up my makeup later.

"I promise," I'd said and put on my most cheerful face, the one I knows Ben likes—the one everybody likes. But secretly I'd thought, *You don't understand what this means to me.* Fun is just fleeting, a momentary pleasure. It comes in on a cloud and evaporates before you can even recognize it for what it is. Success is different. It is something you can hold on to, something you can count and that goes with you everywhere like a designer handbag. Being on *Bake Week* is everything to me. It is my chance—maybe my only chance—to do something important with my life. Something better and bigger than just working at Polly's Diner.

My coworkers threw a party before I left. Brian, Lucille, and Sarah organized it. They'd put up crepe paper streamers and pushed all the tables to one side for dancing and invited everyone I knew from town. Polly even closed the whole restaurant early and everyone came out to drink boxed wine and eat slices of pie from the refrigerated lazy Susan. "I just knew Hannah's pies were something special, didn't I?" Polly said that night to anyone who would listen, trying to steal some credit. From the moment I got the call I was accepted, everything changed. They all wanted to be around me now that they knew I was going to be on *Bake Week*. I feel guilty knowing that, if I do everything just right, I will never serve a slice of pie to anyone at the diner ever again.

It's not that I hate working at Polly's, but I mean who wouldn't want *Bake Week* to help make them a career? I've seen the massive

Instagram following the past winners have, the successful YouTube channels, the cookbook and the endorsement deals they've scored. One winner even has her own line of cookware—pots and pans with her name embossed in gold cursive along the handle—sold in stores all around the country and on QVC. *Bake Week* changed their lives. It's not wrong that I want it to change mine too.

The SUV finally pulls off the main highway and onto a narrow road flanked by a dark pine forest. I try to calm my nerves. I take a deep breath, telling myself to get a grip. I would hate to show up looking frazzled, but I'm so excited I can hardly handle it. More excited than when I graduated from high school—the first one in my family to walk that stage in June and not later with a GED—and more excited than I was before my first date with Ben. *Bake Week* can take me farther in life than school or Ben ever could. As long as I don't mess it up. I can't bear to think of myself as one of those contestants who leave in the first couple days, only to be forgotten quickly, their fame snuffed out before their social media accounts even have the time to be verified.

I look down at my hands. I've tried so hard not to, with the filming coming up and all, but on the ride from the airport I've ripped my cuticles to shreds with my teeth. I hope I remembered to pack a nail file in my bag. I take a small compact out of my purse and look myself over in the mirror, checking that my bangs are hanging just right. The makeup I'd put on during the flight over hasn't budged, but I top up my lipstick with a fresh coat of gloss anyway.

The SUV comes around a bend and out of the woods. As we pass through a tall stone gate Grafton Manor comes into view. I look up at it through the car window, my jaw hanging open. Even though I've seen it on TV a million times, I feel my chest seize up. It is even more impressive in person, the pale gray stone with all those giant windows and chimneys. It looks like something out of Harry Potter.

We come to a stop in front of the main entrance. It's the staircase with the two lions, the one they always show Betsy next to in the beginning scenes of *Bake Week*. Now a slim brunette woman stands on the top step holding a clipboard. It's hard to believe I'm actually here at Grafton Manor and not hallucinating. After all that practicing, so many years of my life devoted to cakes and pies and tarts. So much time spent on fondants and days upon days of piping icing onto sheets of torn cardboard, until every line, every green frosted petal and sugary pink rosebud is just perfect. It's all actually paid off. Hannah Severson of Eden Lake, Minnesota, is a contestant on *Bake Week*.

I get out of the SUV and have to crane my neck all the way back to see where the roof meets the sky. The driver pulls my suitcases from the trunk. I've never seen such a big place. It reminds me of my high school French class when I learned about Versailles. I have the impulse to twirl around on the front drive and do cartwheels, but I remind myself to stay calm. I don't want to look like a child. Little kids don't win *Bake Week*, and winning is what I am here to do.

I wince as the driver drops one of my bags onto the gravel drive. All my makeup is in there. I can't have it shattering. There are no Sephoras around here, and I need everything to be perfect. *I* need to be perfect. I gather my belongings and try to stand up extra straight. I walk as confidently as I can toward the woman on the stairs, fighting back the feeling that I don't deserve any of this. There is no room for dumb errors now. Mom always says there's only one chance to make a first impression, and I am not going to mess mine up.

PETER

Grafton Manor's arched windows stare blankly down at me as I arrive in my pickup truck. I take in the elaborate stonework on the façade. I love this kind of architecture. It's Victorian but nods to the Jacobethan style the English were so fond of in the mid-1800s. This is an incredible specimen. Of course, I've seen it on TV a thousand times—I've watched every episode of *Bake Week* at least twice—but then it was just a backdrop. In person you get a totally different sense of the place. For one, it is in the middle of nowhere. There is a tiny village—really just a gas station and a diner along the road—about a mile away but the closest real town is at least forty-five miles through the woods. You really feel how disconnected it is driving up here. Literally. On the way in, my service kept cutting out and I doubt there's a good connection anywhere close by.

As if to illustrate my point, a man is standing at the front of the house talking on his cell phone, leaning against one of the marble lions on the staircase. "Do you know where I should park?" I call out to him. He points to where the drive curves around the side of the building.

I follow the road around to a small strip of spaces and park next to a flashy white BMW. Most of the rest of the lot has been taken over by a large trailer. Camera equipment, I realize, as I grab my duffel bag from the bed of my truck and amble around the corner back toward the main entrance. Ivy grows up the outer wall on this side of the building, winding its way up the brick around the windows all the way to the slate roof. It flutters in the breeze, making the whole side of the building look ephemeral, alive.

I nod to the man, still talking on his phone, and pass between the lions, pushing open an iron-studded door. I blink as my eyes adjust to the dim light inside. I'm standing in a large open entryway. In front of me a grand staircase rises like a mahogany waterfall, curving elegantly up in either direction at the landing.

A woman hovers near a suit of armor guarding the foyer. She wears a formfitting skirt, her shiny brown hair twisted into a thick knot at her neck, the kind of put together you don't see much where I live. She is staring down at a clipboard, a pencil bobbing between two fingers. Her face twitches nervously when she finally sees me. "Sound guys use the back entrance," she barks.

"I'm here to bake," I reply, "if that's okay."

She frowns and looks at her papers, flipping through a few pages. I see each of them has a headshot on it. She lands finally on a giant photo of my face, embarrassment filling hers as she registers the match.

"So sorry about that . . . Peter! Welcome!"

"It's all right, I'm used to it," I say. It's true, kind of, except in the work I do I normally *am* the guy who is supposed to use the side door. I know that I'm not going to win any awards for best dressed or anything, but I am wearing my newest flannel and I did get a haircut before I left. Not that it's easy to tame my curls. My hair has its own ecosystem, Frederick likes to tease.

The woman is effusive now, trying to make up for not recognizing me. She smiles, but her face looks almost pained, as though it's a look she isn't particularly practiced at. "I'm Melanie, *Bake Week*'s lead coordinator. I keep things running on time, and it's my job to make sure everyone is where they need to be at exactly the right moment. You'll be seeing a lot of me this week. As per *Bake Week* rules, I'll need you

to hand me your cell phone. And then I can take you to your room so
you can relax before dinner."

I hand over my dinged-up phone somewhat reluctantly and watch
her put it into a box, placing it on top of another phone with a glittery
pink case.

"Shall we?" She smiles again, the muscles in her neck straining as
she gestures toward the staircase. "Leave your bags. Someone will take
them up later."

"It's okay. I've got it," I say, patting the side of the duffel, still dangling from my shoulder. Her lips tighten, but she nods in surrender. I
follow her up the massive central staircase, admiring the smoothness
of the wooden banisters, the detail in the carvings on their spokes.
There are many Victorian houses in Vermont, but the size and quality
of the craftmanship at Grafton are unlike anything I've seen. We come
to a large landing where the staircase splits off into two smaller sets
of steps, which wind elegantly up in opposite directions to different
wings of the house.

"You'll be staying in the West Wing," Melanie says, leading me up
the staircase to the right. She pauses, gesturing back across the landing
at an identical set of stairs and doors. "The East Wing is Betsy Martin's private quarters, and it is completely off-limits to guests. If you
need anything, be sure to contact one of the staff from the telephone
in your room. There is a list of our names in the dossier."

Ah yes, the dossier. It came in the mail, in an overnight package I
had to sign for, practically in blood. This was of course *after* I signed
the stack of nondisclosure forms, promising not to spill any of *Bake
Week*'s secrets before it airs. The show is extremely protective of itself,
which makes sense. For just over a month of each year, it is the most
popular program on television, inspiring fanatics and copycats. People
have even been known to peek through Grafton's gates to try to catch
a glimpse of the action. The rules are there to protect the integrity of
the show, and I'll respect them. If I can remember them all, that is.
The official *Bake Week* dossier is a behemoth spiralbound packet cov-

ering the rules and offering helpful "suggestions" for how to look and act on camera. I've done my best to soak it all in, but maybe I should read it over one more time tonight just to be sure. I'm feeling anxious, like I might forget something. I would be so embarrassed if I put the show in jeopardy.

We continue down a long dim hallway until Melanie stops abruptly at a doorway on our right. She double-checks her clipboard and swings open the door, letting the glow of afternoon light into the hall.

"Here you are, hope you're comfortable."

I blink as I step past her. My room makes up for its modest size with an impossibly tall ceiling that arcs upward from the corners and a window that stretches up from near the floor, coming to a point at the top like something you'd find in a church. There's a dressing table and tall chest of drawers along one wall. Most of the room is taken up by a large bed with carved wood posters spiraling up to the ceiling. Above the head, a painting of the manor in its younger days hangs on wire from the crown molding.

I love these Victorian houses—with all their quirks they feel almost human to me, like they could be old friends. More than anything I relish learning all their stories, uncovering their pasts. I've never had the patience for academia, or I'm sure I'd have become a historian. It's probably why I went into restoration work. I notice a crack in the molding that follows the corner of the wall. It's a thin crack, not structural or anything. Nothing I couldn't fix if given the chance. Seeing flaws in buildings is a force of habit, like how a dentist must notice the imperfections in everyone's teeth when they smile. I have to remind myself that I'm not here to work, I'm here to bake. Still, I'd jump at the chance to help restore some of Grafton Manor—the scuffs in the hardwood and cracks in the parapet where I noticed it crumbling.

"I'll be great." I smile, putting down my duffel on the floral duvet.

After she leaves I sit on the bed for a moment taking it all in. Then I open my suitcase and transfer some of my shirts to hangers in the wardrobe. Don't want them to get too wrinkled before tomorrow. Our first day of competition already. I feel around into the bottom of my duffel for the picture, my hand wrapping around the frame. It's my favorite photo of Frederick and our daughter, Lulu, at the park. I'd tied a T-shirt around it to protect it and I unwind it now gingerly, using the shirt to polish the glass before placing it on the bedside table.

I go to the window and look out, resting my forehead on the cool leaded glass. The tent is almost directly below me, the manor casting a bluish shadow over its white peaked top. It's incredible to me that they film *Bake Week* in Betsy Martin's actual home. What other TV personality would ever allow that? I suppose it helps make the show that much more intimate. *Bake Week* is a special kind of entertainment. It's not just a show for bakers, though obviously that is the main activity. It is something else too, an escape of sorts, a glimpse into a simpler way of being where people are kind to one another and sugar isn't thought of as junk food, but as something special to be shared and cherished. Where you can say "I love you" with a slice of cake.

The thrill of it all creeps up my chest. I've really made it. Who'd have ever thought a hobby as silly as baking could bring me to something like this? Frederick did. He has always believed in my baking, to the point where I've sometimes wondered if it was not so much my incredible baking skills so much as he is just blinded by his affection for me. He was there cheering me on for my first rather pitiful attempts at layer cakes. I was alone in the house the day I got the call from the adoption agency. There was a baby girl waiting for us to take her home. I remember looking at the clock, and it was only 11:30. Frederick is an optometrist who would be with his patients, unreachable for the remainder of the day. Unsure what to do with all my pent-up excitement, I baked a confetti sponge cake and topped it with a whipped buttercream. All the while trying to picture her. Our little Lulu. It's hard to believe there was ever a time I didn't know every bit of her. Every lopsided smile and petulant scowl, every pale half-moon on her fingernails. When Frederick came home that evening, he saw my cake sitting slightly lopsided on the kitchen counter. He looked from me to the cake, and all I had to do was give a small nod for his eyes to well up. We were going to be parents. Of course, now I make treats for the three of us all the time. Baking is among my favorite ways to care for my little family. I feel my chest tighten with a surge of gratitude for Frederick and look for my phone to text him, until I realize that I no longer have it. The idea of being unreachable, of not being able to text to see how Lulu is doing, even though the producers assured me I would be contacted if there were any real emergency, fills me with a strange feeling, like I am very far away from everyone.

I guess that is kind of the point, though, to keep us focused on *Bake Week*. I take a quick shower and change into a different plaid button-up shirt for dinner, one of the ones I've bought specially for the occasion. I catch a glimpse of myself in the beveled mirror hanging above the dressing table. My hair's a mess, but that's not unusual. Otherwise, not so bad for forty-two. I try to let myself give in to the experience of just being here. What is baking, I remind myself, other than a way to show others you care about them. I focus on how Frederick and Lulu will be able to watch when the show airs. Even if I manage to stick around all week, I know this experience will be fleeting. I need to just embrace it. Besides, I feel lighter and happier than I have in a long time. It's time to go downstairs and meet the competition.

STELLA

I look at myself in the ornate mirror in the door of my wardrobe. I've put on a silky slip-style skirt and a stylishly baggy sweater, both in shades of blush. I clip in some hoop earrings. Behind me, my room at Grafton is a gorgeous garden paradise in hues of green. The wallpaper is printed with a grid of vines that climbs up to the crown molding. My bed's canopy is stretched with a deep emerald damask that makes me feel like I'm in an enchanted garden. Beyond the window is even more green, a long lawn bordered by thick woods and farther off, Vermont's rolling mountains on the horizon. It's more nature than I've seen in years. The view from my Brooklyn apartment has one tree and a few pigeons. This is something else entirely. The word that springs to mind is *majestic*.

My stomach rumbles anxiously. Tomorrow at this time the first bake will be over. I try to keep myself from getting attached to the idea of making it too far into the competition. I haven't even unpacked my bag yet, just left it propped open in the corner, as I don't want to jinx myself. There are five other bakers after all, and it's already been made clear that I don't have as much baking experience as them. Not even remotely. It was on the dossier they handed out. Our bios were right there for all to see. All the others with their incredibly polished photos and long list of baking expertise, and then there is mine with the headshot I made Rebecca take of me in the park, and below that a description of my next-to-nothing experience. I'll be lucky to last through the first day.

I go to my dressing table and take my time putting on my lipstick. Shaking my hands through my hair, I scoop it up into a messy bun and secure it with a silver pin. I have promised myself to try to take care of my appearance, maybe not in the way I used to but at least to make a true effort. I am going to be on television after all, not sitting around my apartment where no one will see me. So far, so good. My head is still fuzzy from my nap earlier. I'd had the most delicious dream where I was friends with Betsy Martin and she and I were sharing recipes.

When I leave my room to go down to dinner, the house feels surprisingly quiet. I look up and down the empty hallway and worry suddenly that all the other contestants must be downstairs already. I shouldn't have fallen asleep; then I could have spent more time getting ready. It's bad form to be late to a dinner hosted by Betsy Martin, even if she's not in her judging capacity tonight, or so the itinerary says. She may not be judging our baking, but she will certainly be watching us closely. I try to suppress a naive hope that she will form an instant liking to me. I feel a sharp pang of anxiety at the thought that her first impression of me might be that I'm someone who can't show up on time.

I pick up my pace, walking quickly down one long hallway to the end, then turning down another. I'm trying to retrace my steps from earlier. But that was pre-nap, and I clearly wasn't paying enough attention when I arrived. Now I'm having trouble remembering exactly which corridor is which. I come out onto a tiny landing. It is decorated with a giant oil portrait of a man standing in a field. He is handsome, a bit of an arrogant tilt to his head, which reminds me of some of the men I've dated in Brooklyn. He holds a hunting rifle. In his slender arms it looks more like a prop than a tool made for killing. At his side a brown retriever looks loyally up at him, a pheasant dangling from its mouth. A small gold placard affixed to the bottom edge of the frame reads: *Richard Grafton, 1945*.

I take the stairs down to the first floor but find myself trapped in a sort of odd basement with one door that looks like it leads outside. I turn back the way I came, continuing up two flights. Here I am confronted with another empty hallway. I follow until it ends abruptly at three closed doors. Feeling claustrophobic, I impulsively choose the one on my left, wishing I had a piece of string to lead me back in case I've made the wrong choice. The room I enter is dim and the air feels dense and stagnant, as though the oxygen inside is just as old as the furniture. I walk through another room containing a billiards table. I listen for the murmur of voices, the scuff of footsteps, anything to let me know I'm not alone, but everything is deathly silent. I remember an old *Twilight Zone* episode where everyone on earth has disappeared. My armpits prick with adrenaline. I'm grateful I decided against the silk top I'd considered.

Trying not to panic, I start moving a bit more quickly, dashing across to the next door. It opens onto a shadowy sitting room. The curtains are drawn. A trio of overly stuffed chairs gather around an elaborate mantelpiece topped with a large brass clock inside a dome of glass. I listen to it tick. If I could just get to some sort of open space where I could orientate myself or hear other people's voices, I might be able get my bearings, but I'm starting to have the unpleasantly familiar feeling of hysteria creep up on me and am not sure whether to laugh or cry, so I let out a strangled sort of chuckle. It bounces hollowly around the wood paneling. *Where is everyone?*

You're fine, I tell myself. *You're safe. Don't panic.* But it is too late. My vision has started to blur at the edges.

I close my eyes—an old trick my therapist taught me—counting to five as I breathe in. I hold my breath for few seconds, then release the air as I begin to count down *ten, nine, eight, seven, six*. Slowly I feel some of the tension exit my body. As I open my eyes, I hear the creak of a door opening and footsteps through the wall to my left. *There's another person here, thank God!* Relief washes through me.

"Hello?" I call out. I don't wait for a reply. I rush to the door on the left wall and fling it open. The room on the other side is larger than the previous ones, with windows facing out over the woods. A wing-back sofa sits in the center of the room with a coffee table in front holding a large vase with a massive bouquet of fresh irises—another sign of life that brings me comfort. The sun sets a muted pink at the paned windows. I hear a sound on the far side of the room and make my way over to it.

"Hello?" I call out again, edging my way toward the sofa. I suddenly worry that I haven't heard a person at all, that there is an animal loose inside. My throat is dry. I lean over the side, and there is a flurry of movement. It takes me a moment to make sense of what is happening. A scream rips from my chest as I trip backward. An elderly woman with snow-white hair crawls on her hands and knees across the floor. I feel the blood draining from my head. My legs go weak as I begin to lose consciousness.

LOTTIE

Oh, my goodness, I have scared the girl nearly to death! I stand up quickly, my earring in my hand. I must have looked like some sort of wraith, crawling around on the ground like that. I rush over to where she has fallen back against the side of the sofa. I'm embarrassed to have scared her so badly.

"I'm sorry," the young woman stammers. Whisps of shiny strawberry blond hair frame her pale face. She looks absolutely stricken. She reaches one hand to the doorway for support, and for a moment I think she is about to faint. Concerned, I hold my hand out to her shoulder, ready to try to help. I'm not a large woman, but I think I could probably support her weight if need be.

"I didn't mean to frighten you. Just dropped this." I hold up my earring to show her. It's one of a pair of green stones, given to me years ago by my daughter, Molly. I wear them whenever I need a little bit of good luck, and I know I'm going to need all I can get this week.

The woman smiles back at me shakily, her hand still clutching her shirt near her heart.

"I'm sorry. I just get easily startled. Thank you for helping me up," she says, choking out a laugh. "You wouldn't happen to know how to get to the dining room?"

She gives me a strange look, and I can see she is confused by my presence.

"I must have gotten turned around too," I tell her. "But I think I have my bearings now." I smile to reassure her, feeling motherly. If I had to guess, I'd say she's probably in her early thirties, though I am terrible at guessing people's ages. Give me someone between twenty-five and forty-five and I would be hard-pressed to give a remotely good answer. Nearly everyone looks young when you're my age.

"I don't know how I got so lost." She still looks rattled.

I try to make her feel better. "Well, it's not surprising, given how big this place is. I seem to have the hang of it, though. If you want, I can show you the dining room. I should be getting there myself."

"Yes, that would be wonderful." She smiles gratefully, the color returning to her cheeks, which flush a dark pink. She's quite pretty when she smiles, I notice. I want to convince her I'm not an old loon, so I try to strike up a conversation.

"I'm Lottie, you must be another baker?"

"Yes, I am!" She puts her hand out toward me. "I'm Stella, and I really am so excited to be here, even if I don't seem it."

I take her hand in mine, shaking it. It is cold and clammy.

"Lovely to meet you, Stella." Gently I lead her back the way I came, out onto the main landing. Far overhead the ceiling is crisscrossed with carved wooden beams, giving it the feel of a medieval church. A wide central staircase cascades down to the main floor, its wood banister curving elegantly to meet the flagstone of the foyer. Tall windows flanking the main door show a view of the tent, its white peaks set up in the hollow between the house's two main wings, which jut forward on each side.

"It really is stunning here, isn't it?" Stella breathes.

I nod in agreement, feeling a bit uneasy as we approach two menacing suits of armor guarding the front entrance. "I agree. It's absolutely unforgettable."

"So, Betsy Martin lives in that part of the manor?" Stella asks, pointing up to the left side of the landing where the larger staircase splits into two.

"That's what I hear," I say, trying to remember what I've read online about Betsy Martin's personal life. "I guess she wanted her own space during filming. She probably doesn't need the entire place to herself. The stairs to the left are to her private quarters. It's called the East Wing, I think."

As we descend the staircase, I get a prickle on the back of my neck and have the strangest feeling that we are already being filmed. But of course, that's not the case. I don't share my suspicion with Stella, who already had enough of a scare for one evening. I watch as her eyes dart around, taking everything in.

"I kind of can't believe I'm here," she muses. "Betsy is a hero of mine. My only hero these days. I've had one of Betsy's cookbooks since I was a kid. *The Pleasure of Dessert*. It was my favorite book growing up. I mean, what little girl loves a cookbook? But there was something so special about it and it was all because of Betsy. Sorry, I must sound so annoying. Like such a *fan girl*."

I watch her, amused. Her face is still flushed, but I'm relieved to see that her anxiety seems to have given way to excitement.

"Not at all." I brush her concerns away and try to match her enthusiasm. "She's an . . . institution really, isn't she?"

Stella nods vigorously. She leans in to confide to me. "She's a comforting figure to me. Whenever I read one of her books or watch *Bake Week*, I just feel so calm, like the world is a good place and nothing can harm me. You know?"

She turns toward me, her eyes searching, and I realize suddenly that Stella is someone who is unmothered. An ache of recognition forms in my chest. I pat her affectionately on the shoulder. "Shall we continue on to dinner?" I ask softly. "The others are probably waiting."

Stella shakes her head as though to reset it. "Oh, yes please! Look at me jibber-jabbering away about Betsy Martin and making us late to meet her in the process."

"It's just down here, I think."

I guide her through an archway off the foyer and down a short hall. This part of the manor is welcoming and warmly lit compared to where we were upstairs. I tentatively approach a tall set of polished wood doors. I can already hear the pleasant buzz of voices behind them.

"I never ever would have found my way here, Lottie. Thank you."

"Are you ready? I believe this is the dining room," I say, feeling like a tour guide. Stella looks at me, her eyes wide.

"Here we go!"

We each take one of the brass handles and push the doors open. A massive chandelier casts a festive glow above a long table where five people are already drinking wine and chatting. They look up at us as we enter, their faces bright and a bit trepidatious, like children on the first day of school. There are already several open bottles of wine and the remnants of some bread and cheese on a platter.

At the head of the table, I recognize with a sudden lurch in my stomach, is the queen of baking herself, Betsy Martin. I feel Stella's hand squeezing my shoulder.

"Welcome! Come join us," Betsy commands, smiling regally. She gestures to the empty seats. She looks, in a word, wealthy. Swathed in a light pink cashmere sweater, her earlobes punctuated with pearls, she has the kind of glow that at our age comes only with very subtle, very expensive plastic surgery.

I have to say I was surprised to read she'd be joining us for dinner tonight. I'd always assumed she kept a professional distance between herself and the contestants.

A handsome man stands up, pulling out the chair next to him. I hesitate and look to Stella, who gestures for me to take a seat. I watch her sink into the chair across the table from me next to a very pretty and exceptionally young woman with white-blond hair cut in a straight line above her shoulders.

The man next to me picks up a bottle of wine, tipping it toward my glass and raising his brows.

"Just a very small glass," I say.

He fills my wineglass up over halfway, then brings the bottle back to his own glass, filling it nearly to the brim. He passes a tray in my direction.

"You have to try this cracker, it's divine."

I take one and set it on my plate.

"I'll have one of those," a man in a plaid shirt calls from across the table, sliding several onto his palm. "I hear that Betsy made them herself."

"I'm Peter, by the way."

"Pradyumna," the man next to me says.

"I think I saw you out front earlier. Did you bring the BMW?" Peter says, munching on a cracker.

"Ridiculous car, I know." Pradyumna laughs modestly.

"Beautiful car," Peter says, shaking his head appreciatively.

I catch Stella taking a long gulp of white wine. Pradyumna turns toward me, hooking a lanky arm around the top of his chair.

"And what was your name?"

"I'm Lottie," I say, feeling a bit flushed.

"So, what do you do when you aren't baking, Lottie?"

It's been a long time since a handsome young man has taken such a keen interest in me. For a moment I almost feel like it's a line and he's trying to pick me up. Sometimes I forget my age. It's a blessing and a curse, I suppose, to not feel my seventy-two years. Back when I was young, I remember thinking older people were practically a different species. Now I realize we are always the same inside, it's just the packaging that changes.

"I was a nurse, but I'm long retired now," I say. I'm starting to feel uncomfortable with all the attention directed at me, so I deflect by turning the questions back on him. If there is one thing I know to be true, it is that men love answering questions about themselves.

"And what brought *you* to baking, or was it something you've always done?"

A small frown forms on his face, and he looks down into his wine. "Well, I don't know really. I suppose I wanted to impress women."

I let out a surprised laugh. He smiles impishly, pleased with himself. "No, seriously, I just think it's quite fun. Takes my mind off things, takes up time." I wonder how the life of someone so young should be so empty that it needs time taken up, but before I can dig any deeper the dining room doors open and a man rushes in. He's wearing a cream-colored linen suit, wrinkled from a day's travel. He drags his suitcase noisily behind him, coming to a momentary pause he pulls a handkerchief out of his pocket and mops his brow, then carries on, making a beeline for the table. He comes to a sudden stop at the far end of the dining table.

"Hello, everyone, I'm Gerald," he addresses us, but his eyes focus only on Betsy. He gives a small, melodramatic bow in her direction. "I'm mortified that I'm late. It was the trains, you see. The schedules were inaccurate." His voice rises as he says this last part. Across from me, Peter's eyebrows go up.

"Don't worry, Gerald," Betsy says graciously. "Now you are here, and we are delighted you made it. Please have a seat, a glass of wine. We've only just gotten started." Gerald props his bags against the far wall and chooses one of two remaining empty chairs, sliding in next to Hannah. She wrinkles her tiny nose as he settles into his seat, wiping a bit of remaining sweat from his brow. The others introduce themselves to Gerald, who still looks a bit shaken and can surely tell by their empty glasses and crumb-strewn plates that they have not just gotten started.

There is the sound of a glass being dinged with a fork at the head of the table. Betsy stands up and raises her wineglass. The etched crystal catches the light from the chandelier, and it twinkles like a gemstone in her hand. "Bakers! If I could have your attention for just a moment?"

The chatter around the table ceases instantly, heads whipping to watch Betsy. My heart thuds against my rib cage. She beams down at us. Betsy is the only other person at the table as old as I am—older, in fact, by just one year. However, unlike me, an anonymous, gray-haired woman, Betsy has made a name for herself as the absolute authority on baking, "America's Grandmother," they often call her in the press. She's made herself rich enough from her tarts and cookies to own and operate Grafton, the manor house she grew up in and probably a few other homes as well. She is an icon, the Julia Child of home baking. When my daughter, Molly, was a little girl, we'd watch her show in the evenings after I picked her up from day care. It was part of the reason Molly got so interested in cooking. "Can we bake a cake, Mommy?" she'd ask. It was hard to say no. We had so little then, and I barely kept us afloat with the money from my job at the hospital, but with only flour, sugar, butter, and cocoa, we could be happy. What was a little mess, a bit too much sugar?

Behind the table, the doors open once more and Archie Morris swaggers in. I feel a sharp intake of breath from the rest of the contestants as *Bake Week*'s new cohost makes his way to the table. Archie Morris has a reputation as a bit of a bulldog. "Ugh, not him," Molly had said when I'd found out he was joining as cohost. He even looks the part. He is shorter than he appears on television but solidly built. His face is young and full for his reported fifty-three years, his head covered in thick auburn hair that curls in gravity-defying loops straight up from his forehead and around his ears. His smartly cut suit skims his muscular arms and pecs and almost succeeds in hiding the slight curve of a belly under his shirt. His skin glows with a deep tan.

"Hey, team! Aren't you all looking smart? How is everyone feeling? I, for one, am thrilled to be here hosting *Bake Week*!" He smiles at us, flashing a row of teeth so artificially white and straight they are almost blinding. He doesn't look like the sort of person who has spent his career eating decadent meals and desserts and certainly not toiling over dough. He moves confidently to the chair at the foot of the table, unbuttoning his jacket as he sits.

"Pass me one of those, would you? I'm famished." He points at the cracker plate, and Gerald hands it to him, his mouth set in a firm line of displeasure. "Great, thanks," Archie says, taking a noisy bite and giving the rest of us a little salute with the rest of the cracker.

"Now that we're *all* here," Betsy begins again, wresting our attention back to the head of the table. I notice more than a hint of disapproval in her voice.

"I'd like to give a toast. It is an honor to have six of the country's finest amateur bakers in my home for the tenth season of *Bake Week*. As you may know, it is customary for me to join you all for dinner on the first night, not as a judge but as a host. It's a tradition I relish. You all have probably heard that baking came to me early, passed down from the many talented women in my family, as I'm sure is the case for many of you. What you may not realize is that it was in this very home's kitchen that I shaped my first loaf of bread."

Betsy pauses and looks around the table at us as we smile appreciatively. I'm sure we are all happy to be here, but it also feels a bit like a competition already, like we are all vying to be noticed by her. I wonder whether she is actually judging us based on tonight. She is certainly deciding which of us she likes, who is going to be easy to get along with, who is going to be difficult, and who is going to flame out. I press my lips into what I hope is my most genuine-looking smile as she continues.

"Grafton Manor is a special place for me. It is my ancestral home, and I hope during your spare time this week you'll take some time to appreciate it and the beautiful grounds it sits on. As you all know, *Bake Week* is not just a competition. It is also a therapy session, a comfort for those at home. You all have been chosen not only for your exceptional baking techniques but for your unique stories. This is a transformational journey for you bakers in the tent. You may learn things about yourself along the way, so be prepared to accept these discoveries, to learn and grow from them. That said, I will be judging this competition for baking and baking alone. As you all know I am deathly allergic to burnt crusts and doughy centers. So, let's drink up and enjoy the beautiful meal the staff here have created. Tomorrow I take a big step back and resume my role as judge, and you will begin the very important business of baking in the tent for all to see. Hats off to you all for making it here, and may the best baker win!"

I notice several pairs of eyes glowing wetly as we stand. I pick up my glass and lean in to join them. A chorus of "Cheers!" breaks out around the table, and I clink with as many glasses as possible.

"To *Bake Week*!" Betsy says.

"To *Bake Week*!" we shout in unison.

I wonder if anyone can tell my hand is shaking.

Day One

BREAD

BETSY

Betsy Martin looks out at the contestants for the first time. The rows of baking tables are staggered slightly so that from the front she can see each of their faces. They wear identical half smiles to mask their nerves. Each one of them is completely distinct, but she still has trouble telling them apart. It's always like this at the beginning of filming before their individual personalities crystallize, before the cracks and eccentricities start to shine through. Everyone starts out almost the same, all on their very best behavior for the cameras, but it won't take long for a bit of adversity and competition to bring out their true personas. Of course, for one of them it will be too late. Betsy likes to make a little wager with herself about who will go home first. She scans the contestants.

Up front there's Hannah, from the middle-of-nowhere Minnesota. She's very pretty and very young—there's always at least one of those, the producers make sure of it. Likely talented as well, someone like her must be or they'll look like they are just chosen for show. Across from her, Gerald from the Bronx looks stiff and uncomfortable in another linen suit. His fastidiousness may be his downfall in the future, but not today. In the next row is Peter, who is from nearby New Hampshire. With his plaid shirts, he reminds her of a small, handsome Paul

Bunyan. His relaxed confidence makes her think he will do well with challenges and be a good baker as well. Next to him is Stella from Brooklyn, a thirtysomething former journalist who is by all accounts extremely new to baking, not having baked a single cake until this year. It will be interesting to see how she fares. The final row is Pradyumna, a stylish entrepreneur who lives in Boston, and Lottie, an older woman who lives in Rhode Island and, if experience with others like her is any indication, will likely blow her competition out of the water at the beginning and then fizzle out. The older contestants just don't have the stamina, she thinks harshly. For the moment Betsy's money is on Stella going home first. You do not simply teach yourself to bake and then win *Bake Week* all in one year. Next to her, Archie Morris rubs his palms together, bouncing back and forth on the balls of his feet as though he is waiting to start a race.

It is Betsy's first time sharing the front of the tent, ever. She doesn't like it one bit. It had been a shock to her when the producers suggested Archie Morris as the cohost of *Bake Week*. For the last nine years she has been the only one behind the judging table, the sole anchor and mascot of the show. The very concept of *Bake Week* was hers, after all. The idea came to her over twelve years ago. She'd just finished her sixth cookbook and wanted to try something different, when her agent Francis had gotten a call from the producers of a new streaming service. The people at Flixer were looking for new programing, and they'd wondered about Betsy's interest in repackaging her old cooking show. She'd mulled it over. Back when her husband was around, the idea of filming a show at Grafton would never have flown. He'd hated her celebrity and found the idea of televised baking to be a "supreme bore." He may as well have been describing himself. But it had been six years since her divorce from Roland Martin. Grafton Manor needed repairs, and this could help pay for them, she told herself. The idea of making the show a competition had hit her like a bolt of lightning. Back then the concept was fairly novel. But this wouldn't be just any competition. Betsy's show would be gentle, with a focus on the craft, not a bunch of runaway egos forced to bake things you'd never even want to eat, as was so often the case with these things. And most importantly, it would be held at Grafton Manor, Betsy's childhood home.

Archie Morris is known for hosting a very different style of show. Betsy had watched only one episode of *The Cutting Board* and was not impressed. It was the polar opposite of *Bake Week*, a macho, cutthroat competition where the contestants rushed around in a mad panic insulting and undercutting each other along the way. If Archie was anything less than thrilled with their finished dishes, he would push their plates away in disgust and unleash a torrent of abuse. It would be ridiculous, Betsy thought, to make something like baking into a sort of martial art. She was positive that Archie did not have in him what made *Bake Week* so special. To be a good host in her eyes, you need to show you have the right combination of humility and nurturing—two qualities that brash Archie Morris is not known for. When the suggestion of adding him as a cohost first came up, she had set up a meeting with her producers and voiced these concerns. She had expected the idea of Archie Morris to be dropped immediately and for them to, at the very least, suggest other more suitable cohosts.

But later that day she'd gotten a call from Francis. He told her that despite her position on the matter, they'd hired Archie. The show needed "livening up," they'd said. She'd taken that as code for what they were really trying to say: she'd gotten too old, and they were worried she could no longer carry one of Flixer's most streamed shows alone. To add insult to injury, the producers had demanded that Archie stay with her in a guest suite in the East Wing of Grafton. "They want to keep the judges and the contestants separate," Francis had relayed to her. "Then let him stay in a hotel," Betsy had shot back, only to be on the receiving end of *that look*, the one he gives her when she's said something particularly difficult that he prays she won't say to anyone else.

So, she'd tried to accept Archie Morris as gracefully as possible. At least on the surface. Besides, she knew she had no choice. She needed the money the show brought in to keep the manor running. Without *Bake Week*, what would keep Grafton afloat? Her cookbook royalties weren't enough to keep a full manor house alive. Much like herself, an older building must be maintained in order to function properly. There is always something that needs looking into, repairs both small and large to contend with. Along with the aesthetic work—it was unending—there was always a room that needed painting, a floor refinishing. She couldn't hope to keep up without the money from the studio. Aging is not for the weak. Or the poor. Betsy had swallowed her pride and hoped for the best, even though she did not think he was the right fit. Both of them—Grafton and her—would have to endure Archie Morris to survive. Melanie signals from the back of the tent as the camerapeople make their final adjustments.

Watching the bakers come into themselves is one of the joys of *Bake Week*, something that sets it apart from *other* cooking shows where some angry chef barks out insults and orders. At *Bake Week*, the goal was not just to win, not just to bake well, but to be human in the process. *That* is what makes compelling television programming. That is what makes viewers tune in in droves. Not to see how fast you can make a blini while someone barks out the seconds left on a ticking clock. It was one of the tenets Betsy had insisted on when she created this show over a decade ago, that it be truly inclusive. And so far, it has been. She credits *Bake Week*'s massive success to the way it treats people. No yelling, no scolding, just good-natured competition and respectful defeat. Father would have appreciated that part. *You must know how to lose, and to learn when you lose*, he'd always told her. *It's the only way you can come back to win.* She pulls an index card out of her pocket and cups it in the palm of her hand one last time before the cameras start to roll.

Archie has no notecard with names to memorize. In fact, he'd pushed her arm away when she'd tried to give him one the day before. "Don't need it." He'd tapped smugly at the crown of his head and winked. God, she'd wanted to stab him with a cake tester, but she breathed deeply and tried to let it pass, focusing instead on the indisputable knowledge that this is her show.

She can feel the irritation begin to well up again as he starts to work the bakers like the warm-up act at a bad stand-up club. He ambles from table to table, chatting with Hannah and gently poking fun of Gerald's lovely suit, palling around with Peter and Pradyumna. She watches as each contestant he speaks to melts under the gooey warmth of his attention. *Disgusting.* Finally, having made a full round, he comes back around to the front, giving her a cocky little wink as he takes his place next to her, a bit too close, as though he might be trying to inch her to the side of the screen. His head is truly too large in size, like an overfilled balloon.

She looks to the side of the tent where Melanie confers with several of the crew. She points to something on her clipboard, appearing to scold a young woman holding the boom mic. The girl's face falls, and Betsy wonders if she needs to speak with Melanie about her manner. She's noticed a change in the last few seasons that coincided with her climbing rank. Her look has become more intimidating, much more polished and put together. Melanie has always been a bit of a perfectionist, which Betsy appreciates, but sometimes that tendency has her veering a bit too close to control freak for Betsy's comfort. Betsy inspects a gold button on her jacket. They are already a half an hour behind schedule. Time to get started already.

Then a signal finally comes from Melanie. Filming is about to begin. The glow of the lights is familiar on her face, and she steps into them, embracing their warmth. She raises her arms, a gesture welcoming the bakers to the tent and, if she's judged the cameras correctly, blocking Archie's face from the shot entirely.

HANNAH

I lean forward on my toes, my fingers resting lightly on the top of my baking table, ready to launch myself into action when I hear our instructions. I feel my stomach do a little somersault as Betsy begins to speak.

"For our first baking challenge, the bakers are asked to make two kinds of bread. We are looking for one sweet bread and one savory, and at least one must be made using yeast."

"We expect good rises and perfect bakes on these," Archie continues. "Bread can be tricky so stay vigilant."

I focus on the pantry doors to the side of the tent, already planning what I will need.

"Ready . . . set . . ."

One more deep breath. *You've got this, Hannah.*

"Bake!"

I take off, running to the pantry, filling my arms with flour, sugar, packets of yeast, and dumping them on top of my baking station. Bread is hard to get just right. It's fussy. I fumble at first, dropping my measuring cups and spilling flour all over the table. Next, I grab an egg from the refrigerator, and it cracks on the floor. I laugh to cover my embarrassment as the cameras rush to film my first mishap. Getting

used to them watching and recording everything is going to be a challenge. *You can do this, Hannah. You have to.*

I start mixing my dough, finally getting into the rhythm of it as if
I were at home. When I am in the process of baking, I go to another
place. It's the only time I feel this way. Most of the time I am full of
self-doubt and self-criticism. But when I'm baking something, I get
so involved in whatever it is that I'm making that I disappear into it.
The experience feels almost divine, the kind of thing they talk about
at church. It's to the point that if I don't get to this place, if I don't feel
this feeling, I know that whatever I'm making won't taste as good.

For the sweet bread, I've already decided that I'll be baking a spiced
cinnamon roll with chai-flavored icing. I've made this one at least a
dozen times in the past few months, enough that Ben, who usually
can't get enough of my sweets, was literally holding his hands up in
surrender, begging for me to take mercy on him when I brought the
last few tries out to the kitchen table.

Instead, I took the extra rolls to my mom and her sister and to our
next-door neighbors, who agreed they were exceptional, even if most
of them had never heard of chai. Now my hands move almost on their
own, mixing the dough on the countertop. I like to use my fingers
instead of the mixer so I can gauge the texture. You don't want your
dough too dry or too sticky. There's a perfect consistency that I can
find only if I go by touch. I place the first batch of dough on a shelf
inside the baby-blue Smeg refrigerator by my baking table. I wipe my
fingers on my apron and allow myself a quick break to look around
the tent at my competition. Across from me, Gerald has also already
put his doughs in the refrigerator to chill. He'll be a challenge in this
competition, I can already tell. He is as detail oriented as I am and
probably twice as organized. He works at mixing something, his face
intense with focus above the bow tie of his suit. At tables behind me,
Stella and Lottie are still mixing their dough. It looks like Lottie's is
sticking to her hands, which is never a good sign. I remind myself that
this is a competition, and I'd be doing myself no favors by trying to

help anyone out. Stella shapes her dough into a ragged lump on the next table over. Her face is flushed and smeared with flour. She looks up, making eye contact with me, and I break away, turning back to my own table as though I've just been caught cheating on a test. When I swing back around, Archie Morris is standing in front of my table. He has snuck up on me while my back was turned and is surrounded by cameras.

"Hello there, young lady! How are you feeling about your first bake?"

It's crazy being so close to a celebrity. The legendary Archie Morris. My mom used to watch him every night on *The Cutting Board*. She was over the moon when they announced he was going to be the new cohost this season.

"He's so sexy," she'd said back in Minnesota, taking a bite of a butterscotch bar I was testing. "It'll do that Betsy woman some good. She could use some new life in that tent with her. Someone a bit fresher." Mom licked her lips, and I couldn't tell if it was to clear off crumbs or to show her appreciation for Archie Morris. Either way, it was disgusting.

"Betsy Martin is a star, Mom," I'd replied. Mom is nothing if not exasperating. She has always been harder on women. I think it was how she was raised.

"Take these away from me or I'll get fat," she said, pushing the pan across the table, but she made no move to stop eating.

"You know I almost met Archie Morris once." I'd turned back to the counter, rolling my eyes at the story I'd heard at least fifty times already. "I was in a pageant in Tucson, and he was staying at the same hotel as me. I heard from some of the other girls that he was in the bar, but once we got there, he was already gone. Spent too long putting on my makeup. That's why I have the makeup tattoos now! Now I'll never have to miss another celebrity sighting because I am too busy putting on my lip liner!"

And now Archie Morris is standing directly in front of me, looking at me with those huge emerald eyes and asking about my baking. He's so close, I can smell his cologne. It's nothing like the sharp body spray Ben puts on before work when he's too lazy to shower. Archie smells expensive, clean, and masculine, like leather and pine sap.

His head is backlit, surrounded in a halo of light like the saints on the stained-glass windows at our church. His eyes twinkle, inviting me to speak. He must have asked me something, but I don't hear him. The lights are hot on my face. My brain grasps for something to say. I remember what I've practiced alone in the kitchen for ten years now, and I inhale sharply, forcing myself to snap out of it. Angling my best side toward the cameras, I put on my most dazzling smile, the one I hope everyone will like.

"Hi, Archie." I beam. "I'm just so happy to be here."

PRADYUMNA

Bread happens to be my specialty, so I'm elated. I get straight to work preparing my yeast, mixing it with a splash of milk and warming it in a pan as an image of a Swedish cardamom twist comes into my head. With its elaborate plaiting, it's like a cinnamon roll but more complex. I love a bread tied in knots. I'll make mine savory. That will be interesting. I turn off the burner and rush to my designated sage-green refrigerator on the side of the tent. It's stocked to the brim, stuffed full of fresh produce, exotic fruits, and dairy from local farms. I get to work sorting through my options. What is this? Spring onion? No, chives. That'll be perfect. I'll dice them and mix them with olive oil, so they crisp up in the cracks of the bread, along with some mature cheddar. I dig deeper in the dairy compartment and find a log of expensive goat cheese. Even better! Then I'll add a ton of fresh-ground black pepper and top with some flaky sea salt. My mouth is already watering. Pair a few of these freshly baked buns with a crisp, minerally white and aperitivo is served!

This is by far my favorite part of baking, watching the ideas form in my mind. I'm not a planner—all the meticulous plotting, the playing out of different scenarios—what a drag. I make up for my inability to think ahead by being good on the fly. I think I need a bit of pressure to create.

For my sweet bread, I'll start a dough and get it rising so I can think about it more once I've had a break. I work energetically, adding flour to the yeast in the stand mixer, cracking in eggs, a plop of some room temperature butter, sugar, and a generous pinch of salt. I'm not as by the book as most bakers. I think that sometimes too much strict methodology can get you in trouble when it's better to rely at least a bit on instinct. Baking is like playing jazz—once you have the basics down, sometimes it's better to improvise.

Once I have my sweet bread dough in the proofing drawer, I set to work on my bread dough. I watch with satisfaction as it turns from a shaggy lump into something taut and shiny in the mixer. It will need to chill in the fridge before I shape it into knots. It's hot and humid today, which means it's best to let your batter rest for a bit. With my two basic doughs resting and chilling—two of my personal favorite states as well—I take a momentary break.

I wipe my hands on a cloth, tossing it over my shoulder. While I have a sip of water I look around at the others.

Peter is referring to the blueprint he's created as his stand mixer spins wildly next to him. His forehead is damp with anxiety.

In front of me, Stella, whisps of her hair coming loose from the bun on top of her head, aggressively kneads a lump of dough, working it on her counter with expert wrist flips. She attempts unsuccessfully to blow a stray piece of hair from her face. It sticks to her cheek instead, and I'm tempted to go over to her and smooth it. I look away before my thoughts get the better of me.

Melanie is standing along the side of the tent whispering to one of the camera operators, the one with the dark beard. I was surprised to see her when I arrived at Grafton. I don't know why exactly. I suppose I figured her role was less substantial, less hands-on. But she seems to be the control center of *Bake Week*, rushing around in tailored pants and a fitted shirt, an earpiece pressed to one ear. She points a manicured finger at Lottie, whose bread is being pulled out of the proving tray, and the camera guy rushes past me. Her eyes scan the room, looking for other opportunities. It was Melanie who chose me.

I tried out for *Bake Week* as a bit of a joke. Well, maybe not a joke, but I applied the same sense of whatever will be, will be to the application as I do to pretty much all aspects of my life these days. I filled out the forms honestly, telling them that baking was one of the great joys in my life but that I have never had any sort of professional aspirations about the whole thing. I look at baking as a leisure sport, the same way one might look at sailing—something you want to do as a hobby. Nothing you want to be responsible for when it comes to other people's well-being.

I was clear about that in my application video. Clear that I don't need to bake, that I do it for the fun of it. I don't need to do anything really, which is part of my problem. I haven't since I sold Spacer to a billionaire tech investor in 2013. It was a start-up, a service that helped people find open parking spaces. I'd done it on a lark, just a lame idea I'd had that I was telling people about to liven up the conversation at some boring party one day, but a friend from Stanford had overheard and thought it was a good idea. So he'd set up a meeting with some of his investor friends. They'd loved my pitch, and soon enough I was a full-fledged company with a staff of thirty and the buzz surrounding a booming tech sector full of eager hangers-on. When an investment firm swooped in with an offer, I hadn't even flinched. I sold it immediately for a whopping $14 million. Principles be damned. I knew that there was no way something so simple, so stupid frankly, would stand the test of time. Though I had some regret when I told my staff. All were brand-new to the company, all still sold on the lines I'd spoon-fed them about office culture and being part of something bigger *blah-blah*. Spacer was not something bigger, though. We weren't changing the world one parking space at a time, and anyone half conscious could see that. It was a flash in the pan. And if a big company was dumb enough to want to gobble it up while it was still palatable, well then, I was not about to stand in their way.

With so much money in the bank, and investments piling up in a tailor-made portfolio, I was able to just coast, so that's exactly what I did. I took up golf, sailing, and baking. I don't know what exactly drew me to baking. I think I'd always enjoyed making things, showing off when I invited people over for dinner parties. Baking made me seem domestic and accessible, things that are impressive to women. Up until recently, most of my life has been about impressing women. And it just so happened that I found all the kneading and mixing extremely relaxing, an added bonus.

In the *Bake Week* application video, I'd whipped up pavlova in the kitchen of my apartment. While it baked, I sipped a sherry and talked about my life in Boston, gave a tour of my expansive kitchen. Then I topped the meringue with a gooseberry reduction and lemon balm–infused whipping cream. I must have charmed them on some level, because a month later I got called in for an in-person interview and baking challenge. The baking challenge was held at a local culinary school in downtown Boston. I was led to a room with long metal countertops and an industrial oven and instructed to make a perfect quiche with a limited selection of ingredients. It was all very school, and I hated school. The judge was a producer of the show, a scout for Betsy, I was told. I recognize her now as Melanie, skulking around the side of the tent with an earpiece in. She was stern looking then as well, holding that same clipboard on her lap as she scrutinized my cooking technique, which I'll be the first to admit is a bit unconventional. Too many rules just make me not want to play.

That day, as Melanie took a bite of my leek and Gruyère quiche, its crust perfectly flaky and warm from the oven, I knew from the slight flutter of her eyes as they closed that I was going to be a contestant on *Bake Week*. The same way I know when a woman is going to go home with me at night. The next week a phone call confirmed it.

I begin chopping up chives for my filling, stirring them into a bowl with some salt and olive oil. I turn to go retrieve the goat cheese, and it's only then I realize the refrigerator door has been hanging wide open. I rush to it, examining my dough, which is meant to be fully cooled by now. It's warm and gooey. Dammit. Is this fridge broken? I must have been distracted, though it seems like such a strange thing to do. I know I would have closed the door when I put the dough in. Wouldn't I? Now I'm going to be well behind the others. For the first time in the tent, I feel a twinge of pure competition. *The tent*: Am I already drinking the *Bake Week* Kool-Aid? I find all the lingo surrounding the show a bit absurd.

As I glance around the room to see if anyone caught my rookie mistake, I catch Lottie's eye. She starts when I see her looking at me, immediately breaking eye contact and turning back to the dough she'd been scoring. Is it possible that someone could have opened the refrigerator door without me noticing? Intentionally? I look around at them, all so innocently busy with their bakes, and realize that of course, it's completely possible.

LOTTIE

I pull my pan of milk, already frothing, off the burner and stir in a stick of butter as Betsy appears in front of me with her gaggle of cameras and microphones. She is wearing a royal blue jacket with shiny gold buttons. Her matching earrings wobble ever so slightly on her lobes as she addresses me.

"What breads have you decided to make today, Lottie?"

There's a funny way Betsy talks that makes me feel both old and tottering *and* like a small child. I wonder if I am the only one who feels that way, being the oldest here by a long shot, or if it is something she does to others as well. Certainly not Stella, I think, taking a glance across the tent at her. Stella, who practically worships Betsy Martin, is surely treated to a different sort of interaction, one that isn't tinged with pity.

I barely slept last night and can feel the reminder of it pulsing at the back of my eyes. All the anticipation about facing Betsy and Archie and being filmed doesn't help either. I'm not someone who has ever craved the spotlight. Quite the opposite, in fact.

"This is a summer stollen," I say as Betsy scrutinizes the lumpy dough I've shaped into a hefty log. "Made with fresh fruit instead of candied." I know that choosing a recipe this dated and out of style is probably not advisable, but I told myself it's best to cook what I know, and stollen is what came to me so I've gone with it. There's not much time to play around or make mistakes. I don't want to be sent home yet and my stollen is well practiced. I know I can get it right. Despite being served at holidays, stollen isn't a particularly fancy or difficult kind of bread, it's just a kind of fruitcake that had its heyday back when I was young. My mother adored them but rarely baked one, preferring to take me out to share a slice at a German bakery in town. I was never too excited about them back then, to be honest. As a child I found them dense and unappealing, but as I've gotten older, I've come to appreciate their solidity. A hefty slice of stollen, particularly one laced with almond paste as mine is going to be, next to a mug of tea is as comforting a way possible to while away a winter afternoon.

"A stollen in summer? That *is* inventive." The way she says it makes me think she might not mean it in the best possible way. I push through a surge of embarrassment, trying not to read anything into it, though my palms have suddenly gone clammy.

"And this is a pane bianco." I pull back the tea towel I've draped loosely over my second bread, which has almost finished rising, to reveal a loaf that is folded and twisted into an S shape. Its ridges spill over with sun-dried tomatoes, fresh basil, thick chunks of mozzarella, and a generous dusting of fine parmesan waiting to be baked. I see her eyebrows move ever so slightly. Whenever we've watched *Bake Week* on TV, Molly always laughs that it's impossible to ever really know what Betsy is thinking due to all the Botox in her face. But this close I can definitely read her expression. It says "Yikes."

"Using some old-fashioned recipes, aren't you," she says, her tone once again inscrutable. My stomach twists anxiously. The age of the recipe is not what we are meant to be judged on, I want to remind her. But instead, I nervously clear my throat.

"I prefer to think of them as classics," I say quietly, gently replacing the towel. I look down at it, wanting to disappear until I remember the cameras and force myself to look up at her.

A bemused smile appears on her face. "Well, I look forward to tasting them, Lottie. Thank you."

Betsy swishes away from the table and I let out a deep sigh, my muscles unclenching. I hadn't realized I'd been holding myself so still. I pull myself together, turning back to my breads.

It took me so long to get here. I've applied to *Bake Week* every year it has existed. For a decade I've spent nearly all of my spare time practicing every bake I could think of, working my way from breads to pastries to tarts and cookies until my daughter, Molly, told me I had to start finding other people to give them away to or she'd "go paleo," whatever that means, because I was making her sick with so much sugar. Each March I would fill out an application online, my heart in my throat as I pushed send. Then I would wait anxiously for a week, a month, only to become consumed by the slow letdown that comes when you hear nothing back. I didn't let myself give up, though. Every New Year's Day I renewed my commitment to my singular goal, which was to be a contestant on *Bake Week*. And this year, three weeks and four days after I'd sent in my application, I got a call back. I tried not to get my hopes up when I went in to do my live baking demo for Melanie, who is now watching from the far side of the tent. But I knew that this was it, I would have no other chance. I was shaking as she gave me the simple instructions to bake a chocolate cake. I felt as if the gods smiled down on me in that moment, because if there is one thing I know how to bake perfectly, one thing I've made time and time again, which I do still every year for Molly's birthday, it is chocolate cake.

So I am not going to let Betsy shake my confidence when I've worked so hard and long to get here, because baking is not the only thing I've come to do at Grafton.

STELLA

I try not to look at any of the cameras dead-on. Instead I focus on my dough, kneading it, turning it, scoring it. It's hard not to look up when you can feel all those glass eyes are staring at you, recording everything you do, every mistake you make. It's disconcerting. *Focus, Stella.* I take my time braiding ropes of dough, shaping them into a loaf. Using a pastry brush, I paint on a slick of miso and sprinkle finely chopped green scallions across the top. It looks okay. Not perfect but good enough. *Into the oven with you!* I take a deep breath. I am not even meant to be here, I remind myself. It is some sort of fairy-tale miracle. My level of experience is just a fraction of what the other five have. Until last year I hadn't even made a cookie, much less a layer cake.

Eight months before I was accepted to *Bake Week*, I quit my job as a reporter for *The Republic.* At that point I had never really baked anything that wasn't from a mix. For about a week, I wallowed on the couch wearing what I optimistically called my "loungewear," staring despondently at my phone, hoping for some rush of motivation that would bring me back from the brink. Leaving my job felt as much like a breakup as anything else I'd ever experienced, the sudden rush of endorphins followed by the steady decent into isolation and self-pity. Being a journalist was my passion, and I had invested everything I had into it over the last decade. Now I was despondent and directionless. Six days into my new life of unemployment, I was flipping through Flixer, looking for a show or a movie to watch, praying that I could find something that wouldn't give me anxiety, when I stumbled across *Bake Week*. Of course, I'd heard of it. Everyone has heard of *Bake Week*. But before my tenure on the couch, I'd spent what little extra time I had watching things I could talk about or write about at work. I'd watch whichever documentary about a woman's brutal murder was being discussed at the office, or whichever edgy films were up for awards they would obviously not win, so that I could interject that they were robbed when it came up at lunch. A feel-good show about baking wouldn't have given me the kind of adrenaline I needed then to keep watching. But as a thirty-five-year-old woman with a rapidly dwindling bank account who had no idea what she was doing with her life, I was in need of comfort, not thrills. I pushed play and settled back on the couch, expecting the entire thing to put me to sleep. Five hours later I found myself crying as I watched a woman named Alice, who'd just come out of an abusive relationship, win the Golden Spoon with an elaborately decorated Swiss roll.

It was then, my eyes still wet with tears, that the memory of the cookbook from my childhood came to me with a jolt. I went to my closet, pulling up a kitchen chair so that I could reach back into the top shelf, where I stored what few things I had from that time. Pushing away some extra blankets and a stack of notebooks, I saw the cardboard box, far in back, scribbled on one side with marker.

My family was plagued with the kind of dysfunction most people only ever read about. When I was just a baby, my mother left my father and me suddenly and with no explanation at all, or so I was told, not even a goodbye note. My father tried his best for a few years, but I suppose he couldn't handle raising a little kid on his own. I was handed over to the state at the tender age of three and quickly swallowed up by the system, where I bounced around to different foster families, each new address worse and more chaotic than the last. Until I was sent to live with the Finkelmans.

The Finkelmans were the most nuclear-normal family I'd ever met—two parents and two kids, a boy and a girl, already in high school. When I first moved in with them, they took me to the mall. After fitting me for a new school uniform, we wandered into the bookstore. It was maybe the first bookshop I'd ever been to, full of shiny hardcovers in bright colors. The older kids went ahead, disappearing into the teen section. Mrs. Finkelman leaned over and told me to pick out any book I wanted. In my years of being carted around from place to place, I'd never been given such a gift. I remember walking up to a display of cookbooks and seeing Betsy Martin's *The Pleasure of Dessert*. It was as though the book was glowing from the shelf.

Maybe I wanted it only because it was right in front of me and there was a picture of an elaborate birthday cake on the cover, but I still remember the feeling I had when I saw that book. It signified something big and good, something that could be mine. In my imagination the cake on the cover was for me, and beyond it, smiling as they waited for the candles to be blown out, were the friends and family who I didn't have but wanted. Mrs. Finkelman was confused by my choice and attempted to steer me back toward the children's section. But I dug in my heels. I was so rarely allowed to choose anything for myself that I was not about to squander this opportunity. It had to be mine. I reminded her of her promise, that I could have any book I wanted. She relented, rolling her eyes as she took the book up to the counter.

Later, alone in my new bedroom, I pored over it, getting lost in meticulously decorated cakes, glossy fruit tarts, streusel-topped sweetbreads, friendly pies with slices neatly cleaved out. I'd never eaten anything like the desserts in these pages, never even seen anything so beautiful. I memorized the book. I had favorite recipes that rotated depending on my mood. I knew which one I'd bake for my best friend's birthday, the best friend who I didn't have yet, and which would be my wedding cake. They promised celebration, a lifetime of familial love and togetherness. It was as though the recipe for my future happiness could be found within the book's glossy pages.

As I got older, I forgot about the cookbook. I hadn't ever baked anything from it anyway. Mrs. Finkelman never was one to let anyone into her kitchen, and besides, I was shuffled off to live in another home with another temporary family the next school year, and the book got put into a box of my things and forgotten about. It wasn't until quitting my job at *The Republic* and sitting on the sofa for a week in numb shock that I remembered it existed.

I pulled the box down. Inside were all the things I'd collected during my childhood years. A stuffed bunny, a beaded bracelet I'd made in kindergarten, and a notebook full of stories I'd made up. They were mostly things I'd found inside free boxes on the curb. One picture book had a sticker on the spine indicating I'd stolen it from the library. But there at the bottom of the box, still as glossy as the day Mrs. Finkelman bought it, was Betsy Martin's *The Pleasure of Dessert*.

I brought it back to the couch, where I'd made a pathetic nest for myself with blankets, and paged through it, taking my time as I absorbed the soothing images from my childhood. And then, with a surge of energy I hadn't felt since the last time I wrote a particularly explosive tell-all article for *The Republic*, I put on some real clothes and went to the grocery store. Even though it wasn't close to my birthday, I decided I was going to bake myself a birthday cake.

Before I started baking, writing was the only thing I ever was good at, the only thing I'd ever wanted to be good at. *The Republic* was my dream job, or so I'd thought. *The Republic* wasn't straight journalism—what is these days—but it was a news site with guts. I'd wanted to work there since its founder, the iconic Hardy Blaine, came to talk to my college journalism class. He was edgy and smart. He'd built the site from the ground up and ushered in a new thing: journalism with a point of view. It all made him and *The Republic* very attractive.

It took me years to get there. I took an unpaid internship at a competing publication out of college, working two other jobs to pay the bills. I slowly, painfully made a career for myself in journalism, but it wasn't until a position opened at *The Republic* that all my struggling paid off. Well, not monetarily. It didn't pay even close to enough. Most journalists come from money to offset this. I did not. But I had wanted to work at *The Republic* for a decade. When I got the job, I thought my entire life was set. I understood what *The Republic* was trying to do, and I believed in it. Even though I was told by my advisor that I was inexperienced and not to overstep my bounds, I went around her and started pitching stories directly to Hardy. The first thing I published was a piece about creative thinking. I loved forming connections in my mind, noticing what people gravitated to. I remember watching that first story go viral, following the conversation as it jumped from the comments section to Twitter and Facebook and finally to my email inbox, where other publications clamored to quote me, and radio shows begged to interview me. It was a high unlike anything I'd ever experienced, and all I wanted was more of it. I was quickly promoted to assistant editor, then editor. I got to write about politics for a living, and I loved it. Not that it wasn't exhausting at times; it was beyond exhausting. But mostly it was invigorating. I loved calling up sources and then piecing information together around an idea. I loved watching everything take shape in the form of a story and pairing it with a bold headline and my name just below. The thrill of it never wore off. I loved my work. And then everything fell apart. I still can't bring myself to think about it.

Holed up in my apartment, I watched my savings drain away and I tried not to panic. The only thing I could think of to do was bake. This was not the sweaty adrenaline rush that filing a story brought to me, this was calm and meditative.

Baking quickly turned into my safe place. Now if I'm stressed or anxious or even feeling lonely, I go to the bookshelf where I keep my cookbooks and trail my finger along their colorful spines, looking for inspiration.

On the day of the call, I was standing at my kitchen counter preparing to tackle one of Betsy Martin's most iconic creations: honey cake. I was deep into the planning stage and had an image of how I could decorate it, bees with almond sliver wings and spun sugar made to look like honeycomb.

It was an unfamiliar California number, and I almost didn't pick up. "Hello?" I asked suspiciously, expecting a recording to come on telling me about my plummeting credit score.

"Is this Stella Velasquez?" She sounded amped up, like I'd won something.

"It is. I mean, I am," I stuttered, surprised.

"This is Melanie Blaire, the *Bake Week* coordinator. I've called to tell you that you've got the job, you're going to be a contestant on the next season of *Bake Week*!"

I was so surprised I had to sit down, then stand up, then sit again.

The application had been weeks ago, mostly at the insistence of my best friend, Rebecca, who has eaten far more of my cakes and pastries than anyone else. We'd met for drinks at a new bar in Brooklyn.

"I'm paying," she said immediately as we slid into a plush pink booth. "I owe you for all the cakes and cookies you've given me."

I'd taken one look at the menu of cocktails, each more impressive than the last and priced accordingly, and knew she was taking pity on me.

"Are you paying me back or paying me to stop foisting them on you?"

"Both?" She laughed. "Seriously, though, Stel, you are an amazing baker. Better than anyone I know. You should apply for *Bake Week*."

Of course, I laughed her off. "What are you even talking about? Do you know how many people try to get into *Bake Week*?" I'd asked her.

"I dare you." She smiled her most winning smile. "What do you have to lose? As you said, they will never pick you. We're going to have one more drink, and then you're going to go back to your place and enter! Drinks on me for a month if you *don't* get chosen." I'd poked my straw into the lime in my gin and tonic and said I'd think it over. Later that evening, quite buzzed, I'd looked up the application online.

Bake Week's cheerful spoon and whisk logo popped onto my screen. I recognized the face of my favorite *Bake Week* winner holding the Golden Spoon on the homepage and clicked on the application tab. It wouldn't hurt to just fill out the form, no one had to know.

I was floored when I got the first callback, but by the time I'd made it to the second-round audition at a culinary school in Manhattan, I knew my time had come to an end. Melanie had not looked impressed when she bit into my passion fruit and lemon curd layer cake. I think she may have even winced. After I walked out, I texted Rebecca and told her to meet me at our bar. I'd needed a drink and to tell her how ridiculous she'd been forcing me to apply to begin with.

And then a few weeks later I got the call. Standing against my kitchen counter phone in hand, I wondered if this could really be true? I felt a giddy anxiousness fill my body. It was followed by the strange sensation that maybe, finally, something wonderful was about to happen to me. When I hung up the phone, I realized that I was holding Betsy Martin's cookbook. I knew then that it was a sign. Betsy Martin was truly helping me. She had been there for me these past eight months, in the reruns of her old cooking show, in episodes of *Bake Week*, and in her cookbooks. She pulled me through my darkest spells with her brisk optimism and can-do attitude. "This recipe seems daunting, but you can't look at the whole picture, just go step by step," she said once. I took in all her words as much more than advice for making macarons. "Step by step" had become my mantra over the past year. Betsy was my guide, helping me not become overwhelmed. It isn't an exaggeration to say that the prospect of baking one of Betsy Martin's recipes motivated me to get out of bed on some mornings.

"Fifteen minutes left!" Archie's voice booms through the tent.

I open my oven and feel the panic start to rise in my chest as I pull my bread out and set it on a counter. It will need to cool before I can pull it out of the pan. Will I have enough time? I close my eyes for just a moment, breathing deeply. *You can do this, Stella, step by step.*

GERALD

I have always believed that to truly do something well you need to go back to its essence and learn its basics. Just as Picasso didn't paint in the abstract until he had mastered portraits and still life, I believe it is unwise to skip learning the fundamentals of proper baking and go straight to vanilla-glazed mille-feuilles. I see the others around me attempting filled rolls and braided loafs. They've instantly gone for flashy breads and garish flavor combinations. It's a classic case of style over substance. Why focus on fillings when you don't have the right bake or texture? I suspect that many of their techniques will fail due to lack of basic skill. Bread is not forgiving. You can't hide a bad rise behind a dusting of parmesan or an uneven bake inside an elaborate design. That is why I have chosen breads that are very simple and very classic—a herbed boule, with a fast rise and a good thick crust of sesame seeds and classic cinnamon buns.

I'm deeply focused on perfectly rolling each bun and packing them into a baking tray so they can be pulled apart for serving, when out of the corner of my eye I notice Archie approaching my table. This will be his third time talking to me today. When I budgeted my time at the beginning of the bake, I hadn't accounted for forced host interactions. One of the producers even asked if I would re-stir something

I had just mixed so they could get it on camera. Most certainly not, I thought. Inefficiency is my largest pet peeve, but I knew I needed to be more flexible for the show, so I'd swallowed my pride and pretended I was stirring it for the first time. It's a good thing they were just dry ingredients, or I really would have refused. I will not compromise the integrity of my dough for a cheap shot.

"Gerald," Archie says, drawing out the sound of my name as though we are close friends. "What are you making for us today?"

I don't look up at first. I'm rolling my last bun, and if I lose my grip on the dough, I could cause this section to be uneven. I consider telling him that it's not a good time, but then I remember the guidelines in our dossier which explained that it was part of our work here to interact with the hosts and camera crew when they came by our tables. So I stretch my face into a congenial expression that feels tight and unnatural.

"This is an herb boule." I gesture to the oven where my dough is still proving.

"Can we see it to get a quick shot?" Archie asks. I hesitate but slide the drawer open for just a moment, releasing a warm yeasty plume into the air, and then quickly slide it shut. It leaves behind the fragrance of parsley, cilantro, and basil, some of the herbs I've mixed into my boule.

"And these are my cinnamon buns. I've used my own hand-ground rye flour to balance the sweetness and specially sourced Vietnamese cinnamon and just a touch of cardamom." The people with the cameras hover above my baking pan. They are crowding me, and I worry that one will accidentally disturb the dough I've spent so much time sculpting. I fight the urge to ask them to step back a few paces.

"The cinnamon rolls look lovely. And the rye is an interesting choice. I'm excited to see how that turns out. But a true boule, though, in such a short time?" Archie whistles under his breath, shaking his head as though I'm attempting to do something very dangerous.

"It's a short rise. It works because I use a full tablespoon of yeast and I bake it inside a preheated cast-iron Dutch oven."

He gives me a half smile, which I simply cannot read. Is he mocking me, or is that what his face looks like when he's trying to be nice?

"It looks like a beautiful dough, Gerald, and I like that you used so many types of fresh herbs. I'll be impressed if it works." I feel a stab of irritation. Doesn't he understand? Of course it will work. It was tested. Many times. Anxiously I blink into the cameras, forgetting for a moment another one of the rules gone over in the dossier in addition to our prefilming orientation this morning—*Do not look directly at the cameras.* How easy it was to break rules here even when you didn't mean to.

I quickly look back at my breads. I'll need nearly all the remaining two and a half hours to allow for everything to rise and bake properly. "All the variables have been accounted for," I retort, confident I've put an end to this conversation.

HANNAH

"It's the moment of truth," Archie says, leaning over to check on my bread as I pull it from the oven.

I am aware of the cameras watching me, so I let my hair fall into my face playfully as I pull my rolls out of the oven. They're perfectly baked, golden brown on the edges. The chai-spiced filling bubbling to just caramelized.

Archie looks them over and his head dips approvingly, a smile stretching across his face. "Those look . . . very good."

I laugh, pleased with myself, and pull a bowl out of the cupboard in my baking table to begin my icing.

"What kind of icing will you be putting on these?" Archie asks, his face serious as though it's a problem on a quiz. Out of the corner of my eye, I see Melanie watching from the side of the tent. I know that it's her job to keep track of what's going on at all times, but still, there is something about her that makes me uneasy. She's not a friendly person. I disliked her the moment she introduced herself when I first arrived at Grafton. I could feel her judging me, looking me over with her cool stare. She is so shiny and put together, thinks she is so important. I saw the look on her face as she took my phone away then, how she smirked at my glitter case. She probably thinks I am just some little baby, playing grown-up. I try to brush her opinions of me aside. What does she matter anyway? Right now, I need to focus on Archie and looking good for the cameras.

I put a hand to my heart in mock horror at there even being a question. "Cream cheese frosting, of course! But I'll add some of my favorite spices to make it sing!"

His face breaks out into a full grin. I've passed the test. I can feel my body relaxing. "Well, they smell incredible."

I look at him sideways just to make sure he's not teasing me. But his face is earnest as he gazes down at the cooling rack. Archie is more handsome in person than I'd expected. He's just a bit older looking off- than he is on-screen—a few wrinkles fan out around his eyes and two deeper lines cut through his cheeks and curve around his chin. They all just serve to make him more attractive. His skin is remarkably smooth otherwise, almost pore-less. I wonder what kind of products he uses. Could he have had work done? I know I am in an entirely different world than where I've come from. Back in Eden Lake, no one has had any sort of plastic surgery.

"And they'll be even better once I get this icing on them." I laugh. "You just wait, you won't be able to keep your hands off them!" *Oh my god, was that too much?* I watch as his lips break into a boyish smile. If I've overdone it, he doesn't seem to mind. I'm beyond flattered that Archie Morris wants to eat something that I've baked. I look down at my tray admiringly—this batch did turn out very well. Golden on the edges, soft in the centers. I find myself feeling strangely confident. It's a new sensation, and it takes me by surprise. I can win this.

"I can't wait," he says.

Neither can I, Archie. The cameras move on to gather around Pradyumna's baking table. Before he turns to go, Archie gives me a wink. I feel myself flushing. If it weren't a completely ridiculous idea, I would think that he is flirting with me.

PETER

"Bakers, put down your utensils!" Archie booms from the front of the room, giving me a heart palpitation despite the comforting fact that my bake is already done. I take a step back from my table, putting my palms up just in case anyone should think I wasn't following orders. I've been doing nothing but waiting these past five minutes, confounded that I'm finished ahead of the others and trying to make sure I haven't missed anything as I watch them rush around. It's been interesting to watch the atmosphere in the tent turn, the mood slipping quickly from amiable to anxious. You can practically feel the adrenaline flowing through the tent.

Next to me, Stella scrambles to get a last detail right on her cutting board, and I feel a flash of annoyance. *The time is up, so why do you think the rules don't apply to you?* I think uncharitably. But then, this is a competition, even if it doesn't come across that way on television.

"Please bring your breads to the front of the tent and place them on the judging table," Betsy says. By now things are quiet, the tension in the room heavy as the six of us catch our breath and stare at the judge's table.

I scoop up my tray of bread and bring it forward. I'm proud of what I've done today. My baking tray is piled high with a stack of soft spiraled bread shaped like cornucopias. I've piped them full of a thick chocolate custard. A shiny dark chocolate drizzle crisscrosses the top. Next to them, sliced in even rows is my pepper and cheddar babka. They are both precise, their sizes even, each braid and twist neat and purposeful. I pride myself for my attention to detail. It is what gives me a leg up in my work in restoration and the key to my most successful bakes. I place the tray down on the judging table behind the placard with my name on it. I feel myself brimming with confidence as I peek at the other contestants' breads. With the exception of Gerald's sesame-encrusted herb boule and meticulous cinnamon buns, mine are the prettiest and neatest of the bunch.

I step back, standing in line with the other five, and wait to be judged. Betsy and Archie take their places on the other side of the table. I breathe a long, shaky breath. First breads up on the table are Stella's. She steps forward to the table nervously. I watch as Betsy and Archie put their first bites into their mouths, chew. I am relieved when they don't sigh in pleasure. Betsy puts her fork down and looks across at Stella, who watches her adoringly, her hands clasped in front of her. "I think it's good, but you could have done more with the flavors. Didn't you say you used miso?"

Stella's face falls a bit. "Perhaps I should have used more."

"Yes, I agree," Archie says. "The texture is there, but the flavor just isn't coming through."

They move on to her rolls, which go over about the same. "Technically it's very good, you just need to be braver with the spices," Betsy concludes.

It's not the worst assessment, but I see Stella shrug sadly as she steps back into the line. I hold my breath as they move on to my bread.

"Oh, I love a babka, and this one is very well baked," Archie says, taking a bite.

"And look at this pattern." Betsy taps on the top of the loaf with her fork. "Just beautiful. I love the way this tastes, Peter. Terrific work." I beam. I am proud of how steady my hand has been today.

The result has been even better than any I've done at home without a soul watching.

"Now the chocolate horns." I watch with excitement as Betsy picks one up and puts the chocolate-custard-filled end into her mouth. Her lips close and her eyes open wide in surprise. My heart drops as her face twists into a grimace.

"Oh, gosh, what's wrong?" I ask weakly, instantly regretting saying anything at all. It's a problem of mine, talking too much when I'm nervous.

I get no response anyway and watch in horror as Betsy turns her head away from my bread as though it has offended her. She flutters a hand at Archie, her mouth puckered theatrically.

"Water," she gasps. *Surely it can't be that bad.*

Archie snaps a finger at his PA, who scrambles for a bottle of Fiji. It's passed to Betsy, who takes several long, desperate gulps. I can feel my face flush. My ears are probably bright red. I try not to think of the cameras capturing this from all angles for posterity.

"Did you use salt in this in place of sugar?" Betsy finally chokes out. She says it in as kind a way as is possible for someone who just ate a mouthful of salty chocolate.

"Not on purpose." It's all I can say. I feel the ground opening beneath me. All I want is to curl up and disappear into it. I've just fed Betsy Martin a cornucopia full of creamy salt! I might throw up. She looks like she might too. I've never been so mortified in my life.

Archie shakes his head. "I'm not going to try that then, sorry, man," he says. He puts his fork down onto the table with a devastating clink.

"Such a shame, Peter. It looks so lovely," Betsy says, her voice still a bit hoarse. "You'd never know if you hadn't tasted it."

I retreat from the table, falling back into line with the others. My cheeks are burning with embarrassment. As Betsy and Archie move on to the other contestants' bread, I glance back at the canisters of white crystals on my baking table. They are two different sizes. I'd assumed the larger was sugar and the smaller salt. That's how these things are always organized. I even pressed my finger into some of the grains and tasted them at the beginning to be sure. I should have double-checked and tried a taste of my filling like I normally do at home. Then I would have been able to start over again. But I hadn't wanted to seem like I wasn't confident, or for a camera to catch me grotesquely eating raw batter. I glance at Melanie standing in the shadows at the edge of the tent. Her arms are crossed, and her hair is pulled back into its slick bun. She notices me watching her and gives her head a fierce little shake, circling her finger for me to turn back around to face the cameras. I do as I'm told.

As soon as judging is over, I plunge my hand inside the larger canister on my baking table, grabbing a pinch and sprinkling it into my mouth. My eyes tear up as the sharp bite of salt fizzles on my tongue.

BETSY

After judging has finished and the contestants have filed out of the tent, Betsy makes her way back to the house. She is relieved to be finished with day one, happy to be on her way to an evening of relaxation. As she walks, she already is unbuttoning her jacket, anticipating the feel of putting on a silk pajama set, wrapping up in her cashmere robe, sliding her feet into their soft slippers. She is ready for some quiet, away from everyone, a small early supper and a glass of brandy in her study. Perhaps she'll even watch something inane on television.

As she crosses the foyer, she remembers with dismay the empty brandy bottle on her upstairs bar cart. She could ring the housekeeper and ask her to bring up another, but it would probably be faster to just go and get one herself. She sighs and turns off into a hallway. The wine cellar is just past Grafton's kitchen. This part of the house sits lower than the rest, with stone floors that stay cool even in summer. She used to love walking on them with her bare feet as a child—secretly of course, her mother would never let her run around without her stockings on. She loved the kitchen's cozy stone hearth and the sturdy farmhouse table, which was nearly as wide as the kitchen itself. She loved to run her hands along its worn surface, waiting to feel the dings of knife marks and little dips from years of heavy use. She was allowed to make a mess here as a child, and she spent countless happy afternoons shaping bread dough and rolling out pie crusts alongside the family's cook. Later she used the same kitchen to test out the recipes for her cookbooks. But once the show took off, it gobbled up her entire life and she rarely found herself down here. She couldn't remember the last time she had baked for pleasure the way she used to. The kitchen had once been a place of relaxation and peace. Everything was just so different now.

A man's voice coming from inside the kitchen startles her.

"You think it went all right today?"

Betsy pulls herself back, standing at the edge of the door. She can see Melanie standing in the kitchen. She's leaning back against the table, a mug of coffee steaming next to her. Betsy moves forward slightly and sees she is with that cameraman. The dark-haired one with the beard—Gordon or Graham—she can never remember their names.

"It was fine," Melanie says coolly. "Thanks to me. This would all be a total disaster without me, you realize. The show would be so boring, no one would even watch it." She leans back and pulls at her hair, undoing a pin in her bun and releasing a cascade of shiny brown hair down her back.

"Today was better than all of last season," the man says.

What on earth are they talking about? Betsy has half a mind to march into the kitchen and tell Melanie how little she has to do with the show being good. But then, she stops. She wonders if that is even true, or if Melanie has more to do with *Bake Week* than she'd like to give her credit for. She's allowed Melanie far more responsibility these last few seasons. She's even given her the final say in choosing the bakers, a task Betsy had always prided herself on doing on her own.

"I hope so," Melanie says, picking up her mug. "I wonder why I even chose some of them. I'm glad the idiotic lumberjack is leaving. He was way too fucking nice. It was so boring."

Peter? What would Melanie have against Peter? That he isn't good television? Betsy sees the man's big hand clamp onto Melanie's shoulder. "You're not appreciated like you should be. You do everything around here." She leans into his embrace. Betsy hopes that Melanie isn't having some sort of relationship with him. Surely, she has better judgment than that.

"I have worked my ass off for that woman. But she doesn't even see it. I honestly don't know *what* she notices these days," and as Melanie taps her pointer finger on her temple, Betsy's mouth drops open. When Melanie speaks again her voice is icy and determined. "This year I am going to finally get what I deserve."

Oh, these young people. What does she want? A medal for doing her job? Betsy's teeth clench and she shakes her head back and forth. *No, no, no, Miss Melanie. This is* my *house. My* show. *A bit more respect would be suitable from someone who was a nobody assistant until about five minutes ago.* It was Betsy who had helped Melanie, not the other way around. She had given her opportunities most assistants would only dream of. It was good to know who Melanie really was and that she wasn't to be trusted. Not that Betsy ever really trusts most people anyway. Given half a chance, Betsy knows that just about anyone is likely to disappoint her.

She thinks of her mother. Josephina Grafton would never have allowed such impudence at Grafton. She knew that you had to keep a tight rein on all the house staff, to keep track of what they were up to and with who. Betsy likes to remember the house as it was when both of her parents were alive, before the responsibility of caring for it fell to her. Back then there was a whole staff of people keeping Grafton afloat. There was a gardener on sight, a nanny for Betsy, three different maids, and a live-in cook. Her mother demanded perfection. She was a stickler for detail and never missed when the staff were sloppy or cut corners.

Because of that the house was always spotless, the gardens perfectly manicured for when they'd host the upper society of New England or people her father knew from his banking days in New York. Her parents often had guests stay at the manor. She remembers being allowed into the parlor as a child, wearing starched taffeta dresses and sitting primly next to her parents as they drank martinis and mingled with their guests. Betsy was never allowed to stay for the dinners, but she remembers coming down during cocktail hour and seeing the table laid with silver, the crystal glasses catching the light. Sometimes she would sneak out of bed and down to the landing, crouching on the stairs to listen in on the adults' conversations. Occasionally someone would play the piano and her father would sing some upbeat tune that would make everyone laugh loudly. You could always tell a good party when her father was singing. That was when she was very young, though. The fancy dinners mostly stopped by the time she turned twelve. Times were changing, and trips to old houses like hers were already falling out of fashion. Nothing at Grafton was the same as it had been.

Remembering all this makes her feel even more in desperate need of a drink. She moves away from the kitchen doorway and retreats back through the hallway to the stairs, where she climbs her way to her familiar East Wing. But without brandy. She'll ring for some to be brought up to her instantly. It's what she should have done in the first place.

STELLA

The six of us are gathered around a fireplace in the library. Everyone is holding a glass of wine except Pradyumna, who is enthusiastically drinking scotch from an etched tumbler. I'm sitting in a wingback chair next to the fireplace. My shoes are off, and I'm pointing my socked toes toward the hearth, trying to warm up. It was hot and humid out there today, but the temperature has dropped, something about these thick stone walls and being so deep in the forest. We are truly in the middle of nowhere. It's enough to make a city girl nervous. I push the thought away and take a sip of wine.

"To Gerald! Congratulations on your win," Peter says, raising a glass. He's being so gracious, I think, given the situation. It can't be easy sitting here and knowing he's the first one to go home. Especially considering the circumstances. Salt instead of sugar? It just doesn't make any sense. None of the rest of us had salt in the larger cannister.

"It's really just a matter of making proper measurements," Gerald demurs. His fastidiousness would be obnoxious if it wasn't so clear that he just can't help himself. He must love facts the way the rest of us love people. I hold up my wineglass and lean forward, clinking with the others. The wine at Grafton, just like everything else, is impeccable. I take a big velvety sip.

"I'm really sorry to see you go, Peter," I say. And I realize it's true—I am sad that Peter is leaving. It's amazing how just a day of being in the tent together bonds you to each other. I know that if not for salt-gate, I'd be the one heading home tomorrow. My breads were not up to par. They were not thought out or well planned, and bread doesn't forgive. I take another big sip, attempting to clear my head and forget that look on Betsy's face. Not disappointment, thankfully. I don't think I could bear that. But certainly not the delighted smile I'd been longing for. The others' breads showed me how inexperienced I am. Today was humbling, and I am happy and relieved to make it through to another day, whatever the reason.

I tip the last of my glass back and reach for the bottle sitting on the low coffee table in the center of all of us. I don't know if it is the wine or the relief of today being over, but I have a warm feeling running through me. Whichever way it happened, by whatever miracle, I am thrilled that I've made it into day two of the competition. I promise myself that I'll do better tomorrow.

"I still can't believe I mistook salt for sugar. I swear I even tasted it before I poured it in. Oh well, I guess it's just my time to go," Peter says. He puts on a brave face, but it is easy to see that he is unsettled.

"An easy mistake to make. I'm surprised it wasn't me, to be honest," Pradyumna says from across the circle.

"It's not hard if you look at the grain size," says Gerald, ignoring Peter's irritated glance. Gerald seems to be enjoying his wine as well. His bow tie is undone and hangs loosely around his collar. "Baking salt is generally finer than sugar."

"Duly noted, Gerald! Now let's all let the man celebrate his last night with us in peace," says Lottie kindly.

Hannah is perched on a settee next to Lottie, holding her wine-glass in her lap. She looks uncomfortable, and she's hardly spoken all night. It must be hard being the youngest of all of us. I can see how worried she is about the way people view her; I know this feeling. We always glamorize youth as we get older, but at that age all you want is to look grown-up, even if you don't feel it—especially if you don't feel it.

"So, are we all prepared for tomorrow?" Lottie asks, looking around the group and cringing as her gaze lands on Peter. "Sorry, Peter."

"I'm fine." He hams it up, tipping back his glass of wine, dramatically draining the dregs.

"What do you think the next bake will be?" I ask, the nervous feeling returning to my stomach. I've almost forgotten there is more, that it is going to start all over again every day until I am sent home. It suddenly feels exhausting.

"I hope it's pies, or maybe tarts," Hannah quips.

Pradyumna smirks and sloshes his scotch in his glass. "I love a good tart."

I know it's a dumb joke, but the wine is making me giggly, and suddenly I can't stop laughing. I lock eyes with Pradyumna across the room. His face is crinkled up in amusement. God, he's good-looking. Probably knows it too. *No, you stay away from that one, Stella. You don't need any more trouble in that department.*

It's hard to believe it has been only one day since we arrived. I already feel as though I know this group. Like we've been through something together.

"It's nice to have a break from the real world, isn't it?" Peter says, looking around at us, his eyes shining.

"Here, here." Pradyumna holds out his glass again and takes a sip. It *is* nice to get away. The week is going to fly by, I realize sadly. *Bake Week* has given me something to focus on. I worry what I'll do once it's over. I try to push away thoughts of going home, of the job I'll have to find once this is over. *Stay in the present,* I tell myself. *Pies and tarts.*

"Well, I'm turning in." Lottie stands up suddenly.

"She's off to get a good night's sleep, unlike the rest of us. That's cheating, Lottie!" Pradyumna admonishes her playfully, shaking a fist at her as she goes.

"You all better watch out, I'm a terror in the kitchen when I've slept well," Lottie teases back, picking up her empty glass from the table and heading for the hallway. I feel so affectionately toward her after how she helped me find my way yesterday. I can't believe this woman nearly gave me a heart attack. I do wonder what she was doing up in that room. It seems like an odd coincidence for us to both wander into the same spot lost.

"Good night, Lottie," I call after her. I can feel my lids getting heavy as well. The room grows quiet. I really should stop drinking now if I want to have a decent baking day tomorrow. The wine tastes so good, though, and I can feel its warmth traveling down my body. I'll just finish the rest of this glass.

A log cracks loudly in the fireplace, and I jump. "God, that startled me." I laugh at myself.

"It must be creepy living here all by yourself." I turn to look at Hannah, surprised by the sound of her voice. She has collapsed to her side and is leaning on the arm of the settee. Her eyes look droopy with that heavy liner, and I worry suddenly that we've all encouraged her to drink too much. That's silly, though. As young as she is, she's not a child. I'm sure she's spent plenty of nights out with her friends, and she doesn't need a bunch of older people to tell her what her limits are.

"Betsy isn't technically alone," Gerald chimes in with that paternal voice again. "There are five staff members who live on the premises."

Annoyance flashes across Hannah's face. "But I mean, they're not, technically, her *friends*." She looks around the library. "And don't they leave at night? It's not like there's anyone to watch a movie with, and this house is just so big." The fire is growing low, but no one makes a move to add any wood to it. It's getting late, I realize. We should all go to bed. Tomorrow is going to be another big day.

"I tell you, I won't be sad to leave behind all the weird noises," Hannah says suddenly, interrupting my thoughts.

Pradyumna perks up. "Oh yeah? What noises?"

"I swear I could hear someone walking around above me last night." She talks in a loud whisper, like she's afraid the house will hear her. "But when I asked Melanie about it in the morning, she said no one was staying on the fourth floor."

"I was wondering about the fourth floor," Pradyumna says. His face is in shadow, but his glass of scotch catches the light, glowing a rich amber as though lit from within. "Has anyone seen a staircase that goes up there?"

"Well, there must be one," I say dismissively. I haven't explored the house much on my own after getting lost, preferring to stick to my known routes through the house to the dining room and kitchen. "Maybe it's hidden."

"Traditionally the top floors are servants' quarters," Peter says. "The stairs are usually at the end of the halls, rather than connected to the main staircase. You know, tucked away so that the help didn't have to be seen."

"So gross," I interject, rolling my eyes.

"Victorians." Peter shrugs.

"I looked all over the third floor and didn't see anything," Pradyumna says. "Odd, isn't it? Having a floor no one can reach?"

The corners of the library have grown dark and shadowy as the logs in the fireplace crackle. I feel an unpleasant shudder pass through me and try not to think of getting lost earlier. The room grows quiet. Are we all listening for creaks in the floorboards? Pradyumna's finger traces the top of his empty glass. I see his eyes flutter to the liquor cabinet, trying to gauge if he should pour himself another.

"I renovated a haunted house once," Peter says.

"Improbable," Gerald quips. But the others lean forward in their chairs.

"Really? How did you know?" Hannah asks, her voice so soft that it's nearly a whisper.

I pull my feet in closer on the chair, tucking them under me. The blood rushes in my ears.

"It was the usual stuff at first—things moving, weird scraping sounds. But then there was the shape on the wall."

My heart lurches, and I suddenly wish he would stop talking. I have this thing, this problem. If I feel afraid, I just black out. One minute I'll be fine, and then suddenly my heart is pounding out of my chest and my body just shuts down. It nearly happened yesterday, but talking to Lottie helped pull me out of it.

It's funny because I used to love scaring myself. I considered reading horror novels and watching true crime documentaries about gruesome murders a fun way to pass time. Now I can't watch a scary movie or get into an elevator alone without it happening. Sometimes I even feel it start when my thoughts turn dark on the way through my apartment to the bathroom at night. I know when it's coming because I'll experience a shift. First my eyesight goes fuzzy around the edges and then narrows into a dark tunnel. My body will start to feel very heavy and then like it is floating away from me. The next thing I know, I'm waking up on a floor somewhere, with no memory of what happened.

I breathe in deeply, trying to fight it. I would be so embarrassed if I just passed out in front of these people I barely know.

"What kind of shadow? Where did you see it?" Hannah asks, her voice sounding far away.

Peter leans in. "I was redoing a stairwell of a very old house. I'd removed an old chandelier to clean it. It was a heavy one, loaded with crystals. The shadow was on the landing wall near the bottom set of stairs. It looked like a figure. At first, I thought it was a breeze blowing through the drapes from the window on the landing. But then one completely cloudy day, I saw it. The shadow of a figure swaying back and forth. It looked like it was floating. I jerked around looking for a curtain or something moving that would've been blocking or affecting the light, but nothing."

The edges of my vision start to blur.

"That's too creepy!" Hannah's voice slices through the air next to me.

"Did you find out where it was coming from?" Pradyumna asks.

"Not exactly, but I did do some digging. Turned out a past owner had hung himself in the stairwell. *From the chandelier.* I put the chandelier back up and never saw the shadow again."

"That is wild!" Pradyumna slaps his knee, the ice cubes rattling in his glass.

"Well, I should go to bed," I say as brightly as possible, attempting to hide my strange reaction, but I stand up quickly, too quickly. My head spins, and I grab the back of the chair to keep from falling over.

"Are you okay?" Peter jumps to his feet, reaching out to me.

"Fine, fine! I just probably shouldn't have had that last glass of wine." I wave his concern away with a sweaty palm, a smile plastered on my face. At least I hope it looks like a smile. I suddenly want nothing more than to get into bed. I try to keep my voice light. "Today was a lot. You all are going to crush me tomorrow if I don't get some rest."

"You okay getting to your room?" Peter asks.

"I'm great. Thanks, good night, everyone!" But I'm not okay, not really. I leave the library and stagger down the hallway, trying not to look into the eyes of the creepy portraits staring down at me, lining the brocade-covered wall. *One foot in front of the other, Stella, step by step.* I watch each foot make contact with the polished wood floor. As I walk, I count backward in my head: *Ten, nine, eight, seven, six.* Very slowly my vision begins to return to normal. I go upstairs and walk down the narrow hallway to my room. *Five, four, three, two, one.*

"A reaction to a trauma," a therapist called my blackouts. "Until we address what's happened to you," she'd said gently to me at one of our few sessions, "these spells will continue to occur." I'd stopped seeing her soon after. Counting was the only idea of hers I took with me when I left, and it is the only thing that helps take my body out of panic mode. When I focus on the numbers, it transports me straight into the present moment, jerking me out of whatever fear state I've entered. It is the only thing that works. Well, the only thing besides baking.

I didn't need therapy if I had baking, I reasoned. I avoided applying for new jobs and instead spent my time learning how to frost cakes, pipe filling into cream puffs, and knead perfect bread loaves. With baking you are forced to exist only in the moment or whatever you are making won't turn out. There was no fear in baking, I told myself. A lie, probably.

I get to my room, flinging the door open. I half expect to see some sort of ghost, perhaps a man dangling from the ceiling, but the room is quiet and still except for a curtain moving slightly in the breeze. I rush to the window and shut it, closing the latch, and turn back to the bed with its garden green canopy. I fall into it, leaving the bedside light switched on and tucking the covers up to my chin, counting backward until I fall asleep.

HANNAH

Halfway through my second glass of wine, I realize that every alcohol I've ever tried before was actual swill—the beers that Ben drinks, the flavored vodka that Mom loves mixed with diet Sprite, the hard seltzer my friend Emma keeps in the backseat of her car, and drinks warm from the can.

I always told them how much I hate drinking, but I see now that I only hated drinking crap. I like this wine. I can feel it hitting my bloodstream, mellowing me out. The inside of my head is pleasant fizzy. I never understood the point of alcohol, never felt drunk like this before. But now I have a rising sense of euphoria, a feeling like I'm floating.

I walk back toward my room slowly, swinging myself around on the banister as I climb up the stairs. I allow myself to pretend I live here at Grafton. In my imagination I'm friends with Betsy Martin. On the landing I look to the double doors of the East Wing longingly. Would it be so bad just to have a little peek? I stroll up to the door and peer through the glass at the long wood-paneled hallway. I put my hand on the shiny gold handle. It is cool to the touch. Nothing like the chintzy doorknobs in my apartment. *No*, I scold myself. *Just go back before you get into trouble.* As I spin around to go back to the West Wing, I run full force into Archie Morris.

"Whoop! Where you heading there, champ?" He chuckles kindly as I stumble backward, taking me by the shoulder to keep me from falling. I feel his warm hand on my collarbone. It's broad and steadying. I laugh, the vague realization that I might be embarrassed about this tomorrow sloshes around in my head, but I smile and ignore it.

"Oh, I was just going to my room. Trying to, anyway." The words leave my mouth like balloons.

"I think your room is the other way," Archie says. He's trying to be helpful, I think.

"I wasn't going to go in there, just looking," I say. The wine is making me warm inside. I don't want to go to bed anymore.

"Whoa! Easy there, partner." Archie's grip tightens. I think I must be falling over a bit, because suddenly I'm leaned up against him, my shoulder against his chest. I know logically that I shouldn't be touching Archie Morris. That it would be frowned upon for a contestant to behave this way with a host. This is why people like drinking, I think to myself. It's a shocking realization. Alcohol makes you not care about the repercussions of what you are doing. I like it. I can smell Archie's cologne more strongly than earlier. It's like the wine was—complex. Rich. I just want to be near it.

"Easy, yourself," I say. I look straight up. I can see the stubble already forming on his chin after a day of filming. It's gray in patches. I expect him to set me straight, to send me to my room, but he doesn't move. "What's it like over there?" I stage-whisper, leaning into him. "In the *East* Wing."

"Oh, you know, piles of diamonds, closets full of champagne. You'd hate it." He smiles slyly, only half of his mouth rising up his cheek.

I grin up at him, delighted. "How do *you* know what I'd hate?"

His eyebrows shoot up, amused. I imagine telling my mom about this later, how she will squeal with delight. "No, you did not say that!" she'll shriek.

"Good point," he says. I feel my heart sink as he steps away, cool air replacing the warmth of his arm. Now he's going to tell me to be a good kid and run along. He glances behind him at the door, then runs his eyes up and down the staircase. All are empty and quiet. When he talks, his voice is low and conspiratorial. "I tell you what, I'll give you a peek at the East Wing, but you have to promise me you won't tell anyone. Can you keep a secret?"

I lock my lips with an invisible key and follow Archie up the staircase.

PRADYUMNA

"I'm sorry, man." We are the last two in the library. Several empty wine bottles sit between us on the table. Peter is clearly heartbroken to be going home so soon. I can locate where that feeling would exist, I think, though I've never actually felt it. Heartbreak is for people who don't have my kind of resources.

"I just can't believe I did that to her." He looks down into his empty glass like he's committed a crime for which there will be no repentance.

"What, to Betsy?" I scoff. "She ate a little salt, she'll survive." Honestly, the way these people treat that woman like she is some sort of deity is a bit much. I didn't really watch *Bake Week* before I got here. I never quite understood the obsession. It's a cute enough show but not really my idea of entertainment. I like my television to have a bit more edge, an explosion or two, something to keep me engaged or I'll get bored. I've moved on to wine and reach for a fresh bottle, inspecting the label. "Care for some more wine? This is a lovely Montepulciano."

I open it and offer Peter the bottle, but he shakes his head.

"Suit yourself," I say. He watches the ruby liquid slosh into my glass and shrugs, lifting his glass up in surrender.

"I guess why not have another, right? Might as well enjoy my last night here. It's not like I have to bake tomorrow or anything."

"That's the spirit." I fill him up.

Peter leans back, looking into the fire. "Too bad. I finally figure out the house, and it's no longer useful."

"What do you mean?" I perk up.

He glances behind him at the door and then leans forward as if he is going to impart some sort of confidential information.

"Well I didn't want to tell the others but you know how the stairs don't go past the third floor?" he asks, his voice hushed.

I shake my head eagerly. I have to say, I am intrigued by Peter's little mystery. "Yes, it doesn't make sense. I was noticing that while I was walking around the other night."

"Exactly. Well, I had this theory that the staircase exists, I mean it must. Well, after dinner, Gerald showed me these blueprints he'd brought to Grafton, and I was right. According to the plans, there are stairs at the end of the hall. But now it's just a wall."

"You mean that hallway our rooms are on, the dead end?"

Peter nods.

"You think the stairs might be there still?"

"Unless they took them out completely."

"You think they would've done that?"

"It's possible. But it wouldn't make much sense. You'd want to be able to have a way to reach that floor just for safety. You can't just leave part of a house to decay."

"Do you think there's a way up inside the East Wing?"

"I suppose there could be an entrance there. Impossible to say, really." He looks like he is losing interest. His eyes are glassy and tired. Mentally he is already packing his bags, planning his route home.

In the fireplace the last flame snuffs out, leaving just a few glowing embers. The clock above the mantel says it's just after midnight. The others have all gone to bed, each of them nervous about the competition tomorrow. Funny, I feel no anxiety about it at all. I rarely do. Sometimes I wonder if that should worry me, if I have some sort of deficiency.

"Ughhh," Peter groans. "I better get to bed. Long drive in the morning." He pulls himself up off the sofa. Though I know it is probably expected of me, I make no move to follow.

"You go ahead, I'll be up soon. I'm a bit of an insomniac."

Still, I suppose bed is in the cards for me. I pour just a pinky finger of scotch into my empty wineglass—Betsy Martin really does know how to stock a liquor cabinet—and retreat down the hall toward my room. I may not be a longtime fan of *Bake Week* (even if I do truly enjoy the satisfaction of a well-constructed bake), but this whole experience—temporary lodging in a manor, TV appearances, interacting with a group of strangers—it's too novel to ignore all the trappings for the sake of competition. This is the fun part. Winning would be lovely, but my imperative is to appreciate this experience while I've got it.

I walk slowly, admiring the art on the walls as I sip. Most of it is not my thing, honestly. If I'm going to go mainstream, I prefer edgier work—your Cindy Shermans and Anselm Kiefers. This feels very colonial—lots of sheep in meadows with mansions in the distance, women in unflattering dresses staring pensively out of the canvas.

One painting gives me pause. A smallish canvas painted in rich, dark hues with visible brushstrokes that show the confidence of the painter. At first it doesn't seem like much subject-wise—it's just a portrait of a woman. She sits in a high-backed chair, her fingers long and bony, clutching tensely at the arms. It is her face that is most intriguing. The mouth, heart-shaped and delicate, is at rest, but the eyes are hard and intense, the chin tilted as though in challenge to the artist, almost as if there is cold fury lurking beneath them. Stranger still, I realize, that I find this woman somehow familiar.

I will have to ask the others what they think tomorrow. I carry on to my room, past the vacant stare of the suits of armor and up the main staircase to where the stairs split off in two directions. To the left, the door to Betsy Martin's East Wing quarters beckons me with its twisted brass door handles. I take the steps up toward them, tempted. With a sigh, I turn back to the landing, carrying on to the guest wing. I'm just about to open the door to my room, when I see a figure crossing the hall ahead. The person is wearing a long robe and moves from left to right and back again, zigzagging their way down the hallway. I wonder at first if they are drunk. But their movements are purposeful, not sloppy. Their hands reach out, skimming the wall, then turning and doing the same on the other side.

I move up behind them, ducking into a doorway to better observe. Now that I'm closer I can see the puff of gray hair. I thought Lottie went up to bed hours ago. I wonder for a moment if she is sleepwalking. But she turns her head, glancing down the hallway as if afraid of being caught. I press myself farther back inside the doorframe. She turns back and walks away from me silently down the hallway. Occasionally she stops to just put her hand against a wall and leave it there. I continue to watch her move down the hallway, trailing her fingers on the wall. *What on earth is she doing?* I think of what Peter said about the missing stairwell. Could she have overheard us? I'm tempted to step out into the hall and say something, but I don't want to startle her. Plus, I have a pleasant buzzing in my head, and I know that sleep, for once, will come easy. I'll leave it until the morning. I turn back to my room and tip back my glass, letting the rest of the beautiful scotch dissolve around my tongue.

Day Two

PIE

BETSY

Despite the early hour, the air is already hot and sticky as Betsy walks toward the tent. She feels agitated, uncomfortable and itchy in her skirt with its matching blazer. Betsy looks to the side of the tent where Melanie is doing some last-minute adjustments with the crew. It's going to be a miserable day for baking. Nothing rises or chills correctly in this kind of weather. There will be some difficulties today, she can count on it. Surely the network will love the drama, but that's not what is bothering her. What's really on her mind is the text message she received this morning from Francis.

I'm driving up tomorrow. We have things to discuss. What time can you meet? Francis, her longtime agent and biggest advocate, is a creature of Manhattan. He loathes the countryside, hates driving. He wouldn't come all the way up to Grafton unless it was extremely important. She'd tried to lure more out of him, but he'd demurred. *It's better we talk in person. Away from you-know-who.* It is that last part that makes her nervous. Away from Archie?

She glances over at her new cohost. He's standing at the ready looking fresh and sharp in a slim-fitting button-up shirt, that interminable smile already plastered across his face. She hates to give him any credit, but he's adapted remarkably well to the way things are done here. There's not even a hint of the brutish judge he played on *The Cutting Board*, which makes her believe that Archie is just as good of an actor as he is a baker. The contestants seem to genuinely love him, and he defers to her often, which she appreciates even if doesn't feel quite genuine. His presence in the tent has taken some of the pressure off her, she must grudgingly admit, and she does feel lighter not having to radiate the full wattage of energy that the show requires. Whatever ego issues they had at first seem to have evaporated. If it weren't for Francis's cryptic text this morning, she might even feel almost *good* about how everything was going.

Betsy looks out at the five remaining contestants. They've done well this year finding people with different strengths and vastly different personalities. It should come across well on film. Hannah, doe-eyed and youthful, wearing a dress that is not entirely appropriate for a baking show, is the perfect contrast to Stella's wide-leg jeans and striped mariniere. Pradyumna with his lazy good looks and joke always at the ready, a foil to neurotic and buttoned-up Gerald. And Lottie, well, there always has to be a Lottie. To keep the field balanced, they always cast a senior for the others to look up to. She won't win, of course. They never do. Betsy sees Archie bouncing on his toes, making silly faces at the delighted bakers, and feels a tug of irritation. Her advancing age is a sore spot for her, and Archie's arrival has only made it more sensitive. Has she become too complacent, lost her edge? Before she has time to consider more deeply, Melanie waves, signaling that it's time to take their places for filming. She always has to be in charge. After what she heard yesterday in the kitchen, Betsy wonders if she has given Melanie too many opportunities, too much power in *her* tent. She should never have allowed Melanie to choose the bakers. That was Betsy's job, and it should have stayed that way. Now she wonders whether Melanie's obsequiousness was just an act.

Her transformation to shrewd businesswoman seems too quick to have not been calculated. What was her plan, to get Betsy to depend on her until she had the power to throw her under the bus? Betsy will have to find a way to cut her down to size. She takes a cue from her dear departed mother and vows to keep a better eye on her staff. But not this very moment. Right now, Betsy's task is to be as lovable and magnanimous for the cameras as humanly possible. She smooths her skirt, adjusting the string of pearls around her neck, and gets ready to shine.

"Good morning, bakers. Welcome back to the tent for day two of *Bake Week*. I hope all of you are well rested and ready to go for today's baking challenge."

Archie Morris bares his platinum smile. "Today you will be making us a summer meal in the form of . . ." He pauses, looking around the tent with his eyebrows raised theatrically. The contestants visibly tense as they wait for the final word, and she feels her own chest tighten as well. "Pies! One sweet and one savory. Your pies can be any shape, but as usual they must have at least one decorative element. We want these to reflect your own signature style, so do everything you can, in the time you have, to make them as unique and as wonderful as you are."

For God's sake, she thinks, watching him stand there and turn it on for the camera. It's obscene. She tries to shake it off. She must. She can't let his bluster rattle her. He'd love that too much. This is her show, no matter what Francis is coming to tell her. She's been baking since before Archie was born, and she's beloved for it. She's not going to let a buffoon like him stand in her way. No, Archie isn't the only one who is good at getting what he wants.

STELLA

I find I've been holding my breath, afraid I'll miss some important piece of information. I exhale heavily now as my mind whirs through the possibilities, pictures of different kinds of pies flashing before my eyes like the images on a slot machine.

I rush to my designated lilac colored refrigerator and look over the fresh produce stacked on the shelf. I could do cherry. Is a cherry pie too obvious, though? I wonder about giving it a layer of cheesecake. I discard the idea. I remember trying to bake one in my apartment last summer, and it was a nightmare. There's no way I could get it to set properly. I see a carton stacked with fresh peaches and take them out instead. I'll make it more interesting with a subtle note of fresh thyme. For the savory pie, my mind immediately sees a quiche. I'll make it with goat cheese and figs, like Zineb did in season five, but I'll mix up some za'atar spice and top it with a drizzle of spicy honey to finish.

I can't believe that I'm here another day in the *Bake Week* tent with Betsy Martin. Every time she walks past me, I want to reach out and hug her, to tell her how much she's meant to me. Before I arrived here, I always liked to imagine that we were actual friends. Now I play out a short fantasy in which Betsy invites me into the East Wing to have a drink and congratulate me on winning *Bake Week*. "What will you call your cookbook?" I imagine her asking as we clink champagne glasses. "Whatever you want to do next in your career, Stella, I am here to support you, to help you achieve those dreams." I shake myself out of it. *Focus, focus.* I need to make these pies if I want to get anywhere with Betsy.

It's hard though when there are so many distractions everywhere. For example, the camera operator who is currently filming Gerald. I wonder what his story is. I noticed him yesterday. He is distractingly handsome, broad-shouldered and kind of rugged in his flannel shirt. He most definitely plays music in his free time. Drums. He looks exactly like the kind of guy I would have dated a few years ago. Back when I was dating. He pulls his head up from the camera and glances my way. His eyes rest on me for a beat, and a small thrill shoots through me. *He's not flirting with you, Stella, he's doing his job.* I have got to pull myself together.

I grab some ice from the freezer and bring it back to my station, where I mix up flour, salt, and a pinch of sugar and begin combining it with cold butter. There are many ways to make a pie crust, and every baker will tell you that theirs is the best. *If* they tell you. I'm not someone who has been baking long enough to have that kind of possessiveness of recipes. I just use one that I found online and adapted ever so slightly. I make enough for two pies, mixing the dry ingredients with the butter using a pastry cutter. I work the mixture until there's no dry flour left in the bowl. To that I add ice water a tablespoon at a time until I can pinch off the dough in sticky pieces. I run the dough back to the fridge to chill. I slice my peaches, adding them to a pan on the stovetop with sugar, cinnamon, and a squeeze of lemon juice. I turn it on to low heat, simmering to make my filling. Then I sprinkle flour across my table and roll the cooled dough out into sheets, returning it to my refrigerator.

With the hard part done, I glance around at the others. I know that nothing good will come from comparing myself to them, but it is impossible not to when you are in this tent. Some evil part of you is praying that anyone other than you will have a disaster that will make sure you stay in the running. But looking around at the other four, I see nothing but irritating perfection. Pradyumna is shaking toasted spices over his crust, then working them into the dough with a rolling pin. Hannah is creating two different doughs for one pie, the first a rich chocolate brown flavored with cocoa powder and a tiny pinch of cayenne. Archie had said two different pies, not two different crusts. I'm pissed at myself that I didn't come up with something more interesting. When they said to be creative, I was focusing on all the other components, but a few hours from now Betsy might be saying my crusts are too basic. I think back to an episode from season three when a sweet postal worker named Dave made a batch of tiny cookies flavored only with butter. They were plain to look at, undecorated aside from a sprinkling of course sugar, but the flavors were so divine that Betsy went back in for a second. It's part of *Bake Week* lore that if Betsy Martin goes back in for a second taste of something, it means you've created something truly transcendent.

I would kill to have Betsy take a second bite of something I made. I go to the fridge and remove my crusts, carefully unfolding them on top of a pair of pie dishes. They feel drier than I'd like them to be. As I push the first one down, pressing it into the sides of the pan, Betsy descends on my baking table. The lenses hover above her shoulders. I swallow, trying to fight the tightness that has suddenly gripped my throat.

She watches me, a kindly smile frozen on her face. "What can you tell me about your pies today?"

I try to focus on talking to her, but I notice my crust has crumbled a bit around the edges. It's a bad sign that its texture will be off. I see her take note of it, her mouth flinching downward. I find myself grasping for words. "My sweet pie is . . . peach."

"I see. Anything else you want to tell us about it?" She looks at me expectantly.

"Yes . . . um. Sorry." I laugh nervously and try to regain my confidence for the cameras, even though inside I'm feeling insanely fragile and calculating how I can fix the shitty crust—or hide it. "The peaches are being reduced, they are seasoned with sugar and thyme. I'll dot the top with a sweet ricotta after baking."

Betsy nods approvingly, and my body goes weak with relief. She turns to move along and then stops short. She pivots back toward me and sniffs the air. "It smells a bit burnt if I'm being honest," she says, lowering her eyes to my pan of peaches, bubbling frantically on the stovetop.

"Oh no! I thought I'd turned it off!" With a sinking feeling, I look down at my burner, which is now cranked up to the highest setting. I distinctly remember switching that burner off, but I must not have turned the knob all the way and instead locked it on high. I quickly turn it off and inspect the damage, pulling the top layer of peaches away with a wooden spoon. They've scalded, and charred peach slices are stuck to the bottom of the pan in blackened lumps. There's no saving this. That burnt flavor will have tainted the whole pot. What a stupid, stupid mistake. I can feel my eyes prick with tears.

"Good luck," Betsy says, patting my shoulder for just a moment as she moves away from my baking table. I am rooted to the spot. Betsy Martin touched me. The thrill of it makes me nearly dizzy. *Snap out of it, Stella!* The camera operator follows me as I rush to my refrigerator, capturing my every move as I prepare to make my filling all over again, but all I can think about is how I can still feel Betsy Martin's hand on my arm. It must be a sign that she thinks I can do this. I can't let her down.

LOTTIE

I suppose I should just admit that this isn't my first time in Grafton Manor. It's been hard for me not to tell the others every time I notice something familiar. I want to share with someone what I remember about the place, how the chairs in the library were once faced toward the fireplace, or how the dining room used to have drapes in blue crushed velvet that were perfect to wrap yourself up in during a game of hide-and-seek. Other than a few details, I was surprised to see how little had changed. Grafton is preserved like a museum from my past.

"The help" is what they called my mother. There was no mincing words back then. Not that she ever seemed to mind. Cooking and cleaning for a family as rich as the Graftons was not an easy job to come by. Most housekeeping work didn't come with full boarding by the time I was born, so my mother was even more grateful that I was allowed to stay with her in the upstairs room. Not many families would have taken in a single mother and her child in those days. Whenever I was fidgety or misbehaving, she would remind me that we were so lucky to have the Graftons. They were a bit like gods, hidden away in the East Wing.

All I'm left with are fragments of memories from that time. Some are merely images of my mother in the kitchen or Betsy holding one of her porcelain dolls. They are disjointed, though I try my hardest to find a thread connecting the memories, turning them this way and that in my mind as though they are puzzle pieces that might suddenly click into place with enough effort. It's hard to make sense of them, though I've tried for nearly sixty years, lying awake at night, my eyes flicking across the grainy darkness of the ceiling, replaying what little bits I can remember, over and over again, looking for clues.

I put one of my pie crusts into the oven to parbake and begin chopping rhubarb into chunks. I suppress a yawn. That is why I am here, to put myself back into that time, to search for remnants of my mother. For the past two nights, I've thrown back the covers and crept out into the hall, trying to retrace her last steps. But it's hard when I have no idea what those were. So I have been spending my nights wandering Grafton, looking for something intangible that will bring me back to the night she disappeared.

I make my custard, whipping together sugar, flour, eggs, vanilla, cream, and butter.

Betsy comes by my station as I mix the rhubarb with cinnamon and sugar. "I love a rhubarb pie," Betsy says. I can see she means it. "Nothing better on a summer evening." Of course, I already know that Betsy loves rhubarb. I would spend countless summer afternoons at my mother's side smelling the rhubarb bubble in order to please the young mistress of the house. I smile politely, even though every time she speaks to me my legs turn to jelly. Just as they did when I was a child.

I was always a bit afraid of Betsy. She was only a year older than me, but she was a million times more mature. She was already quite a bit taller than I was and walked around the house like a miniature adult in stiff, buttoned-up dresses and shiny leather shoes. Most of the time I saw her only in passing, often marching purposefully from the front door up the stairs toward her room in the East Wing. Whenever she did see me, if we happened to collide in a hallway or pass each other in the kitchen, she'd frown and tilt her head back, looking down the bridge of her nose at me, a not-so-subtle reminder of who was in charge. Despite our differences, I would occasionally be sent to play with her. Apparently, the Graftons had thought it would be good for Betsy to interact with more children her own age, and I was dispatched to entertain her like an organ-grinder's monkey. Not that I minded one bit. To me these playdates spelled opportunity. Betsy with her mountains of toys and fancy dresses was like a princess hidden away in the forbidden East Wing. I wished desperately to befriend her. I would convince my mother to dress me in my nicest clothes for those rare occasions. She would go along, putting me into my church dress and braiding my hair with ribbons. Looking back, I wonder what she thought of my attempts to fit in with the lady of the house, knowing as she did that there was no way I would ever be accepted into their fold. The Graftons knew who I was, a poor, plain little girl who they took pity on.

Occasionally I would run into an elder Grafton in the halls of the manor. The mother, Josephina, was stern and imposing. She preferred me to stay out of her sight, and if I somehow didn't, if she caught sight of me in the hall or by the kitchen, she would look at me with her mouth pursed, as though she'd just swallowed buttermilk. Richard Grafton was more of an enigma. If I saw him with Josephina, he would gaze past me, as though he had somewhere he'd rather be. But occasionally, when I would see him on his own, often when I was playing outside and he was coming back from a walk with the dogs or parking one of his cars, he was quite nice to me. He would ask me how I was doing and pay me compliments. These conversations always filled me with anxiety as a child. The truth was, Richard Grafton made me quite uncomfortable. I didn't like the way his eye would focus on me, and I always felt I was disappointing him with my monosyllabic answers, like he expected more.

Now Betsy moves on from my baking table, cameras in tow. There was a moment, the first time Stella and I went into the dining room, that I worried about Betsy placing who I was. But I knew as soon as she saw me that she didn't recognize me at all. She practically looked right through me. I always knew it was a possibility, but I figured that after all these years the chance of her remembering me was slim. Is it odd that after all this time I was almost disappointed? After all, I have never forgotten her. It's been over fifty years since I last laid eyes on Betsy Grafton. I bet she's hardly given me a moment's thought. She's a celebrity, and who am I? The daughter of a housekeeper. A little girl she played with from time to time. Nobody.

I pull the crust out of the oven, lifting the parchment paper with a load of tiny, spherical pie weights. It is a light butter color, firm and already a bit flaky. This will help it keep from getting too soggy with such a wet filling. Now I pile the rhubarb and sugar mixture onto the crust and pour the custard over the top. It froths pleasantly as it fills in the cracks. It will thicken into a true custard studded with craggy bits of tart rhubarb. My mouth waters.

Coming back to Grafton after all this time has felt strangely like coming home. After all, it is where my mother raised me. The only real childhood home I ever knew.

The last time I spoke to my mother was *that* night. It was already dark when she came into our room and kissed me on the forehead. I was bleary-eyed, already asleep. She smelled of the outdoors, of crisp leaves and woodsmoke. Pale moonlight slanted in through the window, hitting her side where she sat on my bed. Her eyes sparkled.

"Things are going to get better for us," she'd said, leaning over me. Her hair was loose and tickled my face as she gave me a kiss. I fell asleep against her, and will never forgive myself for sleeping so deeply, because when I woke up the next morning, she was gone.

PRADYUMNA

I've had my spark of inspiration at the beginning of the bake as I normally do—a savory mushroom pie with dough that's infused with thyme and rosemary and a sweet one inspired by my favorite summer cocktail, the Dark and Stormy. The idea is, as always, the fun part, and now, an hour into the competition, I find myself looking around the room, watching the others. I have the intense desire to engage someone in conversation, to shake things up, but they all look so serious. Stella is mixing something on the stove with an expression of pure dread on her face. Gerald is measuring his crust with a ruler. I glance behind me. Lottie is fussing with her pie, her eyebrows pinched with focus. As she attempts to weave a top crust into latticework, a slender ribbon of dough pulls free and flops onto the table. She starts again, exasperated. I wonder what she was doing walking down the hallway last night like some sort of weird Victorian ghost. I will ask her later, if only just to see if she even remembers it. Of the five of us, only Hannah looks like she's enjoying herself, a small smile playing on her lips as she fills one of her crusts with a bright pink custard. She catches me looking at her and scowls slightly, shaking her head.

I jerk my head back to my table, irritated. *Does she think I'm going to copy her?* With a sigh, I turn to the rum-and-lime curd I've been making for the filling. The rum bottle sits open in front of me, letting off tantalizing wafts of sharp alcohol. It is taking all my strength not to reach for the bottle and take a quick slug. Is it terrible to admit that I'm getting a bit tired of baking? I've never had to do it for so long or with such discipline. It's nothing to do with baking itself. Pies and breads are fine enough. It's spending so much time in forced concentration without music or a podcast to distract me that is becoming tedious.

I'm just a bit off today, I tell myself, spreading the curd into the base of a parbaked crust. But if I'm really being honest, it had already started the first day I arrived. The feeling is coming back. I've had it for years, an endless, aching boredom. Generally, when I start to feel the emptiness, my first line of defense is to catch it off guard with a distraction. I've done this more times than I can count with a variety of different activities—tennis, yachting, sky diving, elaborate trips to climb far-flung mountains. I have to say that all of them have worked to varying degrees. There is an art to finding a good distraction, one that will keep you from sinking into the abyss. There needs to be some action incorporated into it, and it needs to involve other people, so nothing too sedentary or isolating. No knitting or chess. But it can't be just empty action. There needs to be some sort of goal, some way of bettering yourself or learning a new skill. Otherwise, you will start to question what the point of it even is, and you will become restless. And if you are at loose ends, you will leave yourself open, vulnerable, and the feeling will find you.

There's a commotion in front of me, breaking me free from my thoughts. Gerald has started yelling. He is waving his arms around above his head as though defending himself from the cameras, which are scattering around him, retreating. "This is not right," he shouts as he runs down the corridor between the baking tables. "Someone is not playing by the rules."

He is such a good baker, so meticulous and controlled, that I'm shocked he could have such an outburst. I watch Archie retreat to the far side of the tent, taking refuge between Melanie and Betsy, the look on his face a hilarious mix of fear and embarrassment.

Honestly, I'm just grateful for the excitement.

GERALD

Though *Bake Week* has a pantry of staples for contestants to use, I've brought my hand-ground pastry flour and orange syrup. I prefer to do the job myself and to make sure it is done correctly. I look at each ingredient, accounting for their whereabouts before I begin. After that disaster with the train, I want to be absolutely certain everything is done right and according to plan. No more mistakes.

I melt butter on low heat, pouring it into a bowl with my sugar and mixing it thoroughly with a teaspoon of vanilla. I crack an egg into the mixture and open my orange essence just as Archie comes up to my baking station surrounded by a small cadre of cameramen. Something is wrong. The orange smell is off; in fact it doesn't smell of orange at all anymore.

"Geraaalllld," Archie croons in his overly friendly way. "Everything going perfectly, I'd assume. Not a grain of sugar out of place?"

I ignore his insincerity. That sort of thing doesn't bother me, but I do wish he'd go away. I am having trouble focusing on the orange essence, which is what I need to think about.

"This isn't a good time for me," I say, trying to be direct, but Archie seems to think I am telling a joke, because he laughs loudly. It's rancid, I realize suddenly. But not rancid orange. Rancid something else? Or perhaps it is not rancid at all. No, it has been replaced by something altogether different. A camera swoops down in front of me, and I fight a very strong urge to shoo it away.

"What is this?" Archie picks up one of my icing bags, specially ordered from Belgium, moving it from its assigned spot. "Looks a bit like a torture device?"

I'm almost able to place the smell. If everyone would just be quiet for a moment, I could think. But Archie won't stop talking, yammering on and on. I close my eyes against the onslaught, willing myself to focus on the task at hand.

"Cooking with his eyes closed, now that's a new one." Archie guffaws.

Panic rises in my chest. I place the smell with sudden clarity. The chemical fumes. My eyes flip open.

"It's gasoline."

I feel my voice getting high-pitched. The lights are hot on my face, and my bow tie is far too tight.

"Someone has replaced my orange essence with gasoline!" I choke out the words, trying desperately to make sense of the situation. Archie's face is frozen with that half smirk. I know what he is thinking—kooky Gerald with his tinctures and measurements. I've known Archie's type since I was a child, and I've invariably been teased and mocked by them.

"Gerald, Gerald, you've got to relax." Archie's hands are touching my shoulders, and I can no longer handle the presence of all the people and cameras crowded around me. I am blinded by the glare of camera lenses and lights.

"Stop, just stop, you're ruining everything!" I shout, thrashing my arms out in front of me. "I could have killed someone!"

HANNAH

I put a look of concern on my face, even though I'm thrilled to see another contestant crack under pressure. I never liked Gerald, with his fancy suits and know-it-all answers to everything, even things no one had asked him. But I hadn't expected him to snap like this, waving his arms around, pulling off his apron and flinging it to the ground, and then stomping off out of the tent. Of course, a cameraperson trailed him, recording the whole breakdown. I wonder if they'll use the footage. I mean, they'll have to. It's too good. Gerald's pie crusts are still sitting out on his table waiting for filling. No mystery who is going home today, I'd say.

I rearrange my expression, putting a small smile on my face as I calmly pull my pie crusts out of the refrigerator and try to appear sympathetic. I wore a blue floral button-up dress today. It's sweet but also hints at something sexy, just below the surface, which is how I'd like Archie to think of me.

As soon as Betsy said the word *pies*, I knew I'd be golden. I have endless amounts of practice baking pies at the diner that I could probably do it blindfolded. There are so many recipes I've created to choose from. I think back on my most successful creations and land on one particular pie that had people driving back through a snowstorm to

Polly's for second slices to take home. My chocolate strawberry chiffon pie was a hit not to be missed: a chocolate crust filled with a pink strawberry custard studded with bits of fresh strawberry. I will make it again and this time I'll decorate it with sugared basil leaves and strawberry hearts. For my savory pie, I'm making a mixed mushroom filling with fresh herbs and taleggio, encased in a double crust that is studded with fresh rosemary and thyme. To decorate it, I've cut out of rolled dough an intricate forest scene and affixed it to the top crust with a wash of egg white. I put my savory into the oven to bake.

After Gerald's outburst, Archie went to the corner of the tent, where he's been having an intense conversation with one of the producers. I like to imagine that it must be such a relief for Archie to film with me after all the others. I am so much perkier, so much more fun. I glance at Archie as he heads over to Pradyumna's table, catching his eye. He winks and smiles handsomely. I blush, looking down and thinking about last night. He'd snuck me up to the East Wing, through the main corridor, where we crouched down running from doorway to doorway, trying to stifle giggles, until we reached his suite. It was just like I'd imagined it would be—a golden chandelier in the center of the room, an iron grated fireplace, floor-to-ceiling windows hung with luxurious drapes, their shutters flung open onto a Juliet balcony. He'd sat in an armchair and watched me take it all in. "We don't have anything like this in Eden Lake," I'd said, immediately feeling silly. But he'd just looked at me kindly. "I grew up in a small town too, a village really," he'd shared. "All of this fancy stuff was such a shock to me at first too. You'll get used to it, though."

I'd laughed. "I hope not." I'd yawned and said I should go to bed before it got too late. I wanted to win, after all. He'd said I was being wise. I can't stop myself from wondering what would happen had I stayed a little longer. Will I have another chance to be alone with him?

I steal a glance back at Stella. She's clearly my only competition in the beauty department. Mom would say that her look is very "natural," which is her not-so-subtle code word for slobby. She is pretty, though.

Annoyingly so. I watch her crack an egg into her mixer. She's wearing a striped long-sleeved T-shirt tucked into wide-legged pants. Not terrible, but certainly nothing memorable. Her thick strawberry blond hair—her best feature—is bunched in a messy topknot. If I had hair like that, I'd put some waves in it, let it stay down. My own hair is thin and won't grow past shoulder length, no matter how hard I try. I make up for it by dyeing it very blond and cutting it in a sharp bob with bangs that skim my eyebrows, and I never leave the house without false lashes and winged eyeliner to compliment it.

Stella's got at least ten years on me, maybe more, I remind myself. Younger is better. Even if it doesn't always feel that way. I turn back to my pies, but thinking about her has shaken my confidence. I wonder if Archie would take Stella to the East Wing too if she asked. The idea of it makes me frown, and I can feel myself losing focus. I shake my head to clear it.

"You have twenty minutes left!" Betsy's voice rings from the front of the tent. I don't have time for petty jealousy if I want to win this. I take my mushroom pie out of the oven. It is golden brown, bubbling just a bit at the edges. Steam curls up from the vents in the crust, letting off the most delectable, savory aroma. I place it on a cooling rack next to my strawberry chiffon pie. Turning back to the sweet pie, I spoon strawberry whipped cream into a piping bag and make delicate peaks across the top. I am delighted. Both pies have turned out exactly as I hoped. I bring my strawberry pie to the refrigerator, leaving it on a shelf for its final chill. As I shut the door and wonder what I'm going to do for the next twenty minutes, I'm startled to see Archie standing right next to me.

"I'm always running into you." I laugh and look around for cameras but he seems to be alone. He smiles back at me. It feels funny seeing him in the daylight. My cheeks warm, remembering how close I'd been to him.

"I'm not complaining," he says. His eyes flick to the other side of the tent, where the cameras and producers gather around Betsy.

Archie leans in quickly, so close that his lips almost brush against my ear. "Meet me at the gate after dinner," he whispers. "Don't tell anyone." The vibration of his breath sends shivers through me. Before I can respond, he pulls away, smiles, and walks back across the tent. I return to my table in shock. Could I have even heard that right? Archie Morris wants a secret meeting with *me*? My mind starts to spin in the happiest of ways. *Is it like a date?* Archie has moved to Lottie's table, and I stare at him as the two share a joke. His head tilts back in laughter. He catches my eye and winks.

I notice Gerald's table is empty, the remnants of his pies sitting undone on his baking table. Pradyumna is leaning back on his table, looking bored, his pies finished behind him. Lottie and Stella are still hard at work pulling their pies out of the oven and maneuvering them onto serving trays.

"Your time is *up!*" Archie finally shouts from the front of the tent. "Bakers, please bring your pies up to the judging table."

I carefully pick up my tray of pies and walk them to the front. I've covered the bottom of the tray with a red-checked picnic cloth and decorated the space around each pie with a scattering of cut daisies, tiny, gemlike strawberries, little twigs, and green ferns unfurling from their buds, all things that I've collected from around the grounds.

I lower my tray onto the judging table. There are a few that are so clever, they take my breath away, like Pradyumna's pie with its towering meringue topped with a storm cloud of gray-blue sugar crystals. Stella's pie looks downright terrible, I notice happily. The top is sloppy, and some sort of unappetizing white puddle has melted on top of her peaches, while the crust is a dark brown on the edges. Stella looks like a mess right now too—her hair sticks to her face, and a smear of something chalky runs across her cheek. She gives me a relieved smile as she places her pies on the table. I turn away quickly before she can catch my smirk.

Archie and Betsy make their way down the line of pies. Pradyumna then Lottie then Stella. I have to bite my lip when I learn that the white stuff on top of her peaches is ricotta. No way can you use cheese in this heat. Terrible idea, and both judges agree with me. Now it is my pie's turn. I watch as Betsy's lips close over her fork. I lean forward in anticipation.

"Look at that crust," Archie says, prodding it with his fork.

"Perfectly flaky," Betsy agrees. They each take a bite as I squirm impatiently, watching out of squinted eyes in mock fear. Really, though, I know these pies are good. But I think the act will make me more relatable. The worry will endear me to the viewers.

"Now *that* is good," Betsy says. I smile wide for the cameras, my body light with relief. Then she does the most wonderful thing. She leans forward and scoops up another bite.

BETSY

"I feel badly for Gerald, I really do. But what a mess." She sits in the gazebo across from Archie, the day's bakes laid out in front of them. The opening behind them frames the tent, set back across the lawn and Grafton Manor rising behind it. This picturesque spot is where Betsy has always done her final judging. Normally she speaks only to the cameras, but now of course she must have an actual conversation with Archie about who will leave the tent and who will be the day's winner. She finds herself bracing for an argument. But Archie agrees with her instantly.

"You just can't get that thrown off by a mistake." He nods solemnly. "You really have to pick yourself up and figure it out." Betsy is pleased to see him giving *Bake Week* the respect it deserves. She finds herself exhaling a breath she didn't know she'd been holding.

Betsy doesn't understand what happened today with Gerald. She'd been all the way across the tent, scolding Melanie about unflattering camera angles, when the yelling started. Gerald had sounded so deeply distressed that at first she'd worried someone had been physically attacking him. As Gerald fled dramatically through the back of the tent, Archie strode quickly over to her and Melanie and in a hushed voiced explained the situation. Well, he'd kind of explained it. Something about Gerald's ingredients being spoiled? She still isn't quite sure what prompted the meltdown. She wonders if Archie had something more to do with it than he let on.

He'd never seemed particularly keen on Gerald, teasing him a bit yesterday about his homemade flavors. She'd even caught him rolling his eyes once as he'd walked away from filming a one-on-one. Maybe he wanted Gerald to fail. It's a shame, Betsy thinks. Aside from whatever it was that happened today, Gerald's bakes were some of the very best, neat and well planned. His ingredients were inspired, a miracle given the limited amount of time they had to work with.

"I just wish he'd finished his bakes," she says honestly. It wasn't good for the show to have people walk off set that way. She suspected she'd be having a long conversation with the producers and Francis about optics. Would it look as though Gerald had been bullied?

"How do you think the others are doing?" Archie pushes through, changing the subject. There is no hint of him being rattled from the conflict, Betsy notes.

"Stella's pies were a bit lackluster," Betsy says. It would be obvious to anyone watching this episode that if Gerald had done well today, Stella would be the one going home in the morning. At the beginning, Betsy had predicted Stella would be the first to leave, but so far she's been saved. *Twice.*

"They were poorly baked is what they were. Not well planned at all," Archie agrees, an edge of his former *Cutting Board* persona creeping into his voice.

"Well, she did have that mishap with the peaches being burnt," Betsy says, trying to appear understanding, though if she were being honest, she's already had it with Stella. Every time Betsy walked past Stella's table, she looked up, following her with those moon eyes. It was unnerving.

"She shouldn't be making that kind of mistake this far into the competition."

Betsy gives a curt nod in agreement. "Who did well today?"

"I think Hannah and Pradyumna both did well," Archie says. "Hannah's pies were really something special. To make two different crusts like that—"

"Pradyumna also made two different crusts," she reminds him.

"Yes, but Hannah's fillings were really top-notch. The decoration too." The way he is talking about Hannah makes Betsy stop and look at him more closely. There's something familiar about it. He doesn't have quite the same tone of voice as he does when he talks about the others.

"She does have very tidy piping, and her flavors were quite good," Betsy agrees, begrudgingly. "We're in agreement then?"

"Yes, I think we are."

"Always so sad to see them go." She says it as wistfully as possible for the cameras.

"You're such a softy, aren't you?" Archie says. It is part of the script, making Betsy appear sensitive, grandmotherly. But there is something in the way he says it that makes her pause. It doesn't sound like a compliment. There's a tone there that implies something else. It's almost as if he is toying with her. Or is she just imagining it? Being around Archie has made her question herself more than she has in years. She hasn't felt this insecure since—Betsy's heart pounds with recognition.

She realizes suddenly that Archie reminds her of her ex-husband, Roland. Not in appearance, since they look nothing alike. Roland is the most blue-blooded WASP Betsy has ever encountered, and Archie, well, it's obvious Archie does not come from of any kind of pedigree. But there is something in their mannerisms, their performative confidence. Mostly it is in the way they both make Betsy feel about herself. Like she's a child who needs to be coddled or a doddering old fool who doesn't deserve their respect. Neither would say it out loud, of course, but Betsy can feel it in the way they speak to her. The subtle inflections. Of course, Roland also cheated on her with a much younger woman. She recalls with painful clarity the way he spoke about *her* as well. The look in his eyes of trying to conceal a lie while also desperately wanting to brag about what he'd done. She gives Archie a prim smile.

"Shall we?" Betsy stands. She is suddenly desperate to talk to Francis and find out what he knows.

"After you."

The cameras follow them as they make their way back to the tent to deliver the final verdict. If Archie is anything like Roland, then Betsy knows one thing is for certain—he is not to be trusted.

STELLA

I walk out onto the front steps, past the stone lions. The sun is still visible over the mountains, but the air has cooled, and the breeze that rushes up across the great lawn has a bite to it. I like how it rushes against my cheeks. I take a deep breath, filling my lungs with clean northern air. I feel better outside. I can walk around freely without worrying about getting lost within the endless maze of rooms and hallways inside. I want to take advantage of being here, away from New York and the problems that will begin to pile up as soon as I set foot in my old life again.

I take off at a brisk pace across the lawn, walking through the space between the manor and the tent. Things are quiet. It seems like I'm the only one out here; the crew must have left for the day. I feel like I'm sneaking around where I shouldn't be and remind myself that Betsy was the one who had suggested we explore. I cut to the left and hug the side of the manor. Over here it is shaded and damp. Tendrils of ivy creep like tiny veins across the stone. They pull themselves around the window frames and up to a stone balcony, which is almost covered by vines.

The house gazes down on me. Its leaded glass windows are uniform and opaque, reflecting the gray sky like the one-sided mirrors you see on cop dramas. Anyone could be looking out at me right now, I think. A shiver takes hold of my back, rattling up through my shoulder blades.

I pass through a trellised archway that looks out over rows of terraced gardens. They are overgrown and wild. Tall weeds mingle with patches of flowers. I walk down a set of crumbling stone stairs. There are several small statues here. A woman holding a jug with a hole in it stands in a shallow basin filled with dead leaves; clearly it was once a fountain. Behind it a sundial is caked with moss. I continue deeper into the garden, reaching a cluster of rosebushes. They've been neglected, but some small roses have still managed to bloom on the ends of their spindly branches. I lean forward to smell one, breathing its powdery scent. In the center of the rosebushes is a lone dogwood tree, its pale green flowers just starting to bloom. The gardens beyond here are wild, and I can go no farther into the tangle of thorns.

I make my way back up to the manor, walking around the other side of the house and emerging near the gazebo on the edge of the front lawn. The front of the house is in stark contrast to the back. The hedges are neat and uniform. The grass a close-shorn emerald green. Everything is tidy and controlled. I'm sure the other gardens were once like this too, manicured and beautiful. I wonder if Betsy has trouble maintaining the house. The thought takes me by surprise. I can't imagine Betsy Martin having trouble doing anything.

I start when I notice a dark figure sitting in the gazebo. It's the camera guy, I realize, the one I'd made eye contact with earlier. He's slumped down in one of the judging chairs, his feet propped up against the other. He is staring down his phone and doesn't see me. He looks out of place framed in the delicate white latticework, a large, muscular man, with a frown creasing his face. Exactly my type a few years ago. *What are you doing?* I feel younger Stella asking me impatiently. *Go talk to him. Shut up,* I tell her. He puts something to his mouth, and a thick cloud of smoke fills the gazebo. I am about to turn around and give him his privacy, when he raises his arm in a wave.

"How'd it go today?" he calls out.

Shit. Now I have to say something. *It's okay, Stella. It won't kill you to talk to an attractive man.* I walk up to the side of the gazebo.

"It was good," I say, lying. My mouth feels dry. All those months at home have weakened my conversational skills.

"Stella, right?" he asks. I nod. I notice a piece of a large tattoo peeking out from the cuff of his shirt. "I'm Graham."

"Today was pretty bad, actually, if I'm being honest," I say. I haven't spoken to anyone about my performance in the tent, and I find I want to say it out loud. "I don't think I'm going to manage to stick around here much longer."

"I'm sure you just have to find your rhythm," he says. "Besides, it can be hard to do your job when you have Betsy hovering over you." His voice turns bitter, and I wonder if he's no longer talking about me. He takes another puff on the vape. What could someone like him have against Betsy? I can't imagine her doing anything bad to him. I've watched her, and she hardly interacts with the camera operators.

"It's a lot of pressure," I say, dodging, while hopefully communicating that I am not the one to commiserate with about Betsy Martin. "You've been doing this a while then?"

"This'll be my fourth season," he says.

"And you like it?"

"Yeah. It's not too bad." He stretches and his shirt rises up, flashing a sliver of toned stomach. "The money's good considering it's just a week's work, and it's great being out here during the summer. And don't tell anyone, but sometimes we get to eat the things you bake."

The idea of them scavenging over our bakes at the end of the day fills me with a strange sick feeling.

He leans over, resting his forearms on the side of the gazebo. His voice is low and gravelly when he speaks. "I've met Betsy's ex-husband."

His eyebrows go up like he knows things. He glances back at the manor and bends closer to talk to me.

"Listen, this place . . . Betsy. Let's just say there are rumors."

I don't know what he's getting at, but I don't like it. "I'm sure her ex would have plenty to say about the place he's no longer allowed to be in and a woman who stood her ground in a divorce," I say in her defense.

"Maybe," he says. But I can tell he doesn't believe me at all. I'm finding his personality extremely off-putting and regret stopping to talk to him at all.

"I thought the crew stayed in town," I say pointedly, changing the subject.

"We do. Gotta secure the equipment before we go, though," he says. "I'm always the last to leave here." His eyes lock with mine uncomfortably.

"Oh, really?" I feel my internal alarm bells starting to go off. I look past him at the front steps of the manor, gauging how long it would take to run if I needed to.

"I better get back," I say, already stepping away. "Don't want to miss dinner."

He grins to himself as though he is finding something funny.

"What?" I ask warily as I back away from him, ready to bolt.

He just raises his hands, smiling like he knows something I don't.

"It's probably safer out here than it is in there."

PRADYUMNA

Dinner tonight has been an unpleasantly quiet affair. The only conversation the four of us have had was speculating about Gerald, who has not come down to eat, hasn't even been seen since his abrupt departure from the tent earlier. I suspect he is embarrassed. Being such an uptight man, so intent on doing things to a certain code, it must have been mortifying for him to lose control like that. Not to mention the incredible letdown of being sent home when he could have so easily won.

"It's a shame," I say. "He probably was the best baker of all of us." Nobody responds to me; each of them seems lost in their endive. I wonder if I've offended them. I suppose they all prefer to think of themselves as the best baker of the group, even if it isn't true. I'm almost envious of how much each of them cares about winning *Bake Week.*

Next to me, Hannah is silent and jumpy, which seems a bit strange given her victory in the tent today. I'd have thought someone like her would be over the moon, full of annoying false modesty and equally insufferable false eyelash batting. But she has barely touched her food or even looked at the rest of us. A clock on the mantel behind me ticks loudly, counting down the seconds until this interminable meal is over.

Stella is the only one who has spoken at all, chattering along rather inanely as usual, but even she seems more subdued than normal. Aside from Gerald's unfinished disaster, her pies were obviously the worst of the bunch, somehow both burnt on the outside and raw and unset on the inside. I realize suddenly that this is the second time she's been saved by an unfortunate error. How lucky she is.

Lottie's eyes flutter slightly, and she nods toward her plate as though she is about to doze off into her boeuf bourguignon. I think of the dinners I used to cook for friends, elaborate multicourse affairs that started civilized and would digress into debauched parties that would end listening to records and smoking cigarettes on the balcony as the sky lightened.

"You need something to wake up, Lottie? Some street drugs? Maybe a tuba lesson?"

"I'd rather something that knocks me out if that's fine by you." Lottie smiles at me under heavy lids. She must be exhausted after all her adventuring. I probably should be as well, though I don't feel it. I take a gulp of wine. It's not hitting quite the way it did earlier in the week.

Dessert arrives on a tray, delivered by the same round-faced cook. It's a custard pie. "That's funny," I say. "Can't say I'm much in the mood for pie right now." Stella lets out a little, bitter laugh.

Hannah suddenly scrapes back her chair loudly. "I have to go. I'm going to, um, practice my piping."

I raise my eyebrows, curious, but neither Stella nor Lottie catches my eye. By the time the coffee has been brought out in its shiny silver urn, I am positively itching to get into some sort of trouble. It is a problem of mine that arises when I find myself with not much to do. A defense against boredom, and worse.

I won't last here much longer with my attitude. I know that. But still, it's hard to stay motivated. Being accepted into *Bake Week* was a wonderful distraction, the weeks leading up to it a fun way to get attention. But I'm finding the routine each day increasingly tedious. I know that everyone wants to win, but does that really mean we must make everything so incredibly dull? Wouldn't it be better to have a bit of fun in the process? I consider that to some of them, this monotony *is* fun. To the rest of them, competing for these two corporate cookie makers might be enjoyable. They've never been on Jay-Z's yacht. Never flown a private plane to the Maldives. Well, Archie probably has.

I can handle Betsy. She might not be my first-choice dinner party guest, but she is who she is, and I appreciate that. But Archie Morris drives me absolutely crazy. I can't stand his swagger and bravado. It reminds me of the kids I went to boarding school with. They were all so self-obsessed, so puffed full of hot air, unaware that in reality they had so little to offer. Archie is so clearly compensating for something with that terrible smirk on his face. Every time I look at him, I think, *Man, your job is to be smug to people who bake cookies*. And when do you suppose the last time he actually baked something himself was? I would bet money it's been years since he's baked a cake for someone's birthday or whipped up a batch of cookies for fun. His entire career is criticizing amateur cooks, and yet he acts like he is the gatekeeper to some elite universe. I get the feeling he isn't my biggest fan either, that he's threatened by me. Surely, he knows who I am, knows I don't need his approval. Hell, I don't need *Bake Week* at all. I already have more money than I know what to do with. I'm not looking for a new career. I just need something to keep me going.

My life has always been a series of goals. I may grow bored with them all eventually, but the beginning is always sustaining enough to keep me going, keep me moving. This is all just something to do to fill in the time and to keep the feeling at bay. But I worry it is returning anyway, seeping through the cracks. I fear the gnawing nothingness that will overtake me if I let it.

LOTTIE

I go back to my room after dinner and try to rest, falling across the bed and closing my eyes. In some ways it's enough just being back at Grafton, knowing that my mother had been here. Walking through the halls following in her invisible footsteps. Memories, small ones, have already begun to reveal themselves to me.

I sink down into the pillow and pull the edge of the comforter over myself. My eyelids grow heavy. I start to slip away toward sleep when a memory comes to me, jolting my brain back to consciousness.

It was Christmas day of the year I turned ten. The first thing I remember is my mother's hands on me, gently nudging me awake. The sun had barely risen as we slipped our coats and gloves on. "Where are we going?" I asked her as she wound a scarf around my neck.

"You'll see," she'd said, excitement shining in her eyes. We crept down the stairs and tiptoed through the house to the foyer. Below us, one of the Graftons' famous Christmas trees was lit up with large glass bulbs. They cast a magical glow through the layer of silvery tinsel on the tree, reflecting smudges of color onto the flagstone floor. My mother pulled open the main door, letting in a gust of cold air swirling with snowflakes. I gasped when I saw the world outside, white like the inside of a snow globe. Mom smiled at me like she was also a child.

We went down the front steps, and I stopped to brush some snow off the faces of the lions so that they could see it too. Outside was a pristine white wonderland. Our feet made the first impressions in the snow, as if the world was freshly made and ours alone.

We crossed the lawn slowly, sinking to the top of our boots until we reached the side of the house. "In here." She led me through the archway, into the gardens. The air smelled of snow, crisp and clean. My mother scooped up a handful of snow in her glove, pinching it between her fingers. "As I thought." She held it out, showing me. "See how it sticks? It's the perfect snow."

"For what?"

"Whatever you want!" Mom laughed, scooping more together and packing it in between her palms.

"A giant bear!" I said.

"Good idea." Mom began to roll the snow into large balls and stack them by her side. I followed suit until we had an arsenal to work with. Together we stacked them into the body of the bear and filling in the cracks. Then we brushed it with snow until it was smooth and added two arms curving around the sides of his body. Next, we carved out the bear's muzzle, making dents for eyes and nostrils.

"I have something that will help bring her to life," Mom said, opening her bag and unwrapping a parcel of food coloring and tubes for piping frosting. We mixed the colors with handfuls of snow and piped them on, working happily until the bear had bright, multicolored streaks of fur, a rosy pink nose, bright blue eyes, and yellow claws. We stood back and admired our bear, Technicolor against the canvas of snow. The sun had risen fully now, it caught on the flurries that danced through the air and made the world sparkle.

Later that afternoon, I'd helped my mother make the desserts for the evening's festivities. The Graftons held a locally famous Christmas drinks party. We rolled out dough, pressing it with cookie cutters. "Look at my candy cane tree," I said, pressing two of the cutouts together and holding them up. "Oh yeah?" Mom said, quickly re-arranging dough on the table. "Is it as good as my reindeer-with-a-Santa hat?"

I was laughing so hard that I almost didn't notice Betsy Grafton watching us from the doorway. My mother stopped smiling right away when she saw her standing there, dropping the dough on the counter. "Betsy, what can I do for you?" she asked. She wiped her hands on a towel and went toward the door. Betsy gazed at us, looking over the scene of cookies being rolled out and cooling on wire racks, and for a moment a look of pure longing passed over her eyes, but it was quickly replaced with a haughty expression.

"Nothing. I was just checking to make sure you were working," she said, narrowing her eyes at us. "Good thing I did, because I can see that you're behind."

She turned and left in a huff. My mother looked back at me. "Just ignore her," she said, but the levity was gone from her voice.

After Christmas, I was brought to the East Wing for one of our playdates. The floor of Betsy's room was littered with expensive new toys and clothes. Unwrapped presents were tossed around carelessly, shiny dresses draped on the corners of a chair, patent shoes with ribbons for laces thrown to opposing sides of the floor. And toys—more toys than I'd ever seen. My fingers itched to play with them. On my own I spent hours imagining what it would be like to have even a fraction of what Betsy did.

"In *my* room you must follow *my* rules," she'd reminded me as soon as my mother had stepped away. "First, go find me a comb. I need to fix my hair." I stepped over a beautiful glass doll, which was missing a chunk of its own hair, as though it had been hacked away with scissors. A piece of its porcelain foot had cracked off as well, a jagged hole revealing its hollow center. I thought of my own tiny box of possessions. *If I ever had a doll like that, I would take such good care of it*, I'd thought bitterly. I spent the next several hours hovering near Betsy doing what she instructed me to do. It was how all our playdates went. I was the obedient and quiet servant, and Betsy was royalty lording over me. All the while I was fixated on the doll. I wanted to rescue it, to take it upstairs with me. Finally, Betsy noticed me staring.

"What are you looking at?" she'd asked me.

"Nothing," I said quickly, too quickly. Betsy smiled and crossed the floor to the doll as a knot formed in my stomach.

"Oh, this old thing?" she asked me, picking the doll up in delight. "My mom bought her for me, but she's not my favorite. Did you want to play with her?"

"Yes," I'd gasped, stretching out my hands, already imaging the weight of it in my arms. Betsy leaned forward, holding the doll out as if to hand it to me. Just as my fingers were about to close around it, Betsy's eyebrows came together, and she snatched it back. Her smile twisted as she smashed the doll's face into the fireplace grate with a sickening crack.

HANNAH

While I run a bath, I lay my clothes out on the bed. I'm so glad I've brought the bodycon sweater dress even though I knew I'd never wear it on-screen. I smooth it out, placing some barely there red underwear and a matching lace bra next to it on the bed. I clip up my hair and lower myself into the steaming water. The tub is so large I could practically swim in it. I carefully shave my legs. With Ben I haven't ever really tried this hard to look good, at least not in a very long time. *Ben.* A small tug of anxiety pulls at my chest as I think of his face, saying goodbye to me in the front seat of his pickup truck. He was so happy for me. Not having my phone to text him has put some things into perspective. It's been surprisingly easy not to think of him while I'm here. In fact, I've hardly thought of him at all. I hoist myself out of the bath and wrap a plush towel around myself. I like the feel of it, soft and luxurious. Our towels at home are scratchy and threadbare. The little apartment I share with Ben in Eden Lake seems very far away. Suddenly I can hardly remember it.

I look at myself in the mirror. The chubby cheeks I've had all my life are starting, finally, to narrow. I don't want to stay with Ben just because I'm comfortable with him. It would be so easy to let him keep me in Eden Lake forever. I could pop out a couple of babies and just keep my job making pies at the diner. Ben would be fine with all that. But what about me? I couldn't live with myself if that is all I ever did. What would my mom say? I imagine her sitting at the kitchen counter, fork in her hand. She'd say, *Don't you miss your chance, Hannah Bear. You go out there and you get what you want.* I open a fresh box of false eyelashes and glue them carefully to my lids, sealing them in place with a coat of black mascara. I blink and look up at my reflection. I am so close to becoming just who I want to be.

The wind has picked up. I pull on the hem of my dress as I walk down the drive toward the main gate, checking behind me to make sure no one has followed. I've put in effort to look good tonight, but I hope I haven't overdone it. Suddenly, I feel a bit dressed up. It's just a walk after all.

I've shown up too early, I think, as I approach the stone arch at the end of the drive. But when I pass through the gate, I see he is there already. He leans casually against the wall in fitted tan pants and a denim jacket, like he's got nowhere else to be. He gives me a half smile. "Hey," he says quietly. He looks relieved, as though he were the one worried that I might not show. I feel a shiver go through me. I've never felt so excited just to be in someone's presence. "Hey," I say back, feeling silly and self-conscious. I notice him eyeing my dress appreciatively.

"I thought we could take the path up through the grounds," he says, pointing to an opening in the woods down the road.

"Sure," I say. I still feel confused. He's given me no explanation, no reason for our meeting. We start to walk silently, cutting into the woods on a trail that winds its way into the forest. It's much darker back here, a thick canopy of leaves blocking out the already weak sun. "Don't worry," he says when he sees me glancing behind us at the bright opening we came from. "I walked it yesterday, it just goes up a bit and then loops back around."

Once again, the Vermont wilderness reminds me of Minnesota, of the north near Hibbing, where my grandma is from. Leaves crackle under my heels. A bird high above caws eerily.

"I'm not worried," I assure him.

We come to a clearing where the path widens next to a creek, and I fall into step with him. I notice his hands, large and capable. They swing by his sides. I have the intense desire to take his hand in both of mine, to hold it, caress it. To restrain myself, I tug on my sleeves, pulling them down over my fingers.

"Are you cold?" he asks. Without waiting for me to reply, he pulls off his jacket. I notice the tag as he drapes it over my shoulders. I recognize the designer. I smile, putting my arms into the sleeves, enjoying the feel of the expensive fabric. The rare walk in the woods I've taken with Ben had often left me ten paces behind him being whapped with tree branches.

"Congratulations on today," Archie says finally. His voice feels especially intimate out here in the woods. "They really were special pies."

"Thanks." I look down uncomfortably.

"You don't like being complimented?" He watches my face closely as I respond. I feel as though this is a test of some sort.

"Oh no, it's not that." *I love being complimented.*

"It's just that the others are great bakers too," I say, fishing.

Archie lets out a snort, as I'd hoped he would. "Not like you. And they don't have the drive."

I bloom under the attention, suddenly more confident than I've been all week. And why shouldn't I be? I am today's winner—my pies were leagues better than the rest. I'm the second-youngest contestant in *Bake Week* history. And Archie Morris, *the* Archie Morris, has taken a special interest in me and my career. I have everything going for me. I feel invincible. I am suddenly certain I will win *Bake Week*. I turn to face Archie, looking up at him in the dim forest light.

He reaches out and takes my face gently between his palms. "Listen, you're a great baker, Hannah. I think you could be famous like Betsy Martin even," Archie says. The trees are dark, their leaves rustling around us.

"Ha," I say, trying to keep my cool, but a smile creeps across my face in spite of myself as I allow myself to imagine it.

"I'm serious," he says, stopping and looking at me sternly. "You just need someone to be your advocate."

"Is that person you?" I ask, looking up at him through my eyelashes. I've done smokey-eye makeup tonight. Was I secretly hoping that something like this might happen? I might not have even dared.

He moves close to me. "You really don't know how talented you are, do you?" I love that he sees me this way. I feel so special, so desired. I have never felt this way before. He tilts my face up to see his. The world feels big and surreal and wonderful. Above us the trees roar as thousands of papery leaves are caught in a gust of wind. I am swept into the moment, feel like I am watching myself from above. He kisses me passionately, working his lips against mine. Our tongues find each other. His cheeks are rough. They scrape my skin, but I don't tell him to stop, even though I know my face will be raw tomorrow. I don't want him to stop, in fact I want the opposite. I want to wear the markings of this magical evening. I want it to be our secret tomorrow. We stay there, kissing, until the sun sets, and then carefully we pick our way through the path back to the road. Out of the woods the sky opens up, denim blue against the black outlines of the trees. The beginnings of millions of stars twinkle in the center of the sky. I smile up at them. I feel Archie's fingertips brush my hand, then clasp it firmly. I can see that everything is falling into place. I shiver at my luck. Archie Morris chose me.

PRADYUMNA

I am alone in the library tonight. I've made a pledge to myself: no
brown liquor, so instead I've made myself a gin and tonic. Restless, I
carry it with me out into the hall. As our numbers dwindle, the house
feels quieter, less lived in. The hallways a bit more echoey. In just a
week's time there will be no one left here at all, just Betsy Martin and
her small staff of helpers, slipping through the hallways like ghosts, disappearing each night to their homes in the countryside. I keep thinking
about what Peter said about the missing staircase. I find myself wishing
he were still here. I could use an accomplice. I would love to get my
hands on Gerald's blueprints, but he seems less than amenable after
his catastrophic day. I am tempted to knock on his door. It's not like
he needs them anymore, is it? I could be concerned, ask him how he's
doing. Then pivot and ask him for the blueprints. But something tells
me Gerald would have very little tolerance for my bullshit. As though
to confirm it, his door is tightly shut when I walk past.

Instead, I amble out into the foyer, looking up at the grand staircase. I climb lazily up to the landing on the third floor. I pause, itching
to turn to the left and sneak into the East Wing, but I force myself to
turn right and go into the West Wing. I walk down the now-familiar
hallway, passing the door to my room on the right, then continuing

down the hall. At the far end the hallway ends abruptly at a large wardrobe. It is a hulking piece made of unfashionably dark wood, its legs curved out at the bottom, a decorative scroll-shaped carving out-lining the top. I pause, take a sip of my drink. There is a creak behind me and I turn around, but the hallway is deserted. I turn back to the wardrobe and pull on the handles. They stick at first but then give way noisily, echoing down the hallway. I wait but hear no signs of life behind me. I give the handles one last yank until they pull all the way open. A moth flies out at me, and I wave it and a cloud of dust par-ticles away, coughing.

The hallway is dim at this end, the wardrobe too dark inside to see properly. I remember the lantern I passed sitting on a hall table and go back to get it, creeping once again past the rooms of the re-maining contestants so as not to wake them. I pick up the oil lamp. It is clearly decorative, probably worth a fortune. A slim drawer in the table holds a matchbox embossed with the name of an old hat company. I pull back the glass cone and light the wick. It glows fes-tively. I bring the lamp back with me to the end of the hall. Now I walk around the side of the wardrobe, inspecting it from all angles. It is pressed tight against the wall, but when I shine the light near the back, I think I can see something behind it. Is it the dark outline of a space cut from the wall? Going back into the cabinet, I reach past a wool blanket that's been decimated by moths. It turns to a fine powder in my hands. *Disgusting.* I shove it to the side. I reach out and tap on the back of the wardrobe—solid wood. I move the lantern around the corners, and the light catches on something metallic on the left—a silver hinge, flush with the corner. I move away a stack of sheets and find another one, this time lower down. They are new, shiny, at least compared to the rest of the wardrobe. I scrape my fin-gers along the back right side until I catch on a small hole, drilled to the size of a finger. I pull on it and the back swings in, scraping along the bottom of the wardrobe. Behind the false back is a dark hole. I hold the lantern out. The light bounces dimly around the space, revealing a set of narrow stairs heading steeply into a black void. My heart flutters.

The staircase is so narrow that my shoulders bump up against the walls, my shirt catching on the peeling white paint. My forehead brushes against cobwebs. I hold the lantern out in front of me as I make my way up. The steps end finally at a hallway. I think not for the first time about how poorly designed old buildings are; they seem to be nothing but hallways. The ceiling is low here, the floors merely painted boards instead of the grand finishes found in the other parts of the house. A row of white doors hang open at different angles, as though the rooms have all been left suddenly. I make my way down the hall, the floor creaking loudly. The rooms are nearly identical, each furnished sparsely with a wooden dresser, two single beds—still crisply made—with a shared bedside table between them. This is clearly not somewhere the more privileged Graftons spent their time. Peter was exactly right that they were the old servants' quarters. I shine the lantern into one of the rooms. The wall is angled sharply, in line with the slant of the roof. The windows jut out into narrow dormers. My heart lurches when I see something move, then realize it's just my reflection in a small mirror. I set my lantern down on the bedside table and slide open the drawer. Inside is a brown embossed Bible and an old piece of ribbon still tied in a bow. I shut it and sink onto the mattress, sending a plume of dust up into the darkness. I've left my drink downstairs, I realize. I wish I had it now.

I look around the tiny room. Aside from the mirror it is plainly decorated, the walls empty of any life. I wonder what could possibly be so secret about this floor that it's accessible only via the wardrobe. I lean back on the mattress, throwing my arms above my head and over the pillow in surrender. As my hand goes back it brushes against something stiff and papery.

I pull it out from under the pillow and move it under the lamp. It's an old black-and-white photograph, a spiderweb of cracks spread along its surface. In the picture a man and woman stand close together on a grassy hill. The woman is wearing a fitted dress with a skirt that flares out like a bell. She has one leg bent up flirtatiously and is smiling broadly. She looks into the camera while the man gazes at her lovingly. Behind them is a dogwood tree in full bloom, its white leaves an attractive backdrop to their merrymaking. I sit up, hunching over the lamp to study it more carefully. I take in the man's mustache and his tweed suit. I recognize him. It looks like the paintings I've seen around the manor of Richard Grafton. But this does not resemble the dour man in all the oil portraits holding his rifle and staring stoically into the distance. This man looks alive and vibrant, his head tilted ever so slightly.

There is a sound in the hall. A sharp creak in the floorboards. My throat goes dry as I wait to see if there are more. Another creak—there it is, another step, this time with the scrape of a shoe in the hallway. Someone is out there, coming closer. I panic, looking around the room for a closet or someplace else to hide. Maybe if I moved right this second, I could squeeze myself under the bed, but I find that I'm frozen in place. Another scrape of a foot coming down on the floor, and it is too late. As the footsteps grow closer and closer, I stand up, balancing on the balls of my feet, and look around the room for some sort of weapon. At the last second, I blow the lantern out and tuck myself back against the wall next to the doorframe. There is one more heavy step as the person comes to stand in the doorway. I hold my breath as the beam of a flashlight hits the back wall, bouncing around the far side of the room, reflecting against the window where I can suddenly see the outline of a person. Who is it? My heartbeat roars in my ears.

The figure steps inside, past me, shining the flashlight around the room. The beam lands on the lantern, catches the plume of smoke still rising off its wick. My pulse quickens as the flashlight spins around, hitting me in the face. I raise my arms, shielding my eyes.

"Pradyumna?" a woman's voice asks, timidly.

She lowers the flashlight, and I can finally see her small frame. "Lottie?"

"What are you doing up here?" She sounds frightened.

"I could ask you the same question," I say. She stays near the door, looking as though she is ready to flee.

"I'm . . . I couldn't sleep, so I went for a walk," she answers tentatively.

"You really are a terrible liar, Lottie."

She doesn't say anything. A prick of fear dances in her eyes.

"Seems like a strange thing to be doing alone at twelve a.m."

"Oh, *does* it?" She gives me a withering look, then glances toward the door, making an invisible calculation. We are having some sort of standoff, I realize. Both of us are not where we should be in the middle of the night.

"Point taken." I step back, sink once again onto the side of the bed, showing her that she has nothing to worry about. She can leave if she wants. I have no skin in this, no interest in getting anyone in trouble. My morals are slippery enough as it is, I wouldn't dare impose them on anyone.

"This area is off-limits to guests," she says, as though I wouldn't know that based on how I got here.

"What, you think you are the only one who should get away with sneaking around because you're old, is that it?" I ask.

"Well, shouldn't age count for something?" She sniffs, and I can tell she is no longer afraid. "What's that?" She gestures with the flashlight to the photograph I'd set on the bedside table.

"Just a photo I found. I think it might be Richard Grafton and his wife. Living the high life from the looks of it." She hesitates and then reaches for it, holding it under the beam of the flashlight. I watch her mouth fall open. She sinks onto the side of the bed opposite me, clutching the photograph.

"That's not his wife," Lottie says, her voice wavering.

"What? How would you know that?" I ask, incredulous.

Lottie shakes her head in disbelief. "It's my mother."

LOTTIE

I can't stop staring at the photo. Trying to make sense of it. My mother and Richard Grafton smiling, pressed close together. She's wearing the dress I remember, the one I only ever saw on a hanger in her closet but never on her body. I can recall the color of the fabric, baby blue, and the feel of the damask, the stiffness and slight sheen. It's incredible to be seeing her in it. The bodice is fitted and the skirt flairs out jauntily. Her legs are bare, shapely. Her feet clad in heels. High heels! I try to remember my mother ever wearing high heels, but all I can picture are the clunky soles of her work shoes. They look beautiful. So happy.

"Now care to tell me what *you* are doing up here? And what's this about your mother?" Pradyumna raises an eyebrow at me. I was so stunned by the photograph I'd almost forgotten he was in the room with me.

"I'm . . ." I stop short. I've been caught, it's true, but I can't afford to be exposed. What if Betsy finds out and doesn't understand? What if she sends me home? Fear grips at my heart. I've finally made it here. I can't bear to think of losing this chance. God knows I won't ever get another opportunity to come to Grafton.

"Oh, your face. You're terrified. Lottie, relax. *Please.* I'm not going to rat you out if that's what you're worried about," he says, leaning back in the bed across from me. "You think I care about any of this? I'm mostly impressed that you managed to sneak in here after me like some sort of assassin."

I exhale. I believe him. He seems honest, if a bit odd. Can I really trust him, though? Can I tell him the whole story? It might be safer to let him in on the secret than risk him taking offense. What choice do I really have? He already knows too much.

"My mother was a maid here at Grafton."

"That's an amazing coincidence." Pradyumna considers this a moment. Then he sits bolt upright, planting his feet on the ground. "I'm an idiot. It's not a coincidence, is it?"

I give my head a tiny shake.

"I knew it! I knew there was something going on with you!" He is grinning as though he's just won a bet.

"I lived here as a child. In this room, actually. I slept where you're sitting now. My mother was right here." I pat the bed I'm on, feeling something stir in my chest.

Pradyumna looks around the room, taking in the information.

"It's incredibly lucky you got chosen. You know how hard it is to get onto *Bake Week*, don't you? The odds are like one in a million," Pradyumna says.

"It wasn't my first time applying." I feel myself starting to relax. I hadn't done anything wrong, after all, hadn't committed a crime or anything. I did get chosen for the show. "Once Betsy started *Bake Week* and I read she was filming it here, I realized this was my chance. But it's taken me ten years to get here."

"So did you know Betsy Martin?"

"Oh yes. Of course, she was Betsy Grafton then. At the time I would have said we were friends, but that was silly. Sometimes my mother brought me to up to her room to play with her. Richard Grafton even encouraged it from time to time. The Graftons were progressive in that way, letting someone like me mingle with their daughter.

But I think that there's no way her parents would have ever let her truly be friends with me, someone so poor and from a broken home."

"Weren't you worried she'd recognize you?"

"Oh, it was a gamble, but I figured once you've lived as long as we have, cataloging a lifetime of people in your head is nearly impossible. Besides, I was just a child. I looked much different."

"But why did you do all this?" Pradyumna sputters. It's as enthused as I've seen him about anything. I take a deep breath.

"My mother, Agnes, disappeared one evening. I was only eleven years old. I waited and waited, but she just never came home. The Graftons said that she'd gone out to meet someone. And that something must have happened to her on the road to town. They even implied she might have run away. But I knew my mother would never leave me. It was just the two of us, after all. I was quickly sent away. A great-aunt who I barely knew collected me the following day. They didn't even wait to see if she'd return, and they never allowed me back into the house. I was never able to see where my mother spent her last moments, never able to retrace her steps, to figure out what happened. Something happened, and I need to know. It has haunted me all my life."

Pradyumna takes this in, frowning. "You thought maybe if you came back to Grafton, saw her old room, walked the halls, you could have closure?"

I nod. It feels surprisingly good to share my secret with someone. I feel lighter, almost giddy with relief. "Yes, but I also want information. I need to know what she was doing right before she disappeared."

He plucks the photograph out of my hand again, studying it closely.

"Well, from the looks of it she was having an affair with Richard Grafton."

I know that he is right. It's the only explanation for the photo. "I don't know how she could have kept it from me."

"People do ridiculous things when they're afraid of getting caught," Pradyumna says. "You don't remember seeing them together? Or maybe she told you something about him?"

"I wish there was a way for me to go back in time and ask her," I muse. It is something I've wished for decades. I have so many questions.

"There has got to be a way to find out more about why she left. Maybe his wife found out and she was fired?"

"But she would have brought me with her," I insist, knowing I'm right. There's no way my lovely mother would just walk out on me as the Graftons implied.

"Maybe there was some reason she couldn't mix you up in all of it," Pradyumna says. I know he is trying not to say the other option out loud. The other, far worse and much more likely scenario: that something terrible had happened to her.

"No offense, Lottie, but you're not going to figure anything out wandering aimlessly around the manor at night. Rich people always keep paperwork, especially in old places like these. I'm sure there must be documents, old employment records, even more photographs from that time? If we had more information, maybe we could piece it all together, create a timeline."

I shake my head. "They'd be kept in the East Wing, though, and the East Wing was always off-limits to non-Graftons, even back then."

"We'll just have to find a way in." It is dark on the other side of the room, with only the faint glow of the flashlight that I've propped on the bedside table. Pradyumna is leaning back again on the tiny bed, his arms tucked leisurely under his head. He is looking up into the shadows on the ceiling. I can tell he is smiling.

"*We?*" I'm not sure what he's implying. Certainly, he doesn't want to get mixed up in my family drama while he's trying to win *Bake Week*. "I don't expect you to get involved with all this. It's my past, my issues to resolve. Getting tangled up with something like this could ruin your chance to win the Golden Spoon."

"Lottie," Pradyumna says. "With all due respect, I think this is exactly the kind of project I need right now."

STELLA

It is obvious to everyone that I barely scraped by today in the tent. Believe me, I'm mortified by my performance. My peach pie was burnt, nearly inedible on the bottom with a gooey filling that hadn't had time to properly set before judging. If I hadn't burnt my first filling, it would have turned out okay, I try to comfort myself, but I'm honestly not sure if that's true. I cringe, remembering the look on Betsy's face as she bit into it. The slight pause and purse of her lips in displeasure. If Gerald had stayed and finished his pies instead of storming off set, there's no question that I would be packing up right now. I'm going to do better tomorrow. I know that I can. The thought motivates me. I dig a creased school notebook out of my bag and go to the small desk pressed up against the window of my room. I look at my shadowy reflection. My face looks sad and sunken, and my eyes are dark holes in the windowpane. I'm good at starting over. I think back on all the foster families I lived with over the years. Somehow, I never really minded the upheaval. Each time I moved with a new family, began a first day of a new school, it felt like I was given a fresh slate. I must have always held some optimism inside that my life could still surprise me. I guess I had just always hoped that things would change for the better.

I look away from the window, flipping the notebook open. I once used these notebooks to write down ideas and take down quotes for articles I was writing, but ever since I stopped working at *The Republic* I have just used them to record my baking inspiration. I brush off today's mistakes and start fresh. In my imagination I begin to pair different flavors so that whatever bake is announced in the morning, I'll have a head start on my ingredients. I tap my pen on the paper as I think. I want to be inventive but not off-putting. My mind swirls with images of tarts and pastries drizzled with icing and topped with tempered chocolate. I begin to write out plans for as many desserts as I can come up with. I fill up the page with trifles, croissants, tarts, cupcakes, pavlovas, and madeleines. I want to be prepared so that no matter what dessert they throw at us tomorrow, I will have my wits about me. I won't panic like I did today. The planning calms me, as it always does, and I lose track of time until I hear a sound outside. It is the thin murmur of a voice, barely audible through the glass. I stand up and stretch across the desk to peer outside. The light from my bedroom window casts a long rectangle of yellow light across the grass fading into the inky darkness of the woods. The rest of the lawn is dark and motionless I don't see or hear anything. Maybe the sound was coming from inside the house. Then I wonder if I imagined it and there was no sound at all. I do have trouble trusting my own perceptions the way I used to. When I draw back from the window, my heart is pounding, fearful. I count down in my head. *Five, four, three, two,* until I find myself calming down again.

I move away from the window and sit on the bed. My travel alarm clock says 11:04. I should be getting some sleep anyway. I put my notepad on the bedside table and turn off the light. The faint sound of laughter travels through the glass, and I leap out of bed, rushing to the window. Two people emerge from the woods, darting across the lawn toward the manor. One of them stumbles, leaning on the larger one. Their hands are entwined. The moonlight catches on the smaller one's bright white-blond hair and slim shoulders. It's Hannah, I realize with a start. Her strappy sandals dangle from the fingers of one hand. Next to her, his arm now disappearing around her small waist as if to push her along, is none other than Archie Morris. They pick up speed as they get closer, running silently across the lawn toward the manor until I am looking almost directly down on them. Archie casts a furtive glance up and I dive to the side of the window. Good thing I'd turned my light off or he'd have definitely seen me. I shiver. It felt as if he'd looked right at me. I peer out again over the edge of the curtains just as they disappear into a door in the side of the building. I stand in the darkness, heart thudding, listening for Hannah's footsteps in the hall, the gentle click of her door coming to a close. But I hear nothing.

Day Three

CAKE

GERALD

I stand in front of Grafton Manor waiting for my taxi. The sun hasn't fully risen. Next to me my suitcase and attaché case are neatly packed. The blueprints rest on top of my suitcase in their cardboard roll. At home they'll go into the closet where I catalog all my important documents. I check my watch. It's 6:13. The taxi will get me to the train station at approximately 7:50, giving me plenty of time for a coffee before the Vermonter arrives at 8:35 to take me back to Manhattan. I have double-checked the app, and it shows the train has left St. Albans and barring any unforeseen disaster will be arriving on time. It is still several minutes too early to expect the yellow cab to pull up the drive.

That I have left without saying goodbye to any of the others makes me feel heavy inside. This shirking of the rules of civility tugs at my chest. I should have at the very least gone down for dinner last night, but I was not at my best then. I am still upset by the events of yesterday and embarrassed by my reaction. Sometimes it can be difficult for me to process when things don't go as planned. Up until yesterday's competition, I had been very much enjoying my time away at Grafton, despite all the changes I'd had to make to my daily schedule in order to come. But it wasn't fair what happened yesterday. I stand by the absolute quality of my ingredients. Every tincture had been prepared and stored with the utmost attention to detail and quality.

A flash of yellow appears on the road as the taxi arrives. Right on time. A relief. I instruct the driver on how to load my suitcases into the trunk and settle into the backseat. I brush the wrinkles out of my trouser legs as we start back down the drive, glancing behind me as the gables of Grafton's roof recede into the distance. Soon I will be back in my apartment, back to my routines. I imagine my morning coffees and long walks. The thought should soothe me, but instead I find myself growing agitated. This wasn't how I'd planned on things going. It isn't losing the competition that upsets me. It's the unfairness of the whole situation. If I had lost because of an error I made, then everything would be fine. But I am certain I didn't lose due to an error. Someone tampered with my orange essence. It's the only plausible explanation. I recall page forty-three of the *Bake Week* dossier, which states that it is strictly against *Bake Week* policy to intentionally sabotage another contestant's bakes. I suspect I am not the only one whose bake was meddled with. Peter's salt and sugar containers were stored in inverse of everyone else's. It would be very unlikely that the person in charge of setting up and storing ingredients wouldn't have known which cannister each ingredient went into if they were filling the others as well. And Peter said the night before last that he'd even tasted them at the beginning to make sure, which means someone would have had to swap the containers while we were baking. I stop to think about what that would mean. Could someone have actually switched them up *during* the competition? It would be difficult given the cameras and the lack of privacy but certainly not impossible.

We pass through the stone gate. My mind is whirring. Someone at *Bake Week* isn't playing by the rules. And that person needs to be brought to task so that the game can be restarted and, this time, played fairly. It's only right. My watch lets out a *ding*, letting me know my pulse is elevated. I wipe my forehead and am surprised when my hand comes back damp with sweat. Through the taxi's front windshield, I watch the woods begin to clear at the intersection with the state highway.

"Excuse me, sir," I say, my voice rising sharply. "Stop the car. I'll get out here."

BETSY

Betsy's phone buzzes on the coffee table.

Downstairs whenever you're ready.

George is outside with the SUV. She pulls on a cardigan and rushes out to finally meet Francis.

Normally she'd just instruct him to drive to Grafton, but having Archie here complicates things, so instead they'll be heading to the only restaurant open, a diner just a few miles down the road. As she walks across the gravel drive, she looks back at the manor. The window to Archie's room is black, the curtains drawn tight against the pleasant morning light. The thought of Archie is being left alone at Grafton without supervision fills her with a sense of unease, but she tries to push it away. She won't be gone long. George opens the back door to the SUV and she gets in, allowing herself to be swallowed up by the plush leather seating and climate control.

"Temperature okay back there, Betsy?"

"Yes, fine."

As they drive through the woods and turn out onto the state highway, she becomes increasingly nervous. Francis has driven up all the way from New York, which must mean it's something serious he wants to hash out. What could he possibly be needing to tell her in person that he couldn't just say over the phone? Finally, they pull into the parking lot of the Bluebird Diner. Betsy has never been here to eat, though it's been around for nearly forty years according to the date on its sign. Growing up, the Graftons didn't really *do* diner food. Francis is already here. She can see his back through the window. He's inspecting an oversize menu, the top of his head shining like a worn teddy bear with the beginnings of a bald spot.

"Wait for me here. I won't be long," Betsy tells George.

"Yes, ma'am."

A bell dings as she pushes the diner door open. Bright fluorescent lights vibrate overhead. A woman with hair the color of dishwater stands behind the counter with a rag in her hand. She glances up as Betsy walks in and Betsy watches her register who she is. Her eyes widen in surprise. Her mouth drops open. *Oh dear.* Sometimes Betsy really doesn't have the time to be famous.

"I'm just meeting him." She points across the empty restaurant to where Francis sits in a booth.

"I'll be right over to take your order," the woman says, her voice wavering excitedly.

"Just a tea, cream and sugar please," Betsy tells her briskly as she begins to walk across the diner, clutching her Chanel bag. Betsy doesn't have the patience for all this interaction right now. She'll hear Francis out and then get the hell out of this place.

"Yes, of course! Coming right up!" The woman scrambles for a mug.

Betsy walks up to Francis's booth, stopping abruptly. "Well, here I am." His shoulders jump, startled, and he looks up from the menu.

"Betsy." He starts to rise from the booth, but she waves him off, sitting down across from him.

He's looking older, she notices, his cheeks have become hollower, his suit less filled out than it used to be. He drums his fingers together, a bad sign. She swallows.

"For God's sake, Francis, after driving all the way up here, you'd better just come out with it," Betsy says bitterly.

He clears his throat.

"It's Archie." He starts.

Her stomach drops. "Yes, he's dreadful. Have they finally come to their senses and decided not to use him next season?"

"Not quite." Francis tents his fingers. "The press have seen some early footage."

"How? I'm going to murder Melanie. I swear to you, Francis, that woman has it in for me," Betsy says. Nothing is supposed to be shown to anyone until after filming. It is the only way to keep the results a secret. They've had a specific way of doing things up until now. A way that has worked for everyone for a decade.

"It's okay, it wasn't anything that compromised the show. Nothing that will give away who is going home or anything like that."

Betsy nods, relieved as Francis continues, "Melanie may have been the one to share it with Archie first, but it wasn't Melanie who leaked the footage to the press. It was Archie."

"Why would he do something reckless like that?" she sputters. "What possible reason would he have to risk the integrity of the show? Do you know what would happen if it came out who has gone home already? What about the producers?" At least Archie will be fired for this kind of misbehavior, Betsy realizes, calming a bit with the idea of him finally gone.

"They've seen it, of course."

She's breathing heavily, her mind racing. "Well?"

He runs his finger over the chipped white cup in front of him.

"They love him. Apparently, they are willing to forgive him. He said he did it to 'generate buzz' and 'save' the show." Francis puts his fingers up in air quotes, a gesture that makes her want to slap him. Betsy feels her face growing hot. He leans forward, his face puckered like he has eaten raw flour. "There's more."

"More?" She clenches her teeth.

He pulls something out of his bag.

"It's a tabloid. From today."

She takes the newspaper from him. On the cover is a Photoshopped image of her and Archie. In it, Betsy's eyebrows are arched up and her mouth curved down like a Disney villain. God knows where the press found the photo. Next to the picture of her, Archie is just smiling that smug smile of his. They've done nothing to exaggerate *his* features, to make *him* look bad.

"They've made it look like I'm a crazy old bat and he's just putting up with me."

Francis pulls the tabloid away from her. "He is trying to sabotage you, Betsy. He wants to be the main host of the show, perhaps even push you out entirely. And from what I've heard, the producers are on board."

"No. This isn't happening." Betsy feels like she could break something.

"There's even talk of the show leaving Grafton, moving to LA."

"Here's your tea!" The woman from the counter appears next to them with a mug in her hand. She smiles and places it in front of Betsy. She's younger than she appeared at first, probably only in her early forties. Her hair and makeup are doing her no favors, though. Her skin is rough, like she was once a smoker. She begins to walk away and then pauses. Betsy knows this pause. She is working up the nerve to say something. Betsy braces herself, rage simmering in her chest.

"I just wanted to say, I love your show so much. Made me start baking."

Betsy suppresses her irritation with a dry smile.

"That's so kind of you," Betsy says through gritted teeth. But the woman doesn't read her tone and instead takes it as an invitation to strike up a conversation, coming to stand next to the table.

"I actually made my daughter's birthday cake this year. No mix! But I can't do those fancy decorations like in *Bake Week*. I was lucky enough to get the frosting on without tearing half the cake apart. Did use some rainbow sprinkles, though. Oh no, are those not Betsy Martin approved?"

Betsy has found with these types it is best to just wait it out. The woman will tire sooner if she doesn't engage. As she prattles on nervously, Betsy muses how simple this woman's life must be. Just come to work, clock in, clock out. No mansions to maintain, no competing celebrity egos to stroke. Francis sighs and shifts in his seat, giving his best irritated New Yorker look. Betsy says nothing but smiles in a way she hopes won't betray her irritation but also conveys the message, *please leave me alone.*

"Well, look at me, going on about my silly baking. I'll leave you two to it. Let me know if I can get you anything. Maris makes a good chocolate cream pie. Well, not by your standards maybe, but people do seem to like it."

Betsy says nothing but gives her a withering look. The woman retreats anxiously, her face stricken.

"I'm never meeting you anywhere again," she says to Francis as soon as the woman walks away.

"It's not easy being America's Grandmother," Francis replies, a bit sarcastically. It was the title the press had given Betsy by the end of season one. At first, she was uncomfortable with the moniker, she is rather appalled by children if she is being honest. Their constant needs and terrible messiness—there was a reason she'd never had any of her own. But there is money to be made being America's Grandmother. There is longevity in that title, not like the short season given to so many other women in entertainment. So, Betsy has done what she needed to in order to survive and embraced it.

"*Bake Week* can't leave Grafton, Francis. Where would it go? Some soulless studio, all chrome and glass? No, *Bake Week* and Grafton are inextricably linked. If *Bake Week* left for some prefab set somewhere, it would destroy the show."

It *might* destroy the show, Betsy realizes, but it would *definitely* destroy Grafton Manor. The only thing keeping the place going is the money from *Bake Week*, and even with that Grafton is just barely hanging on. The expense of keeping up an entire manor is endless. There are rooms, whole floors, Betsy has had to completely abandon. Without the allowance from *Bake Week*, Grafton would surely fall into disrepair. Or worse, Betsy would be forced to sell. And there is no way she can let that happen. Not after all she has done to preserve it.

"I know. I've told them that of course," Francis says.

"I can't sell Grafton, Francis." Betsy leans across the table, jabbing her finger into the grimy Formica between them.

She can tell from the look on his face that he doesn't understand. But who could possibly comprehend her attachment to the place? How could she ever explain what Grafton is to her—all its flaws and beauty—creaks and groans and slanted light in the afternoons. It is practically human. She feels almost wedded to the manor. All the history there—her own, her family's. It needs protecting. Grafton is even more important to Betsy since the divorce. Roland had never loved the manor and had convinced Betsy to move to a modern high-rise in Manhattan for much of their marriage. He didn't understand why Betsy would keep such a huge and valuable piece of real estate that she couldn't afford to care for. It was a drain on both of their resources, he argued, even though both of their resources were earned entirely through her cookbook empire. Eventually she was strong-armed into telling him more than she wanted to. The things Roland knows about Grafton keep her up some nights.

"So now what are we supposed to do?" Betsy can feel her temper rising. It takes every ounce of self-control not to pick up her mug and hurl it at the floor as her dream of more restoration work slips from her grasp. She sees her mother's face suddenly, her lips pursed in disappointment.

"We'll need to be . . . strategic," Francis says carefully. "I have a plan." She leans in to listen.

Minutes later Betsy is barreling back to Grafton in the back of the

SUV. She feels a sense of dread weighing heavier on her the closer they get. She wants to be done with it all, the show, the baking. She wished that they would all just go away and leave her alone. She pictures Archie's wide jaw. His clever repartee and fitted suits. She is stunned that he's had the audacity to go behind her back and change *her* show. That he's tried to take the reins away from *her*, *Bake Week*'s creator. Betsy is furious, absolutely boiling with rage.

"It's too damn hot in here, George. Open a window!"

PRADYUMNA

It's early still, just past six a.m. I've slept my typical five hours. As soon as my eyes flutter open, I shower and get dressed. Then I must immerse myself in some sort of activity. I know from experience that the only way to keep the feeling away is to keep moving. From my bedroom window, I watch Gerald pack his belongings into the back of a yellow taxi, his shoulders looking small inside his rumpled suitcoat. He doesn't look at the manor at all as he gets into the backseat. I feel a pang of sadness as I watch him disappear.

I'm about to turn away from the window when I see the black SUV pull into the drive. Betsy Martin toddles down the front steps in her signature high heels and gets into the backseat. A thrill shoots through my chest as it silently whisks her down the drive and out of sight.

I finish getting dressed quickly and tiptoe into the hallway. With any luck the others will stay in their rooms for at least another hour, giving us just the right amount of time. I creep down the hallway to Lottie's room. I can't risk waking the others by knocking, so I open her bedroom door just a crack and peer in. The shades are still drawn tight across the windows, and the room is dark.

"Lottie," I hiss.

There's no answer, so I open the door a bit farther, slipping inside. As my eyes adjust to the dim light, I make out the form of tiny Lottie lying back on the pillow. Her frame is so small, it barely makes a dent in the blanket. She is motionless, lying on her back, peaceful. She looks . . . I lean over closer to her and look for the rise and fall of her chest but see nothing. My heart palpitates.

"Lottie!" I call out in my full voice this time.

Her eyes flip open, and I stumble back, startled.

"Who's there?" she says angrily, swinging her arms, pawing at the air in front of her as though trying to fight off an invisible attacker.

"Lottie, it's me. Jesus, I thought you were dead. You almost gave me a heart attack." I approach the bed again tentatively, my hand clutching my chest.

"Pradyumna? Why on earth would you think that?" she says irritably, glancing at the alarm clock by her bed. "And what are you doing here? It's six-thirty in the morning."

"Yes, I know. Get up!" I am already crossing the room, yanking open the curtains so that golden early morning light spills into the room.

She blinks, struggles to push herself up against the mountain of pillows on her bed. "What is going on with you?" She watches me rush around the room, looking more amused now than annoyed. I pause at the foot of her bed, bouncing from foot to foot impatiently. I don't want to take the time to explain, so I lay it out for her as quickly as possible.

"Listen. I saw Betsy leave in a car just now. I think this is our chance to go explore the East Wing and see if we can find anything else about Agnes. But we have to move fast."

I grab a bathrobe that's hanging off the side of her chair and throw it to her. She is fully awake now, sitting up in her striped pajamas, her feet on the floor.

"Really? You're sure?" She takes the robe.

"Positive. But I don't know how long she'll be gone so we'd better hurry."

Lottie thinks for a moment. I can see the resolution settling on her face as she decides to follow me. She throws the covers back and slides her feet into a pair of slippers as I rush for the door. "Wait!" she calls out. I stop and turn back toward her, my hand resting on the doorknob.

"Are you sure you want to go? This is *my* thing, *my* crazy journey. You could risk your place in *Bake Week* if we were to get caught."

I think of my place at *Bake Week*, of the tent and the competition. How little it matters to me. How little anything matters lately. I shouldn't even be here. Winning would mean next to nothing to me, would give me no prize I don't already have. I am the fraud here, not because I'm no good but because I don't care.

"Yes, you old loon. Now let's hurry."

"You really are something speaking to your elders that way. Ageism is not attractive," Lottie tuts as we creep out into the hallway and make a run for the landing. We cross slowly. One of the cleaning staff comes up the stairs carrying new bed linen, and we stop to casually look up at a painting of Richard Grafton. As soon as the woman has passed, we make a break for the East Wing.

"The important thing is not to wake Archie," Lottie whispers as we tiptoe up to the double doors. Through the glass I see a long empty hallway. I look to Lottie, who gives me a small nod, her eyes wide. I push down on the latch, and it clicks open. I wave Lottie in first, slipping after her into the East Wing and closing the door carefully behind me.

The hallway is dimly lit by oil lamps retrofitted with Edison bulbs. They flicker in a convincingly old-fashioned way as we move down the hall, carpeted with a long Persian rug. My heart rate accelerates pleasantly, relishing the risk. I don't know what we are looking for exactly, or how we will know it when we see it, but the thrill of the hunt is more than enough for me.

Lottie turns back to me and points to the far end of the hall. Wordlessly, we creep up to a set of double doors. We pass through a small sitting area and into a large open room furnished with an oversize wooden secretary and a wall of bookshelves. A large stone fireplace takes up most of another wall with two overstuffed chairs cozied up to it. We scan the walls, taking in the shelves, which are filled with an assortment of books and knickknacks, the kinds of things you'd find on the set of a BBC minidrama—leather-bound books, a brass-handled magnifying glass, a white marble bust of a man, Beethoven perhaps, his hair frozen in close-cropped curls around his head. I open one of the drawers in the secretary. It is filled with old-fashioned pens with metal tips and glass bottles of ink. The others contain similarly obscure bits and bobs, useless for our purposes but interesting nonetheless.

"Oh, I don't even know what I'm looking for," Lottie whispers, sighing with frustration and leaning against the arm of one of the chairs. "This is just a waste of time. I'm so sorry I dragged you into all this."

I ignore her. I've never been one to easily dole out pity, and I continue to poke around the room picking up objects on the shelves. There's a cigar box full of unsmoked Cuban cigars, petrified by age. What a waste. I spin a large marble globe on its axis, noting its borders were drawn from a time far before the sun set on the British Empire. A Victrola record player stands at attention in the corner.

"Maybe we should try her bedroom," I suggest, picking up a non-descript wooden box off the top of the mantel. Before I can open it, Lottie lets out a small cry and snatches it from my hands. She tilts the top of the box back on its hinges, revealing a thick pack of notecards. Lottie pulls a stack of them out, fanning them out across the top of the secretary.

"I'd forgotten all about these." The recipes are written in tilted cursive on white notecards. There are recipes for bread, for elaborate cakes, for pies and cookies. They are worn with use, their edges bent, stained with drops of vanilla, and smudged with cooking oil.

"They're my mother's," Lottie says. "I haven't seen them since she disappeared."

I pick one out and read it out loud. "Special Day Strawberry Shortcake."

"Oh, that one was incredible." Lottie smiles, remembering. "It was like a traditional shortcake, but the biscuit had strawberries baked into it. She sprinkled homemade vanilla bean–infused sugar on top."

Something begins to itch at the back of my mind as I sift through the recipes. They are all unique and lovingly constructed. There's one for a chocolate ganache tart striped with hazelnut and praline, a honey cake with orange marmalade filling, coconut cream–filled doughnuts with meringues in the center. Extra notes have been added to the margins, addendums to use more cherries or to keep it in the oven for five minutes longer. It's what every good baker does: tries to make their recipes better over time. You can tell Lottie's mother was a fantastic baker, and I can see where Lottie gets it from.

"Look, this one is stuck." I gently detach a card, which has been adhered to another with a bit of something sticky. "World's Best Blueberry Buckle." I whistle. "That's quite a claim."

Lottie takes the card from me. "If anyone could make the world's best anything, it was my mother. She was the best baker I've ever met."

Lottie reads each of the recipes lovingly, stroking the handwriting as she reads through them. "Some of these I've never even tasted. She didn't have the chance to bake for just the two of us very often, and I—"

Lottie stops. Outside there is the faint sound of a car door closing. I tiptoe to the window and pull back the edge of the curtain. Below, the black SUV has returned. Betsy Martin has already gotten out. Her arms swing forcefully as she makes her way up the front steps.

"Shit. She's back!" I hiss. We look at each other wide-eyed. Lottie drops the recipe box with a clatter, and we both cringe. Her hands are shaking as we frantically gather the recipes from the secretary. I take a bunch of them from her and stuff them back into the box, closing its lid and tucking it under my arm as I look around the room to make sure nothing else is displaced.

"We have to hurry," Lottie says, her voice thick with fear.

We bolt into the hallway. At the end of the hall the doors are still shut tight. The lights from the landing illuminate their windows. I realize with alarm that there is no way to avoid Betsy if she takes the main staircase. Lottie grabs onto my arm and pulls me back.

"We'll run into her if we leave through the landing," Lottie whispers.

"We have to hide and wait for her to pass." I look wildly around the hallway at the row of closed doors. There is no way to tell what is behind any of them. Betsy's shadow is a smudge on the windows of the French doors, growing darker and crisper as she approaches. I make a split decision, opening a door to my left and pulling Lottie through it with me. I shut it very carefully behind us, my heart racing. The room is dark, the curtains drawn almost all the way across the window, letting in only a tiny shard of silvery light. My eyes finally adjust, and I realize we are in a bedroom. A large four-poster bed takes up the center of the room, and carved wooden poles rise in twisted spears on each corner like some sort of torture device from a medieval dungeon. Lottie sees the shape stirring under the blankets the same time as I do and lets out a gasp. It's Archie. *Shit*. Of all the doors to open, we had to choose that meathead's.

And then I see something else. A slender ankle draped out over the side of the bed. It takes me a moment to process the nymphish outline of a young woman asleep next to him. A loud, snorting snore comes from the bed. I feel Lottie's hand gripping my forearm. I wonder how much she's seen. Out in the hallway the distinctive *click-clack* of Betsy's footsteps grows closer and then recedes down the far end of the hall. I turn my back to the bed, grasping for the handle to the door. I twist it open and release us back out into the hallway. My body buzzes with adrenaline as we run to the end of the hall and out onto the landing. I look down at the grandfather clock standing in the foyer: 7:25. Time to get ready for another day in the tent.

STELLA

I watch Archie Morris swagger up to the front of the tent and am filled with revulsion. He looks around at us, grinning like a shark. Seeing him last night crossing the lawn with Hannah has soured me on him completely. Before, even though I'd found his personality a bit over-the-top, I figured at least his confidence was earned, the product of being good at what he does. I may have even found it a little bit charming to be so sure of oneself. But now I see that Archie's success hasn't just given him self-assuredness, it has given him delusions of grandeur, the idea that he is able to do *whatever* he wants *whenever* he wants to *whomever* he wants with no negative repercussions. In fact, he has probably mostly gotten the opposite and been rewarded for taking what doesn't belong to him.

But now he has made a complete mockery out of what we are all trying to do here. The rest of us are taking *Bake Week* seriously, doing our best. And what has he been doing? Using the show as just a way to pick up young girls. Who the fuck does he think he is? Does he think that just because he's a celebrity it gives him an excuse to prey on women? I glance at Hannah, one row ahead of me today. Each day, as the number of us shrinks, the placement of our baking stations is altered. I've rotated over one space and am now directly behind Hannah and across from Lottie. Hannah's cheeks are unusually pale, as though she'd forgotten to put on the makeup she usually wears. Her hair is lank and parted unevenly, not in its usual pristine bob. I watch as she looks down at her hands, fidgeting as we wait for our instructions. I want to ask her if she is okay and then scold her for allowing herself to get sucked into the bad situation she's in with Archie. Part of me wants to give them away. To point and shout and make a big scene. I want to tell her not to listen to a word he says, that he is taking advantage of her and to stay away from him. I know that it would tear apart the show. As much as I want to expose Archie, I don't want to ruin it for the others, myself included, so I stay silent.

Betsy doesn't look herself today either. She is just as pressed and polished as usual, but there is something off about her, a strange darting of the eyes and twist of the mouth that I haven't seen before. It makes me not want to cross her. As Archie and Betsy step up to the table, something odd and off-kilter passes between the two of them. For a split second, I catch Betsy staring at him with absolute vitriol. The expression is barely on her face for a moment before it disappears, replaced instantly with her signature placid smile. I wonder if Betsy suspects Archie of being a lech. The thought comforts me.

As Betsy steps out in front of the judging table to give us our assignment, my hands go cold and clammy. This kind of adrenaline is exhausting, and yet today I feel more prepared for whatever recipe will be thrown at me. I have an extra sense of purpose now I didn't have before. I glance at Graham, who is behind one of the cameras filming Betsy. I want to keep an eye on that one. It's a real disappointment that even at someplace as seemingly pure as *Bake Week*, there are still creeps to deal with.

Betsy clasps her hands in delight. "All right, everyone, today you will be baking my favorite, everyone's favorite, cakes!"

Archie steps in. "Your cake must be large enough to feed at least thirty people. It must have at least two layers. We want to see you use your creativity and really wow us with your execution. There are only four of you left, and we know you are all excellent bakers, so this will be a difficult challenge."

My mind races to find the cake I'll be making, mentally flipping through the pages of my notebook. An image comes to me fully formed. It is so perfect I can't help but smile even through my lingering disgust.

"Ready . . . set . . . ," they begin in unison.

"Bake!"

I run to my fridge to look for ingredients and nearly collide with Pradyumna, who is doing the same.

"Whoa!" he says, grinning and moving his hands up in surrender as he lets me through. I laugh, but as soon as I've moved past him to my refrigerator, I roll my eyes in exasperation. I don't have time for this today, from him or anyone else. Today I have a plan. Today I am going to win.

We are thirty minutes into the competition when Archie Morris steps up to my table surrounded by cameras. He smiles at me, an acknowledgment of his power in the situation, and waits for me to react accordingly. I stack my spine and return his gaze evenly.

"Hello, Archie," I say, my voice thick with meaning.

Disarmed, the half smile flickers on his face.

"Okay." He laughs awkwardly now, attempting to put me in my place and establish dominance in the conversation by making me look silly, but I won't give it to him. I merely lean against my baking table, blowing hair from my face, and wait for him to get on with it. He is truly confused by my lack of simpering but pulls himself together.

"What can you tell me about your cake?" he asks, leaning over and resting a hand on my workstation. It is large and stubby, his fingers round like cigars. I remember how he prodded Hannah's back, pushing her toward the house. I wonder if he'd even asked if he could touch her. It is unlikely. He has the unearned confidence of someone who has gotten away with this kind of shit for years, possibly throughout his entire career. I look back at him stone-eyed. I'll have to keep my cool for now.

"It will be flavored with honey and orange zest. And I'm planning a sculptural element that I hope Betsy will love." I avoid making eye contact with Archie, working on pouring my batter into a variety of cake pans.

"It sounds gorgeous," he says, smiling. I look away.

"Hard to resist a pretty thing, isn't it?" I say curtly. I can tell he's a bit confused now. *Good.* I'll throw him off his game.

"All right, Stella. Good luck," he says, retreating. I am satisfied that at least for the moment I seem to have won the power struggle.

I'd had an idea last night as I lay awake worried about Hannah. If I can pull it off, it will be my biggest story ever, my return to journalism. I'm imagining it as a reported piece, part exposé and part personal essay. I wouldn't give Hannah's name away, not if she doesn't want me to. But it will be better if I can get her to speak. There must be other women he's done this to. I haven't watched many episodes of *The Cutting Board*, but I do remember some of the youngest, prettiest contestants. As soon as I leave here, I'll do some research. But first, I'll need plenty of evidence. I will collect proof that he is preying on contestants in his shows so that people can see beyond any reasonable doubt what a terrible person Archie Morris is. Today I see none of the flirtation in his interactions with Hannah. He seems almost to be avoiding her, and I wonder, cynically, if he has already had his fun. *I will keep watching you.* Archie furtively glances at me, and I give him a coy smile.

As I put my cakes into the oven, I realize that this experience at *Bake Week* has been about more than proving my worth as a baker. I was a good writer. If I can pull this off, maybe I can be a great one. I grate orange zest for my glaze, and I feel more confident than I have in a very long time. Tonight, I will sit by that fireplace with the others and relish my win. This is my chance to be the journalist, the person, I was before. The one who is not paralyzed by fear, afraid of her own shadow. Someone with a future.

GERALD

After the taxi lets me out, I drag my bags off the main driveway and onto the path that loops around the woods beyond the lawn. There I wait. I have decided that what I need to do next is to sneak back into the house. It is the only chance I have at uncovering the perpetrator who sabotaged me and who clearly has something against *Bake Week*. I'll have to stay put for a while, until filming gets under way, so I pop open the lid on the document canister and tap out the blueprints, unfurling them across the back of my overturned suitcase. I've already studied them well, annotating them to familiarize myself with the places I would pass through each day before and after filming. Now I have a slightly different goal, which is to find the places I'm *not* meant to go, someplace I can hide and watch.

I run my forefinger down hallways, stopping and turning around, testing different pathways as though I'm solving a maze. My eyes land on the cutaway marking of a balcony on the second floor just to the east side of the house. It is off one of the second-floor parlors, a room that shouldn't be in heavy use. Here I would be able to see the tent while remaining concealed.

Satisfied with this option, I roll the blueprint up and slide it back into its tube. I pull out a nutritional bar and munch on it methodically.

Now that I have my phone back from Melanie's clutches, I take it out and look at the time: 10:24. Even accounting for delays, filming will have begun. It is time to get moving.

I stand up and dust myself off, attempting to shake the wrinkles out of my suit, which I notice has already gathered some grass and dirt stains. This kind of sartorial messiness would normally cause me a great deal of apprehension, but fortunately I am too focused on the task at hand to fully give it my attention. I pull my suitcase upright and slide the attaché case over the handle. Tucking the roll of blue-prints under my arm, I begin to drag my things back toward Grafton. I do not like to speculate without sufficient evidence, but I would assume, based on motive, that the person committing these acts is a contestant themself. Who else would have any reason to meddle with someone's bakes?

When I reach the edge of the woods, I stop. Given the time of day, it is unlikely there would be a break in filming for the next hour. Everyone should be deeply involved with their baking. I take a deep breath, focusing on a point in the distance, the corner of the building I must disappear around. Ready . . . set . . . I take off at a good clip, my suitcase bouncing behind me, jerking my arm as it catches on the lawn. Through the clear vinyl windows of the tent, I can make out the bakers at their stations. I am tempted to go closer, to see what the assignment is today, but I remind myself that I have a mission to complete. I must hurry. As I pick up the pace, the wheel of my suitcase catches on something. I feel myself flying backward through the air. I let out an involuntary grunt as I land hard on my back, splayed out like an overturned turtle. Surely I will be caught now. I raise my head and look at the tent. Inside Melanie's back is to me, her head bent to whisper something to one of the camera operators. No one has seen me. I almost feel like laughing. I quickly hoist myself up, pick up my suitcase, and make a final run to the side of the manor.

Out of view, I lean against the cool stone breathing heavily. The sky overhead swirls with cirrostratus clouds. The rain will follow them closely, it's already well on its way. The wall above me is covered in ivy. I look up into its chaotic patterns, admiring how it adapts to the architecture, twisting and turning around windows and stone trim. I step back. I am looking at the balcony with the parapet I'd seen in the blueprint.

On one side of the balcony, a rusted iron storm drain cuts past the parapet and on up to the roof. I take one step up, bouncing my sole on it, testing the strength of the pipe. I put my phone and several nutritional bars into my pocket and push my suitcase behind a row of shrubbery. I approach the drainpipe tentatively, placing one dress shoe onto the bolt that connects it to the wall. This is not ideal. The probability of an accident here is very high. *Please, brain, be quiet for once.* I continue to climb higher and higher until I am level with the balcony. I shift my weight over to the side, throwing myself toward the parapet wall. I feel some of the bricks shift as I land heavily on the floor of the balcony. From here I can lean out just a fraction of an inch and see the action. Now to watch.

LOTTIE

My hands feel light and capable as I mix up a simple batter, cream-ing sugar and butter with eggs and vanilla. Though I have hardly slept I am wide awake, more alert than I've felt the whole time I've been at Grafton. I am invigorated by all that I've discovered in the past twenty-four hours. I still can't believe that my mother and Richard Grafton were together in that photograph. It's an un-thinkable revelation, one I never would have had were it not for Pradyumna. Who'd have thought the young millionaire would have been someone I could confide in, let alone such a help? I'm deeply grateful for his quick thinking this morning bringing us into the East Wing.

Working on my cake, I have a surprising surge of hope. I feel closer to my mother than I have in decades. Finding her recipes so many years later could have made me incredibly sad. Instead, seeing her notecards, her handwriting, feels like a message not to give up. I've thought of my mother's recipes from time to time over the years but always assumed they were just lost in the shuffle of my displace-ment. I had always wondered why the recipe box wasn't returned to me. I think of the carboard box I was sent out into the world with.

It contained my own sparse collection of clothes plus a few of my mother's clothes, a couple of books, a pair of shoes. All that remained of her. I had looked for the recipe box in the folds of her dresses, my small hands coming up against the sides of the box and finding nothing. I assumed that it had gotten lost in the shuffle. But seeing the recipe box sitting prominently on Betsy Martin's mantel was a shock. It makes me realize that she must not have forgotten all about us after all. She can't have.

As I zest a lemon, I replay memories of my mother. It is a common exercise of mine whenever I have a spare moment to think of the times I've spent with her, to recall what she said, what she was wearing, the smells in the air. I do it hoping the repetition will preserve them for me, to keep her alive in what small ways I can. Now I comb through my memories, shake them out, searching them for clues. If I could just discover some new detail that would reveal to me what my mother had been going through, I have the feeling that I could solve the entire mystery of her disappearance. I try to remember any time I saw her with Richard Grafton, a strange look or an intimate word between them, but I can't seem to pull up anything unusual.

I pour my blueberries onto the countertop and pick through them, discarding the ones that are too soft. Then I roll them in flour until each one is coated evenly. As I stir them into my batter, I have a memory of her standing at the tall wooden table in Grafton's kitchen. It is summer, and she is kneading bread, her hands and apron dusted with flour. I am next to her, helping, pulling green beans from a bowl and trimming their ends. We work together, me snapping the beans and my mother slapping the dough down on the table. I remember the rhythm of it, the heaviness of the bread hitting the wood. And how it suddenly stopped. I watched my mother's hands pulling away from the dough.

I stop stirring my cake batter. My heart skips a beat as I recall my mother looking up from the bread, fear freezing her features. I followed her eyes to the kitchen door, propped open to give us a breeze and watched with her as two shadows passed by the door, one tall and imposing and one small in pigtails, Richard Grafton and his daughter Betsy. My stomach drops, my optimism evaporating as I recall looking at my mother's hands and seeing they were shaking.

HANNAH

I pull my cakes out of the oven. The tops are spongy and golden brown. I exhale heavily with relief and set them out on wire racks to cool. I've tried and tried but I am unable get into my baking flow today. I just can't disappear into the rhythm of measuring and mixing the way I normally do. Maybe I'm just too distracted to bake. I keep thinking of last night with Archie, replaying the entire evening over and over in my mind. It was so romantic, I think now, him taking me into the woods like that and then later sneaking me once again into the East Wing, to his bed. I bite back a smile remembering the rest. I've never had anyone act so passionately toward me or say the things he did. I wonder if this is what a real adult relationship feels like, and I have been selling myself short all this time. I know what Archie would say, that I deserve to be treated like a queen.

It's hard for me not to stare at him as he moves confidently around the tent chatting with the rest of the contestants. I try not to feel hurt that he hasn't come by my table yet. *He is just doing his job*, I tell myself. *And you should be too!* But my hands are clumsy, and I struggle to complete each basic step of my recipe.

Stomach full of jitters, I try to carefully pull my cakes out of their silicone molds. My hands are unsteady, trembling as I pull the sides away. I watch with horror as one of the cakes sticks, leaving a jagged chunk in the bottom of the mold as I peel it away. This has never happened before. I am so careful, normally. Panic springs up in my chest. The remaining sponge is a tragedy, with a good portion of its golden crust ripped away, exposing its soft white innards. My eyes sting with embarrassment.

A camera operator catches it all—the worry on my face as I pry the missing pieces out of the mold, my pathetic attempt to salvage it by fitting the pieces together on top of my sponge. I feel them focusing on my every flaw. I try to keep a smile on my face. "No one likes a young lady with a scowl," I hear my mom scolding me. I strain my facial muscles, willing myself to stay calm, look pretty, as they move in closer. I look quickly to make sure Archie hasn't seen me mess up and am relieved this time to see he is engaged in conversation with Lottie. "There we go, just like a puzzle piece," I chirp for them, though even I can hear the strain in my voice. "Won't matter once there's icing involved."

I hope that it's true, but the way things are going for me so far today, I'm not too sure. Though I've managed to fit the cake back together, the seam is still clearly visible, a jagged line of crumbly white cake that threatens to topple off the top entirely. I wonder about trying a different icing to cover up the whole mess but I feel unsteady as well, unsure what to do.

I try not to look up as Archie bypasses my table yet again with two of the camera crew and goes to talk to Pradyumna. As I crouch down next to my station to pull out a new mixing bowl I hear his laugh and feel a sharp stab of jealousy. I try to remind myself that it's silly to compare myself with Pradyumna, of all people. Archie is just doing his job. Remember what he said, I tell myself. I am the one who he thinks is so talented I can be a professional baker, and not just that. *One day you will be as successful as Betsy Martin, Hannah.* I think of him this morning telling me how beautiful I am, murmuring it into my hair as he held me. I almost laugh with relief. I am the one who woke up in his bed this morning, not them.

I'd left while he was still sleeping, slipping through the halls in my stockinged feet and sneaking back to my room so that I had plenty of time to get ready for filming. Just as I'd thought, the scratches from his sharp whiskers had left a ruddy rash across my cheeks and chin. I'd attempted to cover it with makeup, dotting it on with a sponge until I was satisfied that there was nothing that could be seen. I reach up and touch my chin. In the harsh light of the tent, I worry that my face is starting to peel. Still crouching I pull out a shiny measuring cup, angling it so that I can see my reflection distorted in the bottom. I can see some redness but nothing as bad as I'd feared. I shove the cups away and breathe heavily. I worry that by leaving without a word this morning, I may have hurt his feelings. Maybe Archie thought I was the one abandoning him. The possibility knocks me sideways. Suddenly I can hardly handle not talking to him, telling him how much I loved our evening, that I don't regret a second of it and I can't wait for many more dates and to see the places he'd promised to show me out in LA. I look over at him, bantering with Pradyumna about cocoa powder. I try to catch his eye. I want him to acknowledge me so I can reassure myself everything is okay. Then, just maybe, I can still get into my baking flow. But he remains stubbornly focused. I try to let it go for now, to go back to my own bake. I rush to the refrigerator for some heavy cream, then back to my station. As I lean down to pull out a mixing bowl, Archie's voice drifts over to me from Pradyumna's table.

"I'll leave you to it then. Enough distraction."

There is some shuffling around my table, and I breathe a sigh of relief as I feel the heat of the camera lights on my scalp. I stand up, smiling widely in anticipation. But when I pop up at my table, it isn't Archie standing in front of my table, it's Betsy Martin. She leans over the ripped-up sponge, looking down over her nose, inspecting it with a look of disapproval on her face. She says nothing for a moment, and I nervously fill in the gap with an explanation.

"I used silicone molds. I've never done that before. I didn't realize that they would get so sticky."

She frowns. "Can you tell me about the flavors in your cake?"

I swallow.

"Yes, of course. It's a raspberry cream cake. Vanilla and raspberry swirls were my favorite candy flavor as a child."

"So just last year," Betsy smirks. I smile my nicest smile, but inside I'm fuming that she'd made a joke at my expense. If Betsy approves of the flavor pairing, she gives nothing away.

"And what are you using for your raspberry flavoring?"

"One of the sponges has freeze-dried raspberry pieces," I say, my voice rising to a squeak at the end. Her lips press together. I feel like I should offer her something more. "And I'm making a raspberry jelly, actually, to place between the layers and the buttercream. It's in the freezer firming up."

It's a lie. I haven't even considered it until now, but I can't let her look at me like I am some silly kid who hasn't thought things through.

Her eyebrows shoot up. "That's a surprising choice with this weather, but a good idea. Will be hard for a jelly to firm up in time."

"Oh, I think it will all come together," I say, smiling and hoping there is no fear in my eyes to give me away.

She gives me a knowing smile. "Sometimes we must do what we can to keep our mistakes a secret, don't we?"

The words slice through me like a knife. I stop fussing with my cake and look up at her. Does she know about me and Archie? She holds my gaze a moment longer and then turns abruptly from my table.

"Forty-five minutes left!" she calls out sharply.

Archie glances my way, but his expression is unreadable. Before I can even react, he turns away and whispers something in Melanie's perfect ear. I try to push away the feelings of jealousy that bubble up as he pulls back and they smile at each other. I think of the way he looked at me last night. "You're a star, Hannah," he'd said. "I can't wait for you to realize it too." I want to show Archie that I do realize it. I want to be a star. I'm ready for my ascent, and nobody is going to stop me. Suddenly I know exactly what I have to do.

BETSY

The anger has been brewing inside Betsy since her meeting with Francis. She can feel it percolating, bubbling up through her veins, threatening to come out. She hopes she can contain it. She can't afford any further humiliation today. She's already had a run-in on the way to the tent this morning. Melanie had sidled up to her as they walked, shoving that damn clipboard under her nose.

"We want you to come up from the back of the tent today with one of your own cakes as a way to introduce today's challenge."

"But I haven't baked a cake," Betsy dismissed her.

"Don't worry, we've had one made." Betsy looked down at Melanie over her nose. "By a professional." Betsy had said nothing, which gave her the confidence to continue.

"How would you feel about that? Walking up the center aisle with one of your beautiful cakes?"

It wasn't so much the idea that bothered Betsy but the way it was presented, as if she were a child being cajoled. As though she needed hand-holding.

Betsy had stopped short, causing Melanie to nearly trip in an effort to stay on pace with her. "I'd feel just fine about it if it *were* my cake. But I feel like the audience might find it all a bit gimmicky. The spotlight has always been on the bakers, not on me." Melanie had paled at the tone of her voice, which pleased her. "But what do I know? I'm not the one keeping the whole show together, am I?" Betsy had started walking again, briskly so that Melanie had to rush to keep up, sputtering out some sort of apology.

Now Betsy can't tell if the mood has changed or if it is just her own sour feelings infiltrating her perception of everything. The contestants seem more tense than usual, less perky and optimistic. She hopes it doesn't translate to the screen. It would be annoying to have to edit out all their worried little faces, try to force some cheer into it. It never plays as well when it is fake. Archie clasps his hands in front of him, waiting to begin judging. He doesn't look at her. Is it because he suspects she knows what he's done? Or perhaps he can just feel the bad mood radiating from her like a toxic gas and thinks it better to keep his distance? Either way, she prefers him like this—quiet, subservient. If there were any unwanted noise from him, she thinks she might explode.

The bakers bring their cakes up to the front table. There has been a shift in the energy of the four of them. There always is around halfway through the week. It won't be shown on camera—we like to keep it light and heartwarming—but in person Betsy can feel it. They are becoming more competitive, more ruthless. It's only natural when the stakes are so high. They may squeeze each other's hands as they wait for the verdict to be read out at the end of each day, but it's all an act. Each desperately wants the others to lose.

Four cakes stand in front of her on the judging table. Betsy begins at the far left with Hannah's. It is a tall layer cake coated in a thick light pink buttercream that is expertly decorated with drips of white chocolate running down the sides. The frosting cannot conceal that the cake inside is lumpy and misshapen, the top layer bulges giving it away. A mound of raspberries is piled a bit haphazardly on top, but otherwise it is professionally decorated, the piping lines neat as a pin.

Hannah looks down, embarrassed. "I'm sorry! I wanted to do much more with the decoration, but I ran out of time. I hope it's not awful!" Betsy finds Hannah's false modesty a bit tedious, but you do have to give the girl credit—her technical skills are truly unparalleled this year.

She cuts two thick slices and slides them onto both her and Archie's plates as Hannah anxiously twists her hair around a finger. The number of layers is truly remarkable, eight at least, in alternating pale pink and white, all the exact same width, with a thin layer of bright jelly. The cake is held together with thick piped buttercream flecked with raspberry pieces.

Betsy takes a bite feeling her teeth stick rather than glide through the crumb as she was anticipating. She chews as the cameras zoom in closer. Hannah knots her hands under her chin in suspense. "The cake is cooked well enough, but it looks like it has split. Did you try to put a broken cake back together?"

"Just a bit." She winces.

"That'll do it. It's fallen over here." Betsy nods, prodding at the cake a bit more. "And as I'd feared, your jelly hasn't set."

Hannah's ears turn a bright pink, and she looks to Archie for salvation, but to Betsy's surprise he sides with her.

"The sponge is far too heavy," Archie agrees, tapping on the inside of the cake with his fork to show how unyielding it is. Hannah goes pale, and her face strains as though she might start to cry as Archie continues. "I also think that the buttercream is a bit too intense. It doesn't taste like much of anything but is somehow still overpowering. I would have liked some flavor in there to brighten it up. Maybe some fresh berries or even some sort of compote in place of the jelly."

"For a cake with so much raspberry color, I'm not getting much raspberry flavor at all." Betsy hates to agree with him. "Stylistically, it's a beautiful cake, though."

"Thank you, Hannah," Archie says crisply as Hannah's slender shoulders slump in defeat, and she retreats wordlessly from the table.

The next cake is Pradyumna's. It's a slim chocolate tower, with a rich dark chocolate icing. The top of the cake is covered in crushed homemade peanut brittle and tiny chocolate bonbons held in place by expertly piped dark chocolate ganache. It is precise and beautiful.

"It's a dark chocolate peanut butter cake," he says, shrugging almost apologetically. "I know, not the most original pairing."

"What matters to us is flavor and texture," Betsy reminds him. "You can have the most creative flavor pairing, but if it doesn't work, if the bake is off, it will fail." She has seen far too many mistakes with strange combinations of ingredients. No one needs too much almond extract or, God forbid, rosewater in their baked goods.

She takes a bite, making sure to get a good part of the peanut butter filling. "It's rich. Almost too rich," she tells him through a mouthful. She feels as though she needs something to wash it down. Archie reaches past Betsy with his fork, and her eyes flick to him as he takes a bite.

"Oh, man, I disagree. This is so good," Archie says. Betsy breathes in sharply, trying to control her anger. She's noticed how much different Archie is with men than with women. He acts as though they are old pals. It has a strange way of leaving women out in the cold, she thinks, but maybe she's just being sensitive given the circumstances.

"You'll have to take it a bit more seriously if you want to keep improving," she admonishes him gently. Of all of them, her and Archie included, the only one who seems in better spirits today is Pradyumna. She's noticed Pradyumna's stance has shifted a bit. His smile seems more genuine, his shoulders relaxed. He looks happy, unworried.

"Betsy, you've uncovered my terrible secret. I think baking is fun," he says, grinning handsomely.

Stella is next up. Her cake is striking to look at, stacked in graduated tiers, so that it almost resembles half of a bee's nest. It's lightly frosted in that naked style, the icing scraped away to reveal the edges of the sponge, cooked to perfection. A honey-colored glaze drips attractively down the sides, and small fondant bees with almond sliver wings cling to the tops of the cakes; a few are even hovering on wire to look like they are flying.

"I must say I've never seen a cake shaped like this. What are the flavors?" Betsy asks, and Stella beams.

"It's flavored with orange zest and honey."

"It's striking," Betsy tells her.

Stella blushes and smiles broadly, tucking a strand of hair behind her ear.

"I hope that's a good thing."

"It's a great thing," Archie agrees, and does that annoying twinkle thing with his eyes. Betsy watches as Stella looks away from him uncomfortably, delighted to see that some people are immune to his charms.

Archie cuts into the cake with some difficulty given its novel shape and pulls out two staircase-shaped slices. He and Betsy take their bites.

"The cake is melt-in-your-mouth lovely," Betsy tells Stella, savoring the light, fluffy flavor. "I don't mean to sound too full of myself, but it kind of reminds me of one of my cakes."

"Oh yes, your Optimistic Honey Cake!" Stella trips over her words in excitement. "I hope that's okay. That cake is a huge inspiration, all of yours are. I just love everything you do."

Betsy smiles primly, flattered but trying not to show it lest she be called out later for favoritism.

"You can really taste the orange here," Archie says, smiling yet again, as though he is aggressively trying to charm her. He really can turn it on when he wants to, Betsy notes wryly. Out of the corner of her eye Betsy sees Hannah's eyebrows furrow miserably.

"It really is quite delicious," she agrees. "The thin layer of icing, with the tanginess from the cream cheese, pairs perfectly with the honey. Nothing is too sweet. Delicious!"

Lottie's cake is last. This one is layered three deep, impressive for a moist, snacking-style cake, which normally couldn't be stacked. The bottom layers are bound together by a thick cream cheese icing, while the top is coated with a thick streusel crumble held in place by a circle of decorative piping.

"It's a layered blueberry buckle," Lottie says, looking at Betsy hopefully.

"Now *that* is another unconventional choice from you," Betsy says, eyeing the streusel topping, an odd choice for a layer cake.

A buckle is a humble sort of cake—old-fashioned in its simplicity—that she hasn't seen around in years. Nowadays most prefer a thick layer of icing, buttercream they can decorate, or the scraped edge of a naked cake. Something meant to impress on a table or in a photograph rather than just be eaten at a family dinner or on a picnic. Secretly it's kind of a relief to see such a normal person's cake be given its due.

"The decoration is lacking," Betsy tells her flatly, though the completely bare sides show an even sprinkling of blueberries, which is impressive. It can be difficult to keep berries from falling to the bottom of a cake, but these are evenly distributed throughout.

The knife glides into the cake, which has a springy sort of give to it. She cleaves a slice away, leaving a small avalanche of streusel crumbs in its wake. The cake inside is plump and golden, studded with juicy blueberries. Betsy can tell before she even takes a bite that it has been cooked to perfection.

The flavors hit her tongue and bring on a wave of nostalgia so strong that she has to steady herself against the table. It is heavenly, the sweet and sour of the blueberries wrapped in the soft vanilla-y cake. She is instantly transported back in time, back to her childhood. It is unquestionably the best cake of the bunch, simple and satisfying, the kind that if you were to bake it at home would leave you wanting more, taking secret trips to the kitchen to cut another slice. There is something else about it though, something personal. The cake is so intensely similar to one she's eaten as a child that Betsy takes a step backward, dropping the fork on the platter noisily. Betsy suddenly feels sick. It is all she can do to keep from spitting the bite back out into her hand.

The cameras catch it all, zooming in closer as Betsy closes her eyes and forces the bite down her throat. Archie looks at her sideways, startled. He puts his own bite into his mouth. She looks away as he chews, his eyes squinting in pleasure.

"That is . . . an amazing cake. Very well done, Lottie," he says, genuinely impressed. "I want to bring the rest up to my room." Lottie smiles, and the others giggle jealously. Betsy feels dizzy.

"The texture is all wrong," Betsy croaks. She watches Lottie's face fall. "Water," she barks out. Archie looks at her with a patronizing amount of concern, but she barely sees him. She feels instead like she is spinning, falling through time and space with nothing to grab hold of.

"I need to take a break," she waves her arms to signal the crew to stop filming. "I'll be back shortly," she tells Melanie.

"You all right, Betsy?" Archie calls after her as she flees toward the manor, not sounding all that concerned. She ignores him.

Betsy's heart thumps wildly as she rushes across the lawn and past the stone lions into the manor, taking the stairs to the East Wing as fast as she can and finally arriving, winded, at her rooms. She flings open the door to her study. The room is organized, tidy, still. Nothing looks out of place. Her desk is exactly as she's left it—a set of embossed stationery, a jar of pens, a framed photograph of her mother and father at a party hosted by the DuPont family. A stack of fan letters still sits in a basket on her desk waiting to be read. She goes straight to the mantel, but she can see already that the recipe box is gone. Her throat constricts as she spins around the room, her eyes scanning the shelves, the windowsills, even as she knows for a fact that she hasn't misplaced the recipes.

Betsy realizes that she hasn't really focused on Lottie all this time. She has looked at her of course, but she hasn't really *seen* her, not ex-amined her the way she did the others. Perhaps even at her age she is capable of ignoring other older women, of underestimating them. The thought fills her with fear. She thinks of Lottie standing before her at the judging table. She is a humble-looking sort, a green cardigan wrapped around her shoulders. Her brown clogs accentuate her thin legs and knobby knees. Her hands twist together in front of her. Her mind flips through all of the people from her past, decades' worth of them. Her heart skips a beat. The image crystallizes of an insecure little girl waiting in the doorway of her bedroom, hands clasped to be invited to play. The recognition knocks the wind out of Betsy, and she drops to her knees on the floor of her study.

"Elizabeth Bunting," Betsy whispers, her stomach curdling with fear.

PRADYUMNA

While Archie and Betsy retreat to their little gazebo to decide our fates, Melanie instructs us to line up in front of the judging table. It's been like this every day, and I've never quite gotten used to it. You'd think they could give us a chair to sit on or something. It has always felt a bit odd and punitive to have to just stand here, as though we are awaiting something awful like a firing squad. Melanie shuffles us around, sandwiching me between Hannah and Stella and putting Lottie on the far end.

Next to me Hannah shifts uncomfortably, biting at her fingernails. It's annoying me and I'm tempted to grab her arm and tell her to stop. Stella looks equally tense, her arms crossed tightly around herself. Of the four of us, only Lottie looks excited. She leans back behind Stella and gives me a look. Her eyes are shining, exhilarated. I smile back at her. Even if Betsy's reaction hadn't gone the way she'd hoped, it was good Lottie had done this and made herself known. Besides, Archie had loved the cake. I honestly can't wait to try a bite. Stella also did well today. I'm happy for her. She needed this. Hannah, on the other hand, I can't help but have a tiny seed of satisfaction at her lackluster performance. I'm sure that puts her and me in the bottom two. The golden girl herself, down at the bottom of the pile. I have resigned myself to leave if I must. Of course, I'd love to stay and help Lottie out, but I know that I did not bake something so incredible that I deserve to be saved today. I've found my salvation in other ways during this time. This experience with Lottie, it's given me a new perspective on life. I've uncovered part of myself that I always hoped was there but was afraid to try and access in case it wasn't. Being vulnerable has made me feel braver than any sort of cheap thrill I've experienced, and I'm interested in exploring it even more. I've decided that I don't want to drink for a while when I go home. I don't want to be numb anymore.

The camera operators return to the tent, taking their places next to their equipment. Melanie comes by and gives us one last look-over, nudging me an inch to the left, before retreating off to the side. The lights come back on, shining at the entryway to the tent where Archie and Betsy emerge. They stand facing us, their faces plastered with good cheer.

"Well, we certainly had a lot to discuss," Betsy begins. "But in the end, it was obvious the best baking today was from . . . Stella." Next to me I feel Stella's body collapse a bit with shock or relief.

"Thank you," she murmurs.

Betsy continues, "And though we would love to keep you all and just keep doing this forever, you all know this is a competition, and someone has to leave us today."

"The baker going home today is . . . ," Archie begins, his voiced filled with regret. I brace myself, smiling for the cameras to let them know I'm ready. Archie pauses, and his eyes flick to Betsy before he turns them back to us. "Lottie."

I should have expected it with the way Betsy stormed off after taking a bite, but I am still shocked when her name is called. The others are as well. I see their eyes widen in surprise. I shake my head, clearing my ears for a correction. There's been some sort of mistake. Lottie doesn't deserve to go home.

"I'm truly sorry, Lottie, you're a great baker," Archie says, looking back at Betsy. I watch something unspoken pass between them, but before I can sort it out, they are blocked by cameras as everyone crowds around Lottie, hugging her and saying their goodbyes. I hold back, numb. This is odd. Lottie's cake was perfectly baked. I thought it would be Hannah to get the boot today. I wish it were the case. Lottie and I had so much more to do here. I guess I was being naive thinking that I could just go on playing my little sleuthing game indefinitely.

I catch a glimpse of Hannah cooing over Lottie. It's for the cameras, no doubt. I've never seen Hannah so much as say hello to her the past few days. I get a pang of recognition remembering the legs protruding from Archie's sheets this morning. *There's a reason for her to stay a bit longer, isn't there,* I think bitterly. I'm comforted by the idea that someone like Archie won't let her win now. If a relationship of any sort ever came out, it would look far too bad for him giving preferential treatment to the winner.

Later I open a bottle of Chenin blanc in the library. I have drunk my way through most of the best bottles of wine by now, I realize with just the tiniest bit of embarrassment. I bring the open bottle to the sofa and sit down next to Lottie, propping my feet up on the coffee table. My mood has turned, and I feel morose. I wish there were something more I could do, a way to make her stay. She eyes the wineglass in my hand.

"I thought maybe the cake would jog her memory, but . . . nothing." Lottie sighs.

"She really hated that cake," I say. She jabs me playfully in the side with her elbow.

"Maybe I made it wrong." Lottie shrugs sadly. "I hadn't ever baked it before, just followed the recipe the best I could. One of the measurements could have been off."

"I doubt that. Your mother seems like she was quite particular with her notetaking."

Lottie nods. "Oh! I had a memory while I was baking today. I think my mother was afraid of Richard Grafton."

I perk up. "*And?*"

"And what?"

"Do you think he could have, you know . . . done something? Maybe his wife had found out and he had to silence Agnes?"

Lottie considers it. "It is so odd. I can't imagine it. He was such a genteel-seeming man. Though I suppose anything is possible. I could never have imagined my mother having any sort of romance with him until now either."

We sip our wine, and I rack my brain for a way to resolve everything before she leaves in the morning. Lottie's time has run out. She'd have to do something tonight or this whole experience, all those years of practice and waiting, will have been for nothing.

"Why don't you just tell Betsy who you are? Explain the situation. You have nothing to lose really at this point. Maybe she would help you."

She looks at me like I've lost my mind, but then she sits back, exhales slowly. "Fear, I guess." She presses her thumbs into her eyes for a moment, exhausted. "I'm afraid she won't recognize me, or even remember me when I tell her who I am." She looks up at me and laughs hollowly. "I must still care what she thinks of me after all these years. How dumb is that? She was such a big part of my childhood, and then growing up watching her on TV every week. The last time she saw me I was an eleven-year-old. Why *would* she remember me?"

I set my wineglass on the end table and turn to face her. "But you're going to have to face your fears if you want to put this to rest." I reach out and touch her arm. "You can't carry this back home with you." Her hand, cold and smooth, lands on top of mine.

"How did you get so wise?" She laughs.

"I didn't. I just mimic smart people."

"Well. I'm going to go pack, I suppose." She hoists herself from the couch with some effort. I watch her thin form, robed in one of her signature bulky cardigans, heading toward the door, and am filled with a deep sadness.

"Lottie?" I call after her. I'm about to say that I'll help, that I'll continue her search once she's left, that I won't stop until I've found out what happened to Agnes. But my confidence wavers, and I wonder if I would be of any real use.

I picture her back in Rhode Island in a small house filled with knickknacks, her daughter stopping by for cookies and tea. It's such a cozy image that it makes me a bit jealous. Me, the young millionaire jealous of a poor septuagenarian? But it's true. I am. The mystery of her mother may never be solved, but ultimately Lottie will be fine, I realize. Because she has her whole life to return to. But what am I going back to after this? Even if I did manage to win the Golden Spoon, what will that mean? A gleaming, empty apartment full of designer furniture and expensive gadgets that make my life easier. But easier for what? What do I have to save time for? More relationships with women who drive me crazy and who I have no interest in? Who I will eventually disappoint in one way or another?

"Never mind. I'll say goodbye in the morning," I say gruffly. I clear my throat and turn my attention to a book on the coffee table. *Beautiful Brûlés*. The pictures blur in front of me. For the first time in years, decades maybe, I feel as though I am about to cry.

I'll miss *Bake Week* when it's over. But not because of the baking. The real honor of this experience has been trying to help Lottie sort out what happened to her mother. I only wish I could have had more time. I wish I could have actually helped. The clock on the mantel says 5:15 p.m. I realize there is not much else I can do. A dark pit forms inside me, the familiar feeling returning stronger than ever, threatening to swallow me up.

LOTTIE

As I pack up my things, there's a timid knock on my door. I expect Pradyumna to walk in ready to drag me back to the East Wing and confront Betsy Martin, but when I open the door, I'm surprised to see Stella standing there.

"I'm so sorry about today," she says, her chin crumpling slightly as though she might cry.

"No, no. Please don't be. It was bound to happen eventually," I tell her, opening the door wide and gesturing for her to come inside.

She crosses the bedroom, sits down heavily on the side of the bed, looking despondent.

"No, there's no way that cake could have disqualified you. I tried some after the judging. It was absolutely delicious."

I smile gratefully. "Well, thank you, Stella. But you all deserve to stay in the competition. And I'm fine, really I am." I look at her carefully. Her eyes are dark underneath, her face sunken as though she hasn't slept well. It's a look I recognize well. "What about you?" I ask, pulling a chair out from the desk and sitting down across from her near the foot of the bed. "How are you doing?"

"Oh." She waves her hand around vaguely, attempting a smile. "You know."

I lean in, waiting for her to continue.

"Have you ever gotten the feeling like you are suddenly on the right track, like nothing can stop you, and then . . . you just lose your nerve?"

My stomach flips. "Sure, I have."

She leans back on the bed, resting on her forearms. "Oh, Lottie, how do we ever know if what we are doing is the right thing? If we are helping things or just making a big mess?"

I ponder this. "I guess we don't. We have to trust that if we are going the wrong way, something deep inside us will tell us. We have to train ourselves to listen for that inner voice shouting for us to turn around."

Stella appears to think about this for a moment, and then her eyes come to rest on something behind me. She sits up and steps forward, leaning over and reaching past me to the desk.

"What is this?" When she comes back, she is holding the recipe box. Stella opens it before I have time to decide if I want to show them to her. I have the urge to snatch it away from her, to protect them. I have only just found the box. I don't know why I am so scared of anyone seeing. It isn't as though I could get in trouble when I was the one who should have had them all along. I watch as Stella pulls out several of the cards. She is a sweet girl, really, she means no harm to anyone. I suppose there's nothing wrong with telling her the truth, at least the partial truth.

"It's my mother's recipe box."

Stella flips through the notecards, her eyes moving along each line of handwriting. With each one, the furrow in her brow grows deeper, until she turns her face to me, her eyes wide with confusion.

She pulls one up close to her face, inspecting it. It is written in my mother's tilted script: *Agnes's Almond Angel Food Cake*. "Wait!" Stella says. "This is exactly the same as Betsy's angel food cake recipe." What does Stella mean, it's Betsy's? "This pound cake is verbatim from her first cookbook, *Betsy Martin's Seasonal Baking*," Stella says, her voice strained with confusion. "And *this*, this is from the second season of *In the Kitchen with Betsy Martin*." She shows me another recipe for a savory tart of leeks, herbs, and cream cheese. "Lottie, I don't understand." She flips through them again, growing agitated. "These aren't your mother's, they're Betsy's."

My chest goes tight. How had I never figured it out all these years? I'd even paged through one or two of her cookbooks at the bookstore. I'd watched her on television from time to time, but I had never put two and two together. Truthfully, I'd always resented her success in an area she'd seemingly had no natural affinity for as a child, something my mother and I loved doing together. I'd never understood what gave her the motivation to become a professional baker. All this time, I was living in the dark. I'd never realized Betsy was using my mother's recipes because I didn't remember the exact bakes to compare them to. I didn't have her recipe box.

I suck in a breath as I remember Molly and me watching one of Betsy's shows. "Do you think Betsy learned to bake from your mom?" Molly had asked. At the time I'd shaken the idea off. Baking is a common pastime. My mother may have inspired Betsy, but there was no other connection. With how separate the help was kept from the Graftons, I couldn't see how my mother would have given Betsy anything more than a vague, subconscious introduction to baking.

But now I go cold with recognition. "Betsy stole her recipes."

"Betsy wouldn't do something like that," Stella says forcefully, snapping the lid of the box shut.

"I should probably pack," I say, standing up suddenly.

"But what about the recipes? Lottie, there must be some kind of mistake." I can see what made Stella a good reporter. Her curiosity is so strong. She seems to have an insatiable need to figure things out, to cut to the truth. I can't have her getting involved now. There's too much at stake for her. Besides, I've already dragged one person into this mess; it wouldn't be fair to bring another down with me.

"Please don't worry, Stella," I say, opening the door for her to leave. She stands up, and I feel I've betrayed her. As she walks past me out into the hall, her shoulders hunched, I am struck again by how fragile she seems, how vulnerable. There are so many people in this world in desperate need of a mother.

HANNAH

As soon as judging was over, I rushed back to my room and changed into a workout set and sneakers and went outside for a run. Or at least that's what I've told myself I'm doing.

The sky is a dirty gray. A layer of threatening clouds moves quickly across the horizon as I run along the side of the highway toward town. I'm full of extra energy, whether it is from excitement or nerves, I can't really tell, but after being in the tent all day it feels good to fill my lungs and pump my arms even if the air is thick and sticky. I am happy to be taking action. I try to push away the memory of Archie's face as he bit into my cake. That heartbreaking look of disappointment, his eyes avoiding mine as he set down his fork. Instead, I plan what I'll wear tonight when I see him. A sweet floral skirt, or something sexier perhaps. I think of the little black dress I brought on the off chance it could come in handy and am grateful again that I overpacked.

My run brings me to the edge of the town I'd seen driving in. "Town" might not even be the right word for it. This isn't the real town, the one the crew stays in each night, which is forty miles farther down the road. This place is barely a village, consisting of a small cluster of shops hugging the county highway. I slow to a walk, catching my breath as I go past an old gas station, a stubby strip mall with a yarn store, a loan center, and a Goodwill. I finally reach the diner. It is set back from the road with a parking lot. It looks empty, and dark. But most important, what I'm looking for is there, just like I remembered. I exhale, relived. There is the phone booth. I look back over my shoulder at the empty road before I approach it. It is painted blue, a row of perforations on the side outline the shape of an old-fashioned telephone receiver. The sides of the booth are bubbled with rust. The door has been ripped off so that only two jagged hinges remain intact. I step inside, careful not to press up against any of the dirty surfaces, and dig a coin out of the tiny pocket on my yoga pants, the one meant for keys that I've jammed full of all the quarters I could find in my purse. A cord holding the tattered remnants of an old phone book dangles from the bottom of the metal telephone box. I pick up the receiver, and there is a loud buzzing in my ear. I don't know what that means. I've never used a pay phone before, much less a landline. I pray the sound is normal, that it means the phone is working. I push a quarter into the slot, listening to it drop down into the mechanism. I look around again to make sure there's no one watching. The parking lot is empty except for an abandoned shopping cart. I pull the heavy receiver to my ear. My fingers shake as I press Ben's phone number into the metal box. There are several rings, which make my heart leap, and then his voice floods into my ear, familiar as my own.

"Hello?"

"It's me. I'm calling from a pay phone," I reply, keeping my voice low.

"Hannah? Hi! Are you okay? How was your bake today?"

For a moment I want to tell him about the cake, about how the buttercream wasn't flavored quite right and how the cakes stuck in their molds. He knows more than anyone that I struggle with my buttercreams. Ben has eaten so many of my less than perfect bakes without complaining. But I shake it off, reminding myself of what I have to do. I swallow and get on with it, cupping the end of the receiver toward my mouth.

"Ben, I've met someone else."

There's a pause on the line, and for a second, I think I've lost the connection. I picture him sitting at our tiny white Ikea table drinking coffee from his favorite mug with the otter on it, the blinds twisted open to show a view of the parking lot next to our building.

"Hello? Ben."

"I'm here," he says. "I'm just trying to understand you. When you say 'met someone else . . .'"

"I'm sorry." I try to fight back the stinging that has sprung up in my eyes. "I thought it wasn't fair to keep it from you."

"Wow, Hannah." There is a muffled exhalation followed by a heavy silence on the end of the line. Finally, he speaks again. "That was really fast. Is it another contestant?"

I don't say anything. I look out at the restaurant. A battered pickup truck has parked next to the side door without me noticing, and the diner lights have popped on. I slump down along the side of the phone booth, pushing my back up against the glass.

"I'm sorry, Ben. I love you so much, you know I do. It's just . . . things just haven't been good with us for a long time." Is that true? I feel like a fraud even as I say it. Things maybe haven't been good, but have they been bad? I push forward.

"I'll move my things out just as soon as I'm back." I think about how I'll be leaving for New York after this probably, or LA. Archie spends a lot of time there too, he says. He told me I'd love LA, that I'd fit right in there.

"Are you sure this is what you want?" he asks me. He isn't crying like I thought he'd be.

He doesn't even seem too sad. His voice seems . . . concerned.

I try to be confident, but my voice wavers. "It's . . . it's for the best."

"I'm worried about you up there, Hannah. I don't want someone taking advantage of you."

"No one is taking advantage of me." It comes out more shrill sounding than I mean for it to.

This wasn't what I expected. I thought he'd be broken, begging for answers. It must just not have sunk in all the way yet. I push the knife in a little deeper, just to make sure he is understanding me.

"We never would have worked out anyway, not in the long run." I don't know why I am saying what I am. It's like I'm looking at myself talking from above. Inside the diner I watch as a woman ties an apron around her waist. She takes her place behind a long counter and begins setting out fresh bottles of ketchup and jugs of maple syrup. I could have ended up like that, I remind myself.

"Maybe not," he agrees. His voice sounds so far away, and I get the feeling that the space between us is growing wider by the second. I have the urge to make it stop, to reach through the phone to take hold of him and grab him by the collar so that I can look into his eyes and see that I still matter to him.

"We have different goals. We're totally different people, Ben." I imagine him on the couch petting the dog. Will I miss getting slobbered on? I wouldn't have thought so. But I have a pang now, somewhere deep in my chest. An ache that grows more and more acute. I hadn't ever realized how safe I'd felt with Ben. Maybe I took it for granted. *Stop, Hannah*, I scold myself. Where did staying safe ever get anyone?

"I guess that might be true," Ben says. "But I don't think you know my goals. We never really talked about them. We have always been so focused on your baking, there was never much space." The way he says it is just so matter-of-fact. The lack of meanness in his voice makes it all the more heartbreaking.

That can't be true. I scroll back through my memories, all the trips to the store so that I could make some recipe I'd just thought of, the daily tastings around the kitchen table. They're good memories. They must be. But I can't push back the other, less pleasant ones. The tantrums I'd thrown when something didn't go according to plan, the dark moods I would get into when I felt overwhelmed, the angry fits that led to broken dishes. But he'd known that wasn't who I was. That it was just a product of pushing so hard for so long in addition to working long hours. He must have. I would have listened if he had something interesting to say. I would have encouraged it. Wouldn't I?

"Hannah?" His voice is soft, pleading. I brace myself. This will be him begging me to stay, telling me he never has loved anyone more. I lean back on the side of the booth, close my eyes, wait for it.

"Yeah?"

The distant voice again on the other end. It sounds so much older and more mature than I remember. I swallow the lump in my throat, try to contain it before it escapes into a sob.

"Be careful, okay?"

The phone jingles as I return it to its cradle. It is done. The sky is swirling with heavy black clouds that threaten to explode as I jog back onto the main road, my heart pumping. I run faster and faster past the strip mall, past the gas station and back to the safety of the highway, where no one will see me and ask me what I'm doing. No one saw anything, I remind myself. And anyway, I'd look completely innocent to anyone who might see me now that I'm running again. I'm just a young blond girl in a matching yoga set out for a motivating jog. But I can't shake the anxiety that has crept up on me, the taut ache that runs through my chest. I try to remember that it's a good thing it went over so well with Ben. I'm free to be with Archie now. But as I turn onto the narrow road past the sign pointing to Grafton Manor, I feel strange about the whole thing. Be careful? What does that even mean?

I run down the drive, feeling the first few drops of rain on my arms. Suddenly I'm furious with Ben. I was the one calling to break up with him. He doesn't get to turn around and act like he's the one worried about me! How dare he act like I need watching over like some pathetic little baby. I was so worried about hurting his feelings before, but now I'm glad I got to see what he has really thought of me all this time. That I am a spoiled child incapable of making good choices for myself. I'll show him how wrong he is when I come out of this competition completely transformed. He'll see that he had no reason to worry about me when I am a successful TV baker, when I'm Archie Morris's girlfriend.

GERALD

I've been sitting against the parapet for nearly nine hours now, and I may have miscalculated the usefulness of this vantage point. I have not uncovered the saboteurs. The day's bakes are long over, and my plan did not extend this far into the evening. Now I realize this wasn't the most productive use of time. I should have been looking for evidence. If I'd spent my day trying to find a canister of gasoline stashed in someone's room or a duplicate set of salt and sugar canisters, I would have something to go on. But now it's too late. The bakers are back inside now, many likely in their rooms, and the house will be busy for the rest of the evening as dinner is prepared and people come and go. I will have to wait until tonight to search the house. This thought makes me agitated. Absolutely nothing is going the way I'd anticipated. I reach into my pocket for another nutritional bar, which I will eat for dinner, and a tiny flashlight for later. It is comforting being so well prepared, especially when things are not going exactly to plan.

I pull myself up, carefully avoiding the loose bricks, and inch my head up above the edge of the parapet. A figure comes down the main drive, dressed in pink. They come closer and I see that it's Hannah, back from a run. Rain has already begun to fall, spattering in thick drops on the edge of the balcony. I sit back down, lowering myself against the wall to avoid getting wet.

A man's voice drifts up from below. "I couldn't do it. There was never a good time."

"There was plenty of time. I even had them distracted for you," a woman's voice replies impatiently.

"Don't you think there's been enough drama this week?"

"Thanks to me. This season is already so much better."

"What was going on with Betsy today? Sending Lottie home was a bit of a curveball!"

I perk up, surprised that it should be Lottie who is leaving next when she has such a good grasp of the basics. The probability was much higher for Stella or Pradyumna to go home.

"God, though, nothing can really top Gerald's meltdown."

"*That* was good TV."

I tense up at the sound of my name. I pull myself up and lean forward just a bit, trying to get a look at who is speaking, but all I can see is a puff of white vapor.

"Come on, it's starting to rain."

"Let's go back to the hotel."

"I've just got to check on something in the tent."

"I'll meet you at the car."

I'm going to miss my chance to catch them. If I run now, I can cut through the house and intercept them as they go down the drive. I try the door behind me, the one that the blueprint showed led to the parlor on the second floor, and am surprised to find it locked.

I run to the edge of the balcony and look down. The climb down would be too dangerous in the dark. I begin to panic. The saboteurs are getting away from me. I can barely make out the sleek figure of a woman walking toward the parking area, her hair twisted up in a shiny knot on top of her head. She turns to say something to the man, and her profile catches in the light of one of the windows. It's Melanie. I lean out, pushing my face through a tangle of hanging vines. If I can just see the other one, then I can bring their names to Betsy Martin. I can explain what has been happening at *Bake Week* so that it can be fixed and we can start the competition again, this time fairly.

I push myself out farther still, resting my hip on the edge of the parapet and stretching as far as I can to see. Rain spatters on the back of my head as I crane my neck. There he is. The outline of the man walking next to Melanie. They are moving away from me. Their dark silhouettes disappear around the corner. Only the smallest trace of a white plume of vapor hangs in the air behind him. I need to see the man's face. I must intercept them on their way to the parking lot. I will have to bring them to the others, to explain what they've done. Betsy will make sure they are punished accordingly. The bricks below me shift as I try to pull myself back onto the balcony. I reach down to steady myself, but my hands find only vines that tear away as I try to hold on. The side of the parapet is crumbling below me, bricks sliding off into the dark, and before I can stop myself, I am tumbling down with them, falling over the edge.

STELLA

I am in my room with my ear pressed against the door, waiting for Hannah to make her move. I have been like this for hours now, a chair pulled up to the door, my notebook open on my lap. A low rumbling of thunder rattles Grafton. The rain has already started, a gentle pattering behind me on the window, growing heavier by the second. I'm feeling vulnerable.

That time in Lottie's room rattled me. What did she mean, the recipes were her mother's? They may have different names, but I know those recipes, have them imprinted in my memory from the past year of intensively studying Betsy Martin's cookbooks. None of it adds up. I can feel my reporter brain kick into gear, itching to know more. But I don't have the time to solve that mystery. Not yet. I have way too much else on my plate right now.

I've already started writing the piece, and I have a plan to get the story out there. As soon as I finish it, I'll send it to Rebecca. She is my last friend at *The Republic*, the only one I stayed in contact with when I left. She'll help me publish it. She'll have to with a headline like this one: "Beloved Celebrity Chef Caught Sleeping with Young Contestant." It will be explosive. It will end Archie's career. And I can't stop myself from hoping it will revitalize mine. I try to put the thought out of my head. *You quit, remember?* Besides, my own fame is not why I am doing this. I am exposing Archie to stop the imbalance of power that has gone on far too long.

Finally, I hear the click of a door opening and closing and the swish and tap of shoes as someone passes by me. I wait several beats, then crack the door a tiny bit and peer out into the hallway. It is Hannah, as I'd hoped it would be. She is dressed up in a short black dress and tall, high-heeled boots that make the flash of pale leg between look small and childlike. I hope she isn't going outside. I should stop this, I realize. I could go out there and call out to her before she does anything stupid, before she gets hurt. But I don't want to stop it. I want my story.

I mentally prepare myself, taking a deep breath. The hall feels darker than usual as I step out after her, pressing myself up against the wall, waiting to leave just the right amount of time. She steps down onto the landing, and I pause at the doors, looking down at her. She stops, too, glancing up at the East Wing as though she is unsure for a moment. She wipes her palms along the sides of her dress, combs her fingers through her hair. I take my notebook out of my pocket and jot down a few rough notes.

When I look up again, Hannah is climbing the stairs. She is moving quickly, confidently toward the East Wing. At the threshold she pauses only for a second and then slips inside. *Dammit! I can't lose her now.* I follow after her, rushing across the landing. My heartbeat roars in my ears like the inside of a seashell.

I wait in the doorway for her to move farther down the hall, my hand resting on the top of the handle, my finger pressed against the latch. Another roll of thunder rumbles through the manor. The air feels fizzy and electrical. An uneasy calm before the storm unleashes itself fully upon us. When she has moved far enough down the hallway, I push down on the latch and slip in behind her. I follow her from a distance, pressing myself into the shadowy edge of the hallway ready to dart into a doorway if needed but she doesn't turn around. Hannah stops when she reaches his room. I watch her pull on the hem of her skirt again, arrange her bangs. Then, without even knocking, she opens the door and steps inside.

I start to follow Hannah, but realize if I want to catch them in the act, I'll have to give them some time together first. I can't imagine it will take Archie long to seduce her, given how far they've already gone. It's not like she is the best conversationalist, not that witty repartee is what he is looking for. He'll want to get on with it, I imagine. But I must be a bit more patient if I want real evidence. I tuck myself into the doorway across the hall, crouching in the dark with my notebook, and wait.

I can hear the murmur of conversation and wonder what they are doing now. Has he taken her clothes off already? I imagine Hannah lying there, vulnerable, as the figure of Archie Morris looms over the bed, his hands reaching for her.

With a sickening jolt I realize I am not actually picturing Hannah on the bed. I'm imagining myself, and it is not Archie looming over making unwanted advances, but Hardy Blaine who I had worked for at *The Republic*. Like Archie, Hardy was much older and more senior than I was at the time. He was the man who had started *The Republic*, a celebrity around the office. A hero of mine. I was thrilled when he'd taken an interest in me, making up excuses to stop by my desk, asking my opinion of story ideas he'd been submitted for the website. I'd been flattered. After years feeling invisible, he'd noticed me. I relished it.

Two years into my time at *The Republic*, I was invited on a work trip to Los Angeles to attend a fancy dinner where Hardy would accept an award. I got to sit at a table with him and a few others. I wore a velvet Halston gown, rented of course, and diamond earrings on loan from Rebecca. Only a few other reporters and editors came with. I was the only woman from our company on the trip and the youngest person there. I was so honored to have been invited. At the time I thought it was a sign that my life was about to change. That my career was taking off in a new, prosperous direction. After the ceremony Hardy leaned across the table. "We'll all have to get a drink back at the hotel to celebrate," he'd said, and I had been thrilled that he saw me as someone he wanted to celebrate with, an equal. I felt confident and accomplished, optimistic for my future.

We'd gone back to the hotel bar at the Oriental. All our hard work had paid off, Hardy said as the group crowded around, ordering drinks. "Next time you'll be the one accepting that award," he'd said, nudging me as he ordered a Manhattan, getting me one as well without asking what I wanted. I didn't want to appear ungrateful or difficult, so I drank up even though I hate whiskey. After the wine at dinner, the alcohol hit me hard. At first it made me feel euphoric and chatty. I remember talking and talking at the bar until somehow it was only the two of us. "Do you know how beautiful you are?" he'd asked. "Oh, I probably shouldn't say that." He'd held his hands up. I tried not to notice the wedding ring glinting on his finger. My head was spinning when we took the elevator up to his room. Once we were there, he turned to me, kissing me hard. His mouth tasted sour, repulsed me, but I thought that once he was done kissing me, I could just leave. I vaguely remember trying to go back to my room, weakly standing up to go, but I was suddenly so very, very tired.

"Just lie here until you sober up," he was saying, leaning me back into the bed. My eyes were closing as he touched me. "I feel dizzy," I remember saying. "Here, just lie down," he replied, pulling me with him onto the bed. The blackness was coming on strong. I fought to stay awake. I felt the fear taking hold then, but it was the fear of embarrassing myself, of passing out and not being able to hold my liquor.

When I woke up, I was naked, a sheet around me. I rolled over in bed, clutching it to my chest, confused. My whole body throbbed with the beginning of a massive hangover. He was reading something on his phone, his glasses perched on the tip of his nose. Gray morning light lit the windows. He looked fine, refreshed even. He glanced down at me, curled up in confusion and fear. "You really drank a lot, didn't you? You might want to go clean up."

It sickens me now how fast I'd done what he said. Humiliated, I'd dressed myself quickly, walking hunched around the foot of the bed and slinking into my clothing without looking at him. Then I'd gone back to my room. In the bathroom I rubbed underneath my eyes with a washcloth, trying to remove the mascara that had stuck there in a grayish patch.

My skin was yellow, and my hair was in knots. Several deep blue bruises, the size and shape of thumbprints, were forming on the top of my leg. I took a painfully hot shower trying to erase the hangover and the new kind of fear that had started to bloom in my chest.

We'd flown back to New York as though nothing had happened between us. In fact, he acted more detached and professional with me than he ever had before. Our exchanges became occasional and per-functory. The more he ignored me, the more I started to wonder if it had even happened at all.

Now in Betsy Martin's hallway, I gulp for breath. The fear is back, the way it always comes back, a hot panic that rises up in my chest, consuming me. Once again, my vision begins to tunnel, growing darker and darker until all I'm left with is just two blurry pinpricks of light. The blood roars in my ears. I am not here just because of Hannah. My chest sinks at the realization. I'm here for me. I want to help myself by saving her. I hear something in Archie's room—murmurs, some of them pleading. If I could just expose him. I reach for the door, but I am losing consciousness. I press down on the handle, and the door falls open as the last bit of light in my irises snuffs out like a candle.

PRADYUMNA

It's official. I've drunk all of the good wine. My glass and the last bottle of French red sit on the table in front of me. "This just won't do at all," I say to myself. I pull myself up from the couch by the fireplace, feeling the ground shift below me like the bow of a ship. I swivel myself toward the liquor cabinet. Sure, there is a good selection of scotch, a bottle or two of vodka, and some brandy—honestly, who drinks brandy? But I started out my evening with wine, and I intend to keep it going strong. There is no way that the library has the only stash of wine in the house. It isn't even temperature controlled! No, there must be someplace else it's stored, a basement or wine cellar somewhere. I wander out into the hallway, feeling my legs snap out in front of me. The sensation makes me giggle. I haven't felt drunk like this in a while. I must have had more wine than I realized. *Whoops!*

When I reach the foyer, I am tempted to go upstairs and knock on Lottie's door to make sure she's okay. I could make her go on a little wine-seeking adventure with me. I start up the stairs, but then I remember that she's leaving in the morning. It stops me in my tracks. It's a real wallop to the gut losing Lottie like that, a real humdinger.

I spin angrily on the stairs, turning myself back around. I'll have to go it alone from here on out. Like I usually do. No more sneaking around trying to solve mysteries. Now my mission is simple: wine. A bolt of lightning flashes across the foyer windows, followed by a crack of thunder that rattles the house.

I step down into cool stone hallway that leads to the kitchen. If there were a wine cellar, this is the logical location. I pass the kitchen door, stopping in to poke around. I've been here before. There is often a pot of coffee left on in here during the day for the crew that I partake of. Now it is quiet, dark. Raindrops spatter against the two small windows on either side of the wide hearth. I open one of the cupboards. There is a neat stack of mixing bowls nesting on the lower shelf, and above it a row of pristine cake stands. I touch one, and my fingertips come back coated in dust. I open another cupboard and find it almost bare, just some sugar and a stack of unopened tea boxes. The kitchen probably hasn't been used in years. I think of Lottie's mother down here, doing so much hard work for the Grafton family. I run my fingers over the marks in the worktable. I try to imagine how someone like Richard Grafton could have an affair with the cook and still expect her to make his family's daily meals. I wonder if Agnes could no longer bear it, if that's why she went away. But that wouldn't explain why she left Lottie. If only there were some sort of clue. I find myself opening the rest of the cupboards, searching for something, anything, that would help explain her disappearance.

There is nothing of any use, just some stacks of plates and cobwebbed cooking utensils. There is no note carved into the back of a cupboard door, no hastily written goodbye letter conveniently forgotten about for fifty years for me to uncover. I must resign myself to being useless. I have to let it go. Agnes, the Graftons, even Lottie—they have nothing to do with me. It's best for me to just leave it all alone. I can chalk up this whole thing to experience. I'll go back to my luxurious apartment, maybe take up horseback riding, take a long vacation to Bali. I leave the kitchen behind me and continue down the hall looking for a door that might lead me to the wine cellar. I come upon a glass door on the right. I press my face up to it and see

the edges of a wooden shelf containing cubbies filled with wine bottles, rows and rows of them. How wonderful. I feel my body relax in
anticipation of uncorking a new bottle of something special. Maybe
a white burgundy or something from one of the Macon villages. As
I begin to pull the door open, a bloodcurdling scream echoes down
the hallway.

HANNAH

I am packing. Frantically flinging my clothes into my suitcase, not even bothering to remove them from their hangers. As I shove armfuls of my makeup from the countertops straight into a bag, I catch a glimpse of myself in the mirror. My hair is disheveled, my eyes irritated and pink. Without my false lashes, I look like little a kid. Inside I feel like a kid too. A stupid kid. All I can think when I look at myself now is: *You idiot.*

I've made a terrible mistake with Archie. I can see that now. I shudder as I replay the past hour in my head. I don't know how I could have been so naive, so incredibly stupid to have believed anything he said to me. I don't know which is worse, the humiliation or the disappointment. I'd been so excited to tell Archie about how I'd broken up with Ben, but he seemed distracted, almost irritated.

I'd felt so confident as I got ready. I'd talked myself out of the anxiety I was having earlier. This is your destiny. To win *Bake Week*, to be with Archie. This was all good, I told myself, putting on the black dress and a pair of tall boots. I'd waited until I knew for sure he'd be back in his room. I couldn't risk knocking, so I'd slipped inside. Archie startled when he heard me there. He was sitting up in bed looking at his phone. He was in underwear and a T-shirt. My dress suddenly felt overdone, and I mentally scolded myself for choosing it. I waited for him to grin and pull me into bed, but instead he looked anxiously at the door.

"You probably shouldn't be here," he'd said, rising from the bed.

"No one saw me," I'd assured him, laughing coquettishly.

"I have some things going on, work things. I don't have the time right now."

The smile died on my face when I realized he was serious.

"I can come back later."

"No, no. Don't do that." He'd lowered his voice. "I'm sorry but we can't do this again, Hannah."

I stumbled back as though he'd punched me in the stomach. "But *why?*" I'd demanded to know. "What about bringing me to LA?" I'd asked. He looked away. "What about you being my advocate, helping me build my career like you said?"

"Listen, you're a sweet girl and very talented obviously." He'd avoided looking at me as he talked, his eyes resting on the dark screen of his cell phone.

"Sweet?!" My voice rose, my fists clenched.

He'd rushed toward me, putting his finger to my lips, shushing me. "I made a mistake yesterday. I have my career to think about. And you do too. We shouldn't have done that."

"What? But you said you were going to be my mentor."

He looked toward the door, as though calculating if he could leave me there. Then his expression changed and he took my hands in his. For a moment, I thought he was going to apologize, to say that it was a misunderstanding. He crouched down in front of me, finally making eye contact.

"Listen to me," he'd said, brushing my hair from my face. "We are going to pretend like this never happened."

My eyes welled with tears. "Please, no. Don't say that." I pulled on his sleeve, but he was impassive. Irritated, he tried to shake me off. He spoke to me like I was an unruly child, and he was disciplining me.

"You are going to stop. You are going to go back to your room, *quietly*, and not breathe a word of this to anyone. Because if you don't, I will make sure you are the one who goes home tomorrow. Do you hear what I'm saying?" he asks, his voice cold.

I'd looked at him through swollen eyes, my heart nearly breaking in two as I watched my dream of being Archie Morris's girlfriend disintegrate in front of me. How cruel he had been. How heartless.

"I think you'd better go," he'd said curtly, swinging his hands to usher me out, pointing in the direction of the door. I hovered there, unsure what to do, giving it one last chance to turn in my favor. He'd raised his eyebrows.

"Go."

I ran, stumbling down the hall and desperate suddenly to be away from Archie and the mess I've made of things here.

Now I pull off my dress, balling it up angrily and flinging it into my bag. How stupid I'd been to try to dress up for him when he never cared at all. I pull on my yoga pants and a sweatshirt. It doesn't matter who sees me now, or what they think of me. I'm done with all of it. Now all I want is to go home to Eden Lake. I will beg Ben for forgiveness, tell him I didn't mean any of it. He will be mad at me of course at first, but he'll come around. He always does. I have the horrifying thought that Ben won't forgive me. That I will be forced to move in with my mother. I will turn into an old woman working at Polly's Diner who people will whisper about. "See her," they'll say. "She was once on *Bake Week*, and now look at her." I bend over to pick up an eye shadow compact that's fallen to the floor and find myself crying again, big, convulsive sobs that keep me doubled over.

I attempt to close my suitcase, holding it down with my body weight and straining the zipper. Anger rises up in me, and I find myself kicking the suitcase again and again until it slides across the floor, slamming into the delicate wallpaper. I stand there panting, tears still wet on my cheeks. And that is when I hear the scream.

STELLA

When I wake up I am looking up at a dark sky through an open window. Heavy black clouds swirl above me. Rain pours sideways into the room, accumulating in a puddle around me. I am inside, but I feel outside. I blink, still coming to. I try to recall where I am and what I'm doing, but my brain feels like a clenched fist. If I could just get some sort of bearing, I could piece it all together. I take stock of where I am—on the floor. My shoulder bones press painfully into the hardwood. Nearby on the floor are a pair of men's Oxford shoes, the laces crawling toward my line of vision like little worms. They are soaking wet. So am I. My clothes, my hair. With a groan I hoist my stiff body into a sitting position. My forehead pulses with the beginning of a splitting headache. My arms and legs are slippery with rainwater, and my clothing sticks to me uncomfortably.

A small lamp glows warmly on the bedside table. I take hold of one of the spindles on the four-poster bed and hoist myself up, wobbling a bit and then walking myself onto the side of the bed. Drips from my hair spatter the duvet. It is cool and crisp under my hands, the bed still made. A roll of thunder rumples the air, followed shortly by a crack of lightning. My teeth chatter.

I pull myself up across the bed shivering as I retrace what I can remember, trying to locate myself in the present. I can vaguely recall the previous day, the bake-off, dinner. Hannah. That's right, I followed her. A long-sleeved shirt is draped over the side of a chair. My heart starts to pound faster as I realize where I am. I'm in Archie's room. I wonder how long I've been here. Heat blooms on my cheeks as I consider that I must have made a total ass of myself, opening the door and just fainting like that. But where are they now?

My clothes are soaking the comforter, spreading out in a wet patch on the bed. I try again to see Archie through the dim tunnel of my memory, but my brain is shrouded in fog. Where is Hannah? I saw her enter the room, didn't I? I shiver and close my eyes against a wave of headache pain. That's the thing about my blackouts—they feel annoyingly like a hangover. I wake up and am left with a fuzziness and a dull body ache that lasts for hours. I think of the Tylenol in my room. I visualize the bottle. It is deep inside the pocket of the suitcase I've left packed all this time. I'll go back there now, try to regroup in my bedroom. I will piece everything together. I try to make myself move, drawing up all my strength and hoisting myself up from the bed.

The rain beats heavily through the window onto the hardwood floor. The puddle I'd woken up in is spreading, threatening to take over an Oriental rug. I stagger to the window and grip the shutters. My intention is to close them, but something compels me to look out. I lean out over the ledge into the storm and gaze down. My stomach is suddenly sick. It is pitch-black. Rain obscures the edges of everything. The tent is a shadowy mass below. A weak spot of light flashes through the darkness. It bounces frantically across the lawn. It's a figure with a flashlight, I realize. The person moves quickly, through the dark to the house. From above I can't place who it is. I watch, the rain pounding at the back of my head, dizzy as I stare down over the top of the tent. There is a dark spot in its roof.

Is it a tear? How easy it would be to slip and fall from up here. I strain to see. Behind me, deep inside the house, a door opens, echoing through the manor. And then I hear something else. A long panicked scream that sends shivers through my body.

I jerk myself back from the ledge and slam the window shut.

BETSY

It is as if her body and mind have split in two, and each half is working against the other, paralyzing her. All she can do is stare up at him.
His eyes bulge out at her. His jaw gapes open, a dark hole hanging in a
silent scream. His body is caught facedown on two of the steel beams
crisscrossing the tent. It hangs there limply, contorted in a sickly, unnatural pose, one shoulder twisted up to his ear and the other jerked
down as though he's been thrown off his axis. An ugly black gash near
his temple drips a steady trickle of blood onto the table with a sickening splatter. It mingles with the cake and drains off the side of the
table into a dark pool on the floor.

Beyond the beams, there's a dark hole in the tent, a jagged rip in
the white canvas where he broke through it. She stands below him as
the water pours in through the hole, running off his body and onto the
tent floor. One of his arms dangles straight down. His fingers curve
as though he is reaching for her, pleading for help. Betsy gulps for air
but is unable to breathe. Backing away, she catches the edge of one of
the colanders of baking utensils, and it crashes to the ground. It takes
several more moments to absorb the shock of what she's seeing. When
she emerges from it, she finds herself gasping for air, looking wildly
around the tent.

"No!" she finally pushes out, as her lungs fill and begin to work double time. She breaks into full-throated screams. *I should be finding something to help get him down*, she thinks. But instead she backs away, stepping through the aisle in the center of the tent, keeping the flashlight trained on him as though he might disappear, or worse. She makes her way back through the baking tables, stumbling as she goes. Each stand mixer, each set of bowls, looks like a monster in her peripheral vison. The wind whips the side of the tent, the rain lands like bullets on the sheeting. She finally reaches the back door. Her flashlight beam is weak, but as she takes one last horrified glance at the front of the tent, she thinks she can see his fingers move.

She runs toward the house in a nightmarish daze. Her shoes stick in the muddy lawn, trying to glue her in place. She pulls her feet free and leaves them there, sunken in the grass. Running barefoot up the steps, her arms splayed out to either side, she screams again up into the foyer. Her voice, competing with the rain and wind, is swallowed up by the house.

Shaking, Betsy digs into her pocket for her phone. She punches in 911 as she stands in the center of the foyer with bare muddy feet, rain dripping off her father's raincoat and pooling around her on the floor.

"Nine-one-one, what is your emergency?" a staticky voice comes through the phone.

Archie Morris is dead. The idea is nearly impossible to grasp. Just hours ago, Archie was her worst enemy. And then a thought occurs to her. The show. What would happen to *Bake Week* now? With Archie gone, would everything go back to the way it was? The producers couldn't survive this sort of scandal without her. They'd need her now to steer the show. Perhaps this is a gift to her from the universe. She slips the phone back into her pocket and begins again to scream for help.

LOTTIE

In my dream I'm trapped in a maze of hallways, and someone is screaming. With sudden clarity I realize it is my mother who is in distress. I must go to her, help her, but I am lost. I run and run, turning corner after corner looking for a way to get to her, to help. But the hallway is unending, twisting and turning, taking me farther and farther away from her. I am startled awake, blinking into the darkness, my heart hammering in my chest. I hear something. At first, I think it is the wind battering shrilly against the windowpanes, but then the scream breaks free of the storm, becoming jagged and human. It is coming from downstairs in the belly of the house. I'm afraid to move out from under the covers. Afraid to step into the dark. I inch the covers down and gaze up into the room. The windows are black, vibrating with the assault of the rain. The room is dark and menacing, the hulking outlines of furniture barely visible.

There are footsteps out in the hall. The others have woken and are running toward whoever is in distress. I should join them, go find out what is happening, but a part of me is still inside the dream and I'm afraid, too afraid to move. *Go, go. Get up!*

I force myself to sit and switch on the light. The curtains are drawn, but I can see that it is still pitch-black outside. Now there are murmurs from the hallway, low and urgent. Heart racing, I grab my bathrobe from the back of the chair and rush out to the hall to join them. I reach the landing at the same time as Stella. She is coming from the other side, the East Wing. I pause, confused. Her hair is wet, and her face is twisted in fear. What was she doing in the East Wing? Below us the floor is streaked with wet footprints. The front door stands open and the rain comes in at an angle, pounding on the flagstone. Hannah and Pradyumna are already there, huddled around Betsy Martin.

"Is everything all right?" I call out.

When they turn to look at me, their faces are united in horror. Stella and I continue down the steps, running to join them. Betsy is bent over, gasping for breath. It's alarming to see her undone like this.

"What's going on?" Stella barks. Her voice is low and hoarse.

Betsy points to the open door, where the tent is barely visible through the downpour.

PRADYUMNA

I've always wondered what I'd do if I saw a dead body. I assumed that years of playing video games and watching gory movies would have left me somewhat immune to horrors if I were actually faced with them. And in a way they have. Because I don't react at first when I go out to the tent with the others and look up at his body dangling there.

The four of us stand there stunned, watching as the water rushes off Archie's mangled corpse and onto the floor of the tent. It is odd to see him like this, so still and silent. I find I'm having to convince myself that it is real. He is a heavy man, and the metal beams holding him bow out, struggling below his weight. It is only a matter of time before one gives way.

Hannah cries out first, a low sob that escapes from her and morphs into a sharp wail. Stella turns away from us and throws up violently in the corner of the tent.

"Oh, dear," Lottie says. Her hand grips my arm. "What should we do?"

"Probably just wait for the police," I suggest uselessly.

Stella flinches when I say it. I notice this and the deep gash on Archie's head, incongruous with the angle of his fall through the canvas tarping. I watch myself react, feeling strangely empty. It's like

I've had my insides scooped out. *Typical Pradyumna*, I think, *making a man's horrific death all about myself somehow.*

Stunned, we've shuffled back inside and are gathered in Grafton's kitchen. It is as if, being bakers, we are drawn to its comforting hearth and stacks of mixing bowls, everything in its place. It feels safer in here, with the solid stone walls are holding back the storm. We sit at a long wooden table. Lottie has started a kettle, and it whistles cheerfully on the stovetop, a strangely comforting sign of life in a very dark moment.

"The police should be here soon?" Lottie asks for the second time. I can see she is a doer in a crisis. She is already looking around the kitchen for something else she can busy herself with, a way to help.

"They've been called," Betsy states as though irritated with the question. She is huddled at the far end of the table, away from the rest of us. I find it almost funny that even in a time like this, she feels she must keep herself separate from the contestants.

"Do you think it was an accident?" Hannah asks. Without all the makeup on she looks vulnerable, like a different person.

"I doubt it. Unless he did it to himself," I say. "But with that shiner on his head, I would expect not."

I glance around the kitchen, sizing the others up. None of us exactly fit the profile of a murderer. Clearly Lottie is out. She has no motive or any real relationship with Archie. Stella seems a bit off right now, though she has just seen a corpse. But why was her hair wet earlier? Then there is Hannah and her clearly sexual relationship with Archie. Which would hardly make her a killer, would it? It's hard to ride someone's coattails when they're dead, isn't it?

"There's no use in speculating," Betsy snaps. "It's grotesque."

I have a flash of memory. The look exchanged between Betsy and Archie after judging today. What was that? I am overcome by weariness and lean my head into my hands.

Who'd have known that Archie Morris's death could make me feel so hollow. This place, this experience—it is making me *feel* far more than I want to. I did not sign up for this. It was meant to be only a bit of a distraction, some baking, something to brag about. I don't need to be here, I realize suddenly. I could be at home in my eight-million-dollar apartment with its humidor and walk-in wine cooler, relaxing in front of a nice movie with a container full of weed gummies. I do not need this. If it weren't for the storm, I'd find my keys and drive off into the sunset. *Bake Week* was a fun experiment, and now the party is clearly over. And I *hate* being stuck at a bad party. Maybe I'm reverting back to the shallow, dumb version of myself, but I don't care. Someone is dead. The only thing I want right now is a very stiff drink.

"I'll be right back. Going to look for something." I catch a look from Lottie as I turn to go, a flash of disappointment. *Oh, whatever*, I think. What do I owe her anyway? What do I owe any of them?

STELLA

"Take me upstairs," Betsy orders me. "I need to freshen up." Her hair is lank and damp, plastered to the sides of her face, which is puffy and pale without her makeup. Still, I would think the possible murder of her cohost might be more pressing than her appearance at this moment.

I offer her my arm, but she ignores it. Instead, she moves past me toward the main staircase. I slow my pace, allowing her to take the lead. I can't help but be flattered that Betsy chose me to help her. Just hours ago, alone time with Betsy Martin would have been my dream come true. But the recipe cards in Lottie's room with their frayed edges and instructions for baking cakes that Betsy made famous have confused me. Is it possible that Lottie is the one who is lying? That Betsy was the actual inventor of the recipes?

Finally, we reach the landing. We pause there and look up at the door to the East Wing, and I see a flicker of fear in her eyes. I'm afraid too. I don't want to go back up there, past his room. She reaches for my arm now, her hand gripping my elbow. She is heavier than I expected, her weight like an anchor pulling me back as we climb the stairs, up to the East Wing. Walking back into that hallway, I have a moment of panic. I still don't remember what happened, and it terrifies me. I hold my breath, squeezing my eyes shut as we pass Archie's room, each step down the hall feeling like an eternity. Since seeing Archie's body, time feels like it has slowed down to an excruciating crawl.

There is a tug on my arm, and we stop in front of a set of French doors. Inside is Betsy's office. It is a large room lined with heavy wood bookcases surrounding a massive stone fireplace. Betsy strides across the room and sinks into a deep leather chair, switching on a small Tiffany lamp.

Above the fireplace, mounted on a plaque made from polished mahogany, is the golden spoon. I have never seen it in person, and it is hard not to stare. It is the shape and scale of a full-size mixing spoon and has the shiny-dull look of solid gold. It must be heavy, I think, leaning in closer to inspect it. I imagine holding it in my hands, the other contestants and cameras crowding around to get a better look.

"I'd like some tea." Betsy's voice is sharp, and I jump to, going to the side of the room where a marble countertop holds a set of delicate porcelain mugs and an electric kettle. An angry roll of thunder vibrates through the house. I almost laugh when I realize that this is my fantasy. Tea alone with Betsy Martin. This isn't exactly how I'd hoped it would be, though. I'd imagined something far more joyful.

"You are the first contestant to ever set foot in the East Wing," she says as I put the electric kettle on and struggle to open two paper tea bags. My hands feel weak, disembodied.

"Invited, that is," she adds bitterly.

"Oh?" My voice sounds high. I desperately wish this were my first time. If I had never followed Hannah, then I wouldn't have woken up in Archie's room and I wouldn't have this terrible feeling in the pit of my stomach.

"I've never allowed any of the contestants into my family's personal quarters. My parents kept this area private. You have to protect against the prying eyes of the public. Especially when you are *somebody*."

I am not quite sure what to say in response. "Yes, I'm sure it must be very hard."

"This is just a terrible situation," she says, her mouth puckering like when she tasted Peter's bread. I'm not sure if she means Archie's death or me, a commoner, entering the East Wing.

"It is," I agree.

The kettle switches off, and I pour steaming water over the tea bags. I hand Betsy a cup and fall into the chair facing hers. The adrenaline of the day is wearing off, leaving me weak and shaky. My teeth chatter as I hold my mug with both hands. Since waking up in Archie's room, I have been freezing, unable to warm myself up. Now I put my face close to the steam, trying to bring my body temperature back to normal. Betsy is oblivious to me. Her eyes flick to the wall, and I can see her mind racing. It is like I am not even here with her. She's just had a terrible trauma, I remind myself. We all have. I shudder thinking of Archie's face, his open eyes staring down as though he could see right into me.

"Do you think the police will be here soon?" I ask. It is strange that Betsy is the only one with a phone, with access to the outside world.

Betsy sets her tea down on the table next to her. "Melanie called earlier. Said something about the storm knocking some power lines into the road. It could be a while." There's a concerned pause. "Don't tell the others."

"Of course."

I swallow a sip of my tea. It is far too hot still, and it scalds my throat going down. A thought comes to me, intrusive and terrifying: *If I hadn't followed Hannah, would Archie still be alive?*

Betsy looks at me as though expecting something. "I need some time to gather myself," she says. Her voice is cold. And then I realize that what she wants is for me to leave. I'm embarrassed that I hadn't understood earlier. I thought she'd wanted the company, but she may have just wanted me to wait on her. I put the teacup down, still full, and stand to leave.

"Yes. Yes. Of course."

It has taken me all this time to recognize that Betsy isn't the woman I thought she'd be. She is colder and shrewder than the kindly grandmother she portrays on television. The real Betsy doesn't seem to have a nurturing bone in her body. Betsy's spine is stacked primly, eyes staring ahead angrily. Watching her like this, I realize that she seems more than capable of what Lottie said. She doesn't so much as glance at me as I shut the door behind me.

I flee down the hall, holding my breath again as I pass Archie's bedroom—*ten, nine, eight.* It was stupid of me to ever believe I had a special connection with Betsy. How ridiculous it seems to me now that I'd thought *Bake Week* would be the start of something new and wonderful. I am just as confused, just as messed up as I was before. I burst out onto the landing. *Maybe it's even worse than that.* I squeeze my eyes shut at the thought of it, clenching my fists so that my fingernails dig painfully into my palms. *Maybe I'm a murderer.*

LOTTIE

The storm is still raging outside. If anything, it is even stronger now. Angry gusts pummel the sides of the manor, wind whipping leaves and other bits of debris against the windowpanes. I have no sense of the time, but it must be well past midnight. Morning cannot come too soon.

"I can't believe he's just out there, in *that*," Hannah whispers. It's something I've been trying to push from my mind, but it is almost impossible not to imagine Archie's body out in the elements. I'm relieved when Stella returns to the kitchen. She sits on a stool, looking pale and exhausted. My relief turns to worry when I see she is shaking violently. No one should have to see a body like that, but the shock of it all seems to have been too much on her especially.

"You're cold," I say, surprised. When she looks up at me, her eyes are dark and spooked, haloed in red. I wonder if we all look that way: haunted.

"I'll go find us some blankets," I say, wanting to be useful. "Probably best if we all stay together down here until the police come."

"Are you sure? I can come with you." Stella's voice is weak and distant.

"Don't be silly. I'm fine. You sit, drink some of this tea before it goes cold, and just rest up. Both of you." I look to Hannah, but she says nothing. Her silence is concerning.

I leave Stella and Hannah in the kitchen. I've become accustomed to walking around at night alone, but this is different. Lightning flashes at the windows as I make my way into the foyer. Despite how well I know the place, Grafton spooks me tonight. The walls creak and groan as I make my way up the staircase, quickly, heading through the West Wing. The wardrobe at the end of the hall beckons, and I go to it, tugging open the doors.

I pull out several thin comforters, pausing when I see the silver hinge on one side. But I push the thought of the rooms upstairs out of my head. There's no time for that right now. I fold the blankets over my arm and slam the wardrobe shut, turning and walking purposefully back down the hall.

On the landing, I pause, looking up at the door to the East Wing. I turn to go down the stairs, but something makes me turn back. I stand there, weighed down with blankets. This could be my last opportunity to talk to Betsy alone. I set the blankets down at the top of the stairs and move to the door. I stand at the threshold of the East Wing, my fingers wrapped around the handle. Why am I afraid? I remember these handles, the curve of the latch. I was afraid then too. I press a finger down on it and feel a small click. I slip inside, into Betsy Martin's lair.

I move down the hallway tentatively. The point is to talk to Betsy, to see if there is anything else she can tell me about that night, but as I walk, I realize that I am both looking for and hiding from her. The closer I come to finishing what I've been trying to do all this time, the more I almost want to give up, to take it all back and run away. I remind myself why I've tried so hard to get here. This is not just for me, this is for my mother. To give the story of her life closure so I finally feel like I've honored her.

My foot lands on a creaky board, and I stop dead in my tracks waiting to be found out, heart racing as I listen for footsteps. Hearing none, I venture farther down the hall. The door to my left is open. It is an opulent bedroom. The ceilings are tall and arched in the corners, trimmed with scrolled molding. A four-poster bed in elaborately carved dark wood stands to one side. A delicate sofa and two chairs surround a small fireplace with bronze grate. A man's shirt hangs over the side of a chair, waiting to be worn. Archie's room. I shudder and force myself to keep moving. I pass Betsy's childhood bedroom, moving toward the doors at the end of the hall. I never ventured this far into the East Wing before that morning with Pradyumna. The Graftons always made sure there was a separation between the family and their help. I find myself wishing he were here right now. His teasing good nature would be a welcome distraction.

I pass by a row of oil portraits along the hall. Most are of men in military uniforms, the hilt of a sword bulging out from their jackets. One smaller portrait is of a woman with a tight collar circling her neck. Her face looks weary, hardened. Their eyes seem to plead with me not to go any farther.

The hallway ends at the set of impossibly tall double doors, hanging wide open. I hold my breath as I pass into Betsy Martin's sitting room. The windows here are closed and bolted against the storm. Two plush chairs, their backs to me, face a fireplace that crackles festively. In the corner a record spins on the old Victrola record player. It's a song that takes me back to my childhood.

In the still of the night
I held you
Held you tight
'Cause I love
Love you so
Promise I'll never
Let you go

I walk toward the spinning album, mesmerized. I have a flash of memory from my childhood. I am helping my mother cut potatoes downstairs in the Grafton kitchen. The radio next to the sink is on and she is humming as she cooks, stirring a pot on the stove. A chill goes up my spine.

I remember
That night in May
The stars were bright above—

"Can I help you?" Betsy's voice, sharp as glass, startles me. I spin around. She is sitting in one of the high-backed chairs. She must have been watching me for a while now. She looks entertained, the way she did as a child watching me as I moved toys around for her. The power she wielded was clearly so enjoyable to her. It always had been. Looking at her now, her face contorting into a sinister grimace, it sickens me to think of all those years I wished she were my friend. To her right is a tumbler partway full of a brown liquor. She lifts it to her lips and takes a leisurely sip. The wind continues to shriek at her window. It is now or never. I think of my mother, and I stand as tall as I can, clasping and then unclasping my hands.

"Do you recognize me?" I ask her, bracing for the answer. Finally, she smiles. It is not a warm smile. She takes another sip.

A bolt of lightning flashes in the windows. It is followed by a violent crack, the sound of it striking something close by. The lights flicker off as she replies.

"I mean, I can't say you haven't aged a day, but your demeanor really hasn't evolved much, has it? Still skittering about in those old clothes. Makes it easy to fly under the radar, doesn't it, Elizabeth Bunting?"

PRADYUMNA

I'm standing in the library alone. Torrents of rainwater batter the windows as I pour myself a twenty-one-year-old Balvenie PortWood from Betsy Martin's beautiful teak bar. I need something memorable to get rid of the image of Archie Morris's body twisted in a pose best imagined by Salvador Dalí. It isn't exactly something that is easy to get out of your head. But I'm going to have to try.

But there's something more that's been bothering me, and seeing Archie's body dangling there just crystallized everything for me: I'm not happy. And I haven't been for a long time.

A scotch should help take the edge off all that nonsense. My hand trembles as I bring the glass to my lips. A violent crack of thunder startles me, and I slosh some of the whiskey onto my shirt. The lamps around the room flicker and then go out completely, plunging the library into darkness.

"Well, that's unfortunate," I say to the black room. My voice is swallowed up by another clap of thunder, and a lightning strike meeting its target somewhere in the distance. Muffled voices bounce around the manor. It is the others calling out in surprise as they fumble around in the dark.

The panes rattle against the pounding water. I steady myself and take a large sip from the glass of scotch. It's so smooth, so absolutely perfect, as it travels down my throat. I feel a bit fortified already, *the feeling* is being displaced by the urgency of the situation—I'm better in a crisis than in real life. *I should find a flashlight or something*, I think.

Lightning throws a patch of light across the room, and I take the moment to orient myself. My eyes land on a carved wood desk before the room goes dark again. I move in that direction and hit my toe on the edge of something hard. The glass of scotch falls from my hand onto the floor, shattering.

"Fuck!"

I wave my hands out in front of me, looking for the desk until my fingers find the smooth edge of it. I fumble for the pull on the drawer, yank it open and feel around inside for something resembling a candle, a flashlight, anything useful to see with. My hand catches on the side of something sharp, and I jerk it back from the desk, dragging the drawer all the way out of its track. There is a powerful clatter as the drawer hits the floor.

"Fuck! Fucking fuck! Ow!"

I feel wetness oozing from where the pain is and suck the side of my hand. I can taste the blood but not see it, a strange sensation. I grope for something to wrap it with.

Another strong flash illuminates the fireplace next to me, and I see a tall canister of long, fat-tipped matches on the floor next to the grate. *Of course!* How stupid not to think of it earlier. I lunge for them as the light flickers away. My hands close around the canister, and I pull out a match, striking it several times on the inside of the fireplace. I am rewarded by a sizzle and a tiny flame, enough to see a couple of feet in any direction. I guide myself to the wood bin and begin to build a fire as drips of dark blood from my hand spatter across the hearth. I snatch a piece of newspaper from the tinderbox and twist it around my hand as a bandage, then crumple up a few more sheets and place them in the cracks of the logs. I dab the lit match into the paper, blowing into the flames until they catch on the wood. The fire finally takes hold, and the room around me brightens.

I light another match, tucking the canister under my arm, and go back to the desk to clean up my mess. The contents of the drawer have been scattered across the floor next to it, including a letter opener with a smear of my blood across it. My hand throbs in response. I drop to my knees and, holding the empty drawer like a basket, begin to gather the fallen objects. I pick up a magnifying glass, a selection of folded maps, and an array of heavy pens. I slide one into my pocket for future use.

I raise the drawer to its empty slot and start to line it up with the wooden guides. It catches and slides into place. But as I push it in, something inside catches on it and stops it from going flush with the others. I pull the drawer back out and set it on the ground. I strike a fireplace match, moving it in front of the empty socket. A large paper envelope is taped to the far back of the inside of the desk. It's twisted up in the corner where the drawer snagged at it—probably came loose when I yanked the drawer out of place. I stick my arm back into the cavity and pry it free. It's a flat parcel, light as a feather.

I blow out the match and bring the envelope back to the fireplace. Now that the light is better, I can see it's made of faded yellow paper and bound together in the back by twine. I study the envelope, turning it over in the firelight. Its corners are winged with tape so old it's petrified, crumbling off in flakes when I touch it.

A roll of thunder rumbles through the house as I unwind the twine. Two thin pieces of cardboard hold in place a single pristine document. I read it, trying to make sense of what I'm seeing, and as I do, something horrifying and wonderful clicks into place.

HANNAH

Stella and I are alone in the kitchen. I sit on the floor in the corner, my knees tucked up inside my sweater. Stella sits opposite me, leaning against the kitchen counter. Neither of us has spoken for an extraordinarily long time. We've gone through way too much today. I wish I hadn't followed the others into the tent. I didn't need to see him like that. I shudder to think of Archie's face. Every time I close my eyes he is there, dangling above me. His mouth open in a silent scream. I know I won't be able to sleep soundly for a very long time. Stella looks shell-shocked as well.

"I wish someone would move him," I say finally. "I don't like thinking of him like that."

"I know. But the police will be here soon. I'm sure they will want to see him," she says, wincing.

We go quiet again, listening to the rain pound against the outer wall of the kitchen. My stomach is empty and sour.

"Hannah, I should have asked earlier. But how are you?" Stella's face is full of concern. "Are you okay?"

I try to brush the question off with a laugh, but it catches in my throat and comes out as a short sob.

"I know," Stella whispers, her eyes searching mine.

I feel nauseous. "What do you mean?"

"About you and Archie. I saw you leaving the woods the other night." I jerk my head up at her, surprised. I had thought we'd done such a good job of being secret. I hadn't even considered anyone had been watching. I'm relieved that is all she saw. Even now, the humiliation of Archie's deception tugs at me. I pull my sweatshirt farther down my calves.

"Can you tell me what happened?" Stella asks. I am paralyzed, unable to respond. Can I trust her enough to tell her? I think of what happened with Archie, how I let myself get taken in by his stupid lies and empty promises. It fills me with so much shame I can hardly breathe. I want to push her away and run all the way home to Eden Lake.

A violent crack of thunder rattles the kitchen. The overhead lights buzz loudly, going brighter and then fading out completely, plunging the kitchen into darkness. We sit there with only the noises of the storm—the howling of the wind and chaotic tapping of the rain against the small kitchen windows. The darkness makes me feel like I am alone floating in space, like my body doesn't even exist anymore. Like I am dead.

I start to cry. It is silent at first, but it builds until my body is racked by sobs and I can no longer keep it inside and I am howling. In the pitch-black, Stella's hand finds my shoulder. I resist at first but give in, letting her pull me toward her in a hug. I can't handle it all on my own any longer. The secrets Archie wanted me to keep are making me sick. Now that he's dead, I realize I have no reason to fear his retribution anymore. He can't help me or hurt me. *Bake Week*, Archie, it's all over.

"He'd promised to help me. But it was all just so he could sleep with me. I still can't believe he would go to all that trouble. I feel so, so stupid." I wipe my nose with my sleeve. As she pets my head, I tell Stella about Archie, about how he'd promised me that I was going to be famous, how he'd told me he was going to take me to LA with him, to make me into a celebrity baker.

Stella's voice is filled with disgust. "You have to know that none of this is your fault, Hannah. That kind of man, they just prey on whoever."

I know she is right, but I still feel a pang of sadness. Even now after everything, I still want what we had to be special. I think of his fingers brushing against my cheek in the woods and shiver. I wish that his interest in me had been genuine, different from any that may have come before.

"You know, I had something similar happen," Stella says. I wish I could see her face.

"You did?"

"Yes, that's why I was so worried about you. I could see that Archie was the same as—"

Footsteps echo through the hallway, and Stella goes silent.

"What is that?" I whisper, finding myself reaching through the dark for Stella, our hands finding each other, entwined.

There's a beam of light beyond the doorway that moves like a lightning bug through the air toward us. The sound of heavy breathing follows it. I feel Stella squeezing my hand.

"Hello? Is anyone in here?"

"Pradyumna?" Stella calls out.

"We're here," I say, my voice shaky.

The light comes closer, bright and comforting. It shines over us, and I can see Stella's face. Her eyes are tear streaked, afraid. She stands suddenly, catching herself in the beam of the flashlight. I pull myself up shakily next to her, turning to the doorway. The light is so bright I have to shield my eyes at first, blinking as the person comes closer until finally, I can see that it is not Pradyumna at all.

"Gerald?" Stella says.

He stands across from us. His suit is ripped and soaking wet.

"What are you doing here?" I ask nervously. He approaches the table, limping.

"Are you okay? What happened to you?" Stella's voice quavers.

"I came back. I'm trying to save the show. Someone has been sabotaging *Bake Week*. I know who it is too," Gerald says a bit uncertainly. "Well, I know who one of them is." I feel Stella's hand relax as she realizes what I do, that this is Gerald, not some killer on the loose. Even though I'd found him so irritating before, I am relieved to see him now.

"I think it's a bit late for that," I snort, trying to laugh and then feeling my chin crumple again. Stella's hands grip my shoulders as though she is trying to physically hold me together.

There is another sound at the door, a scrambling of footsteps that makes us all jump. Out in the hallway, someone swears in the dark. There's a scuffing noise, followed by the sound of a match being struck. Gerald turns the flashlight onto Pradyumna. His hair is disheveled, the rapid rise and fall of his chest visible as he tries to catch his breath. His eyes move rapidly between us, widening in surprise when he sees Gerald.

"Gerald? What are you doing here?"

"I had to look for clues—" Gerald starts, but Pradyumna cuts him off.

"Actually, explain later." Pradyumna shakes his head. "As if things couldn't get any weirder. Okay, give me that flashlight, would you?" When Gerald hands it over to him I notice that his right hand is wrapped in newsprint, stained dark with blood. "Look!" his voice a mix of excitement and fear as he waves a piece of paper in front of us. The flashlight catches something shiny, an official seal in one corner.

"Pradyumna, what is it?" Stella asks. But Pradyumna is already backing out of the door into the main house.

"Come with me. We have to find Lottie!"

The way he says it, the fear darting in his eyes, makes me worried that something has happened to her. I don't want to see another horrible thing today. I have had enough of the storm, enough of the spooky old house, enough even of *Bake Week*. I just want to go home. But mostly I don't want to be left alone down here in the dark. So I follow them, leaving the safe feeling of the kitchen and edging out into the hallway. Pradyumna takes the lead, holding the flashlight. He is followed by Gerald, who holds out his phone. We follow these two fragile beams of light down the hallway, slowly picking our way out into the foyer and to the bottom of the stairs. I cling to Stella as we go up the staircase. I know where we are going, though I can't bear the thought of returning to the East Wing. There is a chill at my back as I follow the others up. I do not turn around. I'm certain if I do, he'll be standing there, soaking wet, blood dripping from his head, his mouth parted in a permanent scream.

LOTTIE

"Little Elizabeth Bunting. You've hardly changed at all." Betsy tents her fingers, leaning back in her chair. "I'm not sure how I didn't see it earlier. A terrible oversight on my part." It's that same unreadable tone. No hint of warmth or familiarity. I shudder.

"We were friends, remember? My mother, Agnes—"

Betsy shrugs and turns her face to the fire. I step toward her.

"I didn't want to do it this way," I say, opening my palms to her, pleading. "I tried writing letters to you for so many years. You never answered."

"Do you know how many letters I get, Elizabeth? You must know some would slip through the cracks." The record on the Victrola has stopped playing music but continues to drone with static as it spins.

"You have to believe that I've been wanting to tell you who I am this entire time. I'd always imagined if we were to meet again, we'd have so much to talk about."

The light from the fireplace dances on the side of Betsy's face. "Oh, you expected a big warm welcome from me? I think not, Elizabeth. You tricked your way onto my show to gain access to Grafton for some unfathomable reason? I must say, I don't know what you are playing at."

"But I'm not playing at anything."

She snorts derisively. A log cracks, sending a spray of sparks across the hearth. I am trying so hard to be brave, but I feel shaky and wrung out, like my legs might give out at any moment. It has taken all my strength to confront Betsy, and now I am desperate to sit down. "Don't you see? I'm here to find out what happened to my mother."

"You know what happened, though, don't you?" She sneers.

"No, that never made any sense," I protest.

"She was lazy. She didn't want to work anymore, and she must not have wanted to be a mother anymore either."

"No, she wouldn't have left me. We were inseparable." A bubbling hopelessness tears at my chest. A grief with nowhere to go, no marker or stone to lie at. It's the feeling I've had for fifty-one years.

"Oh yes, you and Agnes were just the perfect pair, weren't you?" Betsy's voice drops to a snarl. "Always running around together, playing and giggling like you were *both* children. It was unseemly, not how a mother and daughter should behave together."

I realize when she says it that Betsy was jealous. All this time, I thought she'd looked down on us when she was secretly envious of our close relationship. The revelation stuns me and I am momentarily unable to speak.

"Frankly, I'm tired of this conversation." Betsy folds her arms in front of her. "I think you should leave."

"But I've waited so long to talk to you. I never got to come back, to retrace her last steps. I just need—"

"What? What do you need, Elizabeth?" Betsy snaps.

"I need closure." I find myself growing angry.

"*Closure?* You did all this for *closure*? Might have been easier to just find a therapist."

I grip the back of the chair. How dare she treat me like I'm still a little girl who doesn't deserve to be here. We are not children anymore.

I've given this bitter woman way too much power over me, and it is going to end now.

"I know about the recipes. I know that you stole them from Agnes to build your first cookbooks. Without my mother you would have been—"

There is a pounding of footsteps in the hallway, and Pradyumna bursts in through the double doors.

"Lottie!" I turn toward his voice as he rushes to the fireplace. Stella and Hannah crowd behind him, their eyes wide with fear.

Pradyumna reaches out to me. His hand is bound with a piece of newsprint that is dripping with blood. He holds something in it, a piece of paper.

"Pradyumna, are you okay?"

"Lottie, you have to see this!" he says, waving the document, a look of pure victory on his face.

"No!" Betsy cries, standing up and lunging for the document. "Where did you get that?"

But Pradyumna pulls it away from her, passing it over to me. I take hold of the paper, turning away from Betsy's grabbing fingers. It is almost transparent in the flickering light. The wavy watermarks of a birth certificate visibly streak across its surface.

"It's wrong," Betsy says. "That isn't real."

The gold seal catches the firelight. It is all written there, stamped in the certain lines of a typewriter: my birthday, the eighth of June, 1952. Elizabeth Bunting Grafton. Born to Agnes Bunting and Richard M. Grafton. It is authorized with the doctor's scrawling signature and an official seal.

"It can't be," I whisper. How had I never even considered the possibility? All those years, thinking I was the product of a random encounter, but it wasn't like that. My father was here the whole time, right in front of me. Had he known? He must have. I think of all the interactions I'd had with Richard Grafton. He was kind to me always, but he hadn't ever seemed like a *father*, certainly not my father.

Gerald steps forward. He has his phone with him and shines the light up through the back of the birth certificate. "This kind of document is nearly impossible to replicate without extremely sophisticated equipment. Note the watermark. Therefore, it is my assessment that this document is original."

"This is obviously a mistake." Betsy's voice is wavering, straining to remain calm. "Richard Grafton was *my* father alone."

"The birth certificate would say otherwise," Pradyumna interjects.

I shake my head bitterly. "She's right, Pradyumna. Why would I even want to be a Grafton? What did they ever do for me? If he was my father, he lied to me the whole time I knew him and then had me sent away."

"My father was an angel. He treated all of you like gold, even your slut of a mother." I reel back as though I've been slapped.

"How dare you talk about my mother like that?" I say through clenched teeth. "You owe her everything!"

"My career was hard earned." Betsy's calm is fracturing, but I can see through the cracks. She is not the only one losing her temper. I clench my hands, press my fingernails into my palms until they dig painful ridges in my palms. "So what if she scribbled some words on some cards? I did this! I built this!"

"You built your whole career on the back of my mother. You stole her recipes. And what did she ever get from any of you Graftons?"

Betsy is standing now, ready to confront me. "Agnes gave me *nothing*. I didn't need her to teach me to stir some flour. I didn't need her at all!"

"I saw the recipes, Betsy," Stella says, her hand clutching her heart like she's physically hurting. "You are a total fake! I can't believe I worshipped you!"

"Oh, get over yourself. All of you! A bunch of nobodies!" Betsy shouts. Her shoulders rise and fall. Her eyes are like pinpricks.

Pradyumna puts his hand on my shoulder. "Lottie, I've just realized something. Agnes wasn't afraid of Richard Grafton. She was afraid of Betsy."

BETSY

They've trapped her, cornered her in her own home. She wants to lash out at them, to scratch and kick. She has been trying to contain her rage for so long. Becoming Betsy Martin, America's Grandmother, has been a way for her to heal, to prove to herself that she's in control, but seeing Elizabeth has shaken something loose in her. She feels herself reverting to that child she once was. That terribly angry little girl.

"I killed her, is that what you want to hear? And I'd do it again," Betsy explodes. White spots flicker in her vision. Betsy sees Lottie's jaw drop open, but she can't stop herself. "She deserved it." The words tear from somewhere inside Betsy, shooting out in a ragged scream. Lottie and the rest lean back from her, afraid. She should stop, pull herself together, save the remaining scraps of her career, her rapidly unraveling reputation. But she finds herself unable to control the torrent of rage. The anger has overwhelmed her now. It feels good to give into it. Betsy is lost, swirling back in time, reliving the injustice of all she endured at the expense of Agnes.

Betsy remembers her father and Agnes stumbling into the conservatory one afternoon when she was playing there. The way they looked, her father smiling back at Agnes as he pulled her into the room with him, told her their meeting was a secret. Betsy had hidden behind a crate and watched as Agnes, flushed and happy, reached for her father's face, pulling it toward her, kissing him on the mouth. It was all Betsy could do not to wretch and give away her hiding spot. Their lips were stained with wine. She'd watched through the slats as her very own father, all smiles, kissing the maid. Her father's face was full of desire, his hands traveling up the bodice of Agnes's uniform. He never looked at Betsy's mother that way. For years Betsy watched as her mother would try to engage with him. "How was your sleep?" she'd ask at breakfast each morning, but her father would shake the newspaper open to a new page, pretend not to have heard. Beyond the pages, her mother's face would drop, the smile fading from her face. As the years passed it hardened there. A mask of disappointment she never removed. There were days before finding out when Betsy had felt an almost uncontrollable anger at her, lying there, letting it happen. Those days she'd go back to her room and break something her mother had bought her. She'd crack a glass doll or rip the seams from one of her dresses. But after seeing her father acting so full of life with another woman, she was no longer furious with her mother. Betsy could see that she was only trapped in the unhappy situation her father and Agnes had created.

Then one night as she crept downstairs for a glass of milk and one more slice of cake, she'd heard her father and Agnes plotting in the kitchen. Her father would move away, it was decided. Agnes and Elizabeth would go with him. What a happy little family. Their plotting was so brazen; they hadn't even left the manor. Her mother could have heard. She couldn't blame her father. It was Agnes's fault. It was her spell he was under. She ran back to her room feeling physically sick. His words to Agnes echoed in her mind. "It is *you* who I love, my darling, and our precious girl deserves more than the life of a servant. You both do." She had to do something. She had to stop them.

The night it happened, Agnes was trying to make things right with Betsy. They'd both come out onto the landing at the same time, Betsy from the East Wing and Agnes from the West. She had an apron around her waist, was heading down to the kitchen to clean up the remnants of the family dinner. As they met on the landing, Betsy turned her head away from Agnes, not wanting to even look at her. It had been like this for weeks. Every time they saw each other, Betsy would twist away angrily so that Agnes knew how she felt. She wanted her to see how much her mere presence hurt Betsy. She wanted to see the hurt in Agnes's eyes when she rejected her. This time, though, Agnes blocked her path, gentling touching Betsy on the arm. "I know that you are upset with me," Agnes had told her, lowering herself to Betsy's eye level. "And I want you to know that I care so much about you, Betsy. You are like a second daughter to me."

Betsy jerked away from Agnes as though being burned, turning back and glaring at her with what she hoped was absolute hatred in her eyes. The absolute hubris with which Agnes, the homewrecker, was trying to appeal to Betsy was too much for her. "Well, you are just the maid to me," she'd spat out, the anger rising up inside, overwhelming her. "I hate you," she'd hissed. Agnes stood up in surprise as Betsy took off at a run and barreled into her with all her might, pushing her head into Agnes's stomach and sending her flying back against the railing. Agnes, gasping, caught herself against the ledge. For a few sickening seconds, she teetered above the foyer. All Betsy had to do was shove her once more, catching her square in the shoulders and pushing with all her might. Agnes's eyes were wide, her mouth open in a wordless scream. Her arms reached out for Betsy as she fell backward, tipping over the edge of the railing, headfirst. She landed on the flagstone with a loud crack. Betsy didn't run for help, didn't budge from the landing. She just waited, watching as a trickle of blood escaped from Agnes's head onto the tile.

It was a cry for help from a neglected child. That's what Betsy's mother had told her father, whispering it forcefully in his ear as he sat on a chair, his head drooping into his palms. "If it wasn't for that woman trying to steal you away from your family, none of this would have happened," she'd hissed. The body was already gone from where it had fallen, the blood scrubbed clean. They sent Elizabeth away to some far-off relatives' house and hired new help, sealed off the fourth floor. But her father couldn't erase it. She never saw him happy again. Betsy still hated Agnes for it.

"They were going to get married! I couldn't let him leave my mother for her. It was preposterous. Agnes was going to ruin our lives! I had no choice, don't you understand?" Betsy looks around the group, searching for a face of reason, someone who can comprehend where she is coming from. But she sees only fear and shock in their eyes. She should have known better than to expect empathy from this bunch.

"What about me?" Lottie cries, her voice sounding like that of a frightened child. So irritating.

"My father knew he had to protect me, or my life would be ruined. So he took care of it. We couldn't have you around asking questions, reminding us." Betsy breathes heavily, winded from the outburst. After Agnes died, her father shuffled through the halls of Grafton defeated, shoulders slumped. "He'll get better," Betsy's mother often said those first years, but she was wrong. If anything, he retreated into himself more as the years passed, engaging with Betsy and her mother only when it was absolutely necessary. Every day the old Richard Grafton faded until there was barely a whisp of the man he'd once been, and then even that vanished. She hated him as well.

After her outburst Betsy's throat feels raw, like she has swallowed glass. Pradyumna steps toward her gently, as if he is coaxing a wild animal from a cave.

"Where *is* Agnes, Betsy?"

Before she can stop herself, Betsy's eyes flick to the window. She looks out at the dark shapes of the lawn just starting to become visible under the early morning sky. Lottie follows her gaze, stepping past her and up to the window, pressing her fingers against the glass. The clouds have broken, and the first morning light catches on a lone dogwood tree glowing a ghostly white in the garden.

Betsy is exhausted now, spent from her outburst. She falls back into the chair in surrender. The rage she'd been feeling is dissipating like a storm. It's funny, she thinks, how anger does that.

There is a low wail of sirens, growing louder. A flicker of blue-and-red light at the windows as a row of police cars and ambulances pulls up the drive.

Gerald holds up his cell phone. "Based on traffic times, even accounting for the storm, I deduced that there was no call put in yet to the police so I did it myself."

ONE YEAR LATER

STELLA

I open my eyes, and for a moment I forget where I am. The bed I'm sleeping on is plush, covered with luxurious pillows. The molding in the corners of the ceiling curves toward a gold chandelier that dangles precariously above me. I throw the blankets back and push myself upright, rubbing my eyes. Sun streams in through the tall paned window. I blearily stand up and wander over to it, looking out onto Grafton's lawn. I'm in a different room than the last time I was here. This one looks out over the vast front lawn where the tent would have been. Now the tent is gone. There's no sign that it ever existed, except for the faintest hint of brighter green from the fresh sod. You'd never know that just a year earlier it had been the scene of such horror. Nervousness creeps up into my chest, but I take a deep breath and it dissipates, quickly. I'm much better at controlling my anxiety now. I don't even have to count anymore.

On the heels of Archie's death and Betsy's incarceration, my story turned out to be so much more than I could have imagined. I focused the article on Archie's seduction of young, female chefs on *The Cutting Board*, leaving out Hannah's experience with Archie. With all the speculation after Archie's murder and Betsy's arrest, it was only fair that she be allowed to get her life back together. She was an

invaluable resource to my writing, though, giving me inside information that helped me pinpoint the way Archie seduced and groomed
women. On the heels of such a big scandal, the story immediately
went viral. I started getting calls from radio and TV programs, wanting me to comment on what happened, to offer my unique perspective being both a journalist and a *Bake Week* contestant. It wasn't long
before I received messages from literary agents wanting to sign me
and then, much to my delight, a book deal. I love being a journalist
again. I can feel myself growing more confident with each day that
passes, building back up a stronger and healthier version of myself.
Now that this project is over, the first draft of the book already with
my publishers, I find myself excited to keep going. I am determined
to tell stories that will help empower people who have lived in fear
for too long.

It is easy to get wrapped up in it all. Sometimes I even have to remind myself that I went on *Bake Week* to be a contestant, not as some
kind of undercover journalist. When I think of Archie, dead in the
tent, or Betsy, stuck in some women's prison with no one to make her
tea, I almost feel guilty at how well everything has worked out for me.
Almost.

The most important thing I've done since last year has been to
start with a new therapist, one who can help me do more than just
count backward when I'm stressed. She has helped me realize that so
much of my stress comes from unresolved trauma that took place far
before my time at *The Republic*. That I suffered from a lack of nurturing and stability as a child. Now when I feel anxious, I know how
to nurture myself. Not that there still aren't times when I struggle. I
almost cried when I saw Lottie again. We'd stayed in touch of course,
but there was something about being back at Grafton, coming up the
main drive yesterday evening and seeing her open the front door, that
knocked the wind out of me. I had to stand in the foyer and catch my
breath, laughing and crying as we embraced. Seeing everyone back at
the house has been cathartic too.

We're all here for the documentary. Hopefully it will explain what happened so that people can move on. I don't think any of us want to be forever associated with something so dark and twisted. I think of Lottie, and my heart breaks for her, being so closely connected with Grafton she doesn't really have a choice. But even she seems more at peace than I've seen her. She's really settled into herself. We've all grown from this in some ways, I think.

Even Gerald is back for the documentary. "I made the calculation that you needed me here to provide my objective take on the experience for it to be factually accurate," he'd said before I threw my arms around him. He cleared his throat uncomfortably, but when I pulled away, he had a small smile on his face.

I never thought I'd be on camera again. I never wanted to much, to be honest. But I could never turn down a request from Lottie, and I wanted to come back to Grafton. It is good for me to put it all into perspective. My new therapist is proud of me for taking this step. But of course, I don't tell her absolutely everything.

I put on a pair of flowing pants and a fitted vest—I want to look like I'm making an effort. Then I go to the mirror, pin my hair back, and put in some silver earrings. I glance at the grandfather clock in the corner of the room. The others will already be downstairs, and I don't want to be late. Not this time.

LOTTIE

The kettle boils, and I direct a stream of hot water over a filter, making myself a fresh cup of coffee. There is coffee already made, a cardboard box with a spicket of suspicious-looking stuff, but I prefer to make mine the old-fashioned way. Molly pops her head around the corner of the kitchen door. "You almost ready, Mom? The crew is all set up."

I turn to look at my daughter. "I'll be right there." We'll be filming in the library today.

I smile, feeling a flutter of gratitude at seeing her there. It's a gift that she can be with me at Grafton, that she can get to know where I come from and have a connection to the grandmother she never met, even if it is only symbolic. I make sure the stove is turned off. Agnes's recipes live here now, in their rightful place on the shelf. It seems strange to me that I had to look so hard to find her, when the truth is I see evidence of my mother every day now. Especially here, in the kitchen. She is in the nicks in the wood of the table where she used to chop vegetables, in the worn surface of the counter where she kneaded bread. And of course, the dogwood. After reuniting with my extended family, I found out that Richard Grafton had often visited their special place, next to the dogwood tree, as he couldn't mourn her publicly. I still have the photo of them standing in front of it framed in my bedroom. Apparently, he never really recovered from her death. My father. It still feels strange to say it. A part of me will always feel like that little girl hesitantly standing at the threshold of Betsy's bedroom, an interloper. There are so many things I wish I could go back and ask them, but sometimes that is how life goes—sometimes you don't get all the answers.

Pradyumna strolls in, casually pouring himself a coffee from the spigot. He looks at home here. Not surprising, given the amount of time he spends at Grafton. It's practically his second home. Without him, I don't know how Molly and I would keep Grafton going. I inherited the manor soon after the investigation into Archie's death was officially closed and Betsy was committed full-time to a mental health facility for violent offenders. The estate fell to me, the only heir not incarcerated. Little did I know the expense of keeping an entire manor house afloat. Pradyumna is a wonderful business partner. As an investor in the estate, I've given him part ownership. He is always coming up with new, inventive ways to keep the manor going. It was his idea to hire Peter to bring it back to life. The first thing he did was restore the old staircase. Soon he will begin restoration of the rest of the fourth floor. When producers from Flixer contacted him about making a documentary about what happened here, Pradyumna was the one who suggested we consider it. Grafton as a place has become far more interesting to people now that it is part of two stories involving murders—my mother's and Archie Morris's, both pushed to their deaths by an unhinged Betsy Martin.

"Are you nervous?" I ask him.

"Nah. Nothing for us to worry about." I detect a hint of an emphasis on the word *us*. I don't know what he means exactly, but I don't push for an answer. Craft services has set up the kitchen counter with food. Mediocre-looking baked goods are piled high on paper plates next to an aluminum tray of raw vegetables. I pick up a fist-size muffin and inspect it.

"Not exactly up to snuff, is it?" Pradyumna laughs. Molly comes in and leans on the counter next to him. I see him discreetly take her hand in his. They think I don't see. But then, people constantly underestimate what I notice. It's one of the many advantages of old age, getting to view people who don't think they're being watched. For example, I've never mentioned to Hannah that I saw her that night with Archie. If she wants to come out with it, she will, I suppose. Still, I'm surprised that she agreed to do the documentary. I didn't think she of all people would want to relive such a tragic day, but she was the first to respond.

"I think Hannah will take whatever attention she can get," Pradyumna had said wryly when I told him.

Stella wanders into the kitchen and gives a wobbly smile. "Are we ready? Is this happening? Oh God, I'm really nervous."

"You'll be great," I tell her.

The producers of *Bake Week* had made the controversial decision to air the first three episodes. Instead of one per week, they were released all at once this past winter. It became the most bingeable three hours of television in the country for a good month, with everyone clamoring to look for clues that Betsy Martin was about to snap. For a while, there were too many articles to count that attempted to pinpoint the exact moment Betsy Martin's insanity took hold.

"The *Bake Week* murders," they've come to be called, and as much as I don't love having my own mother lumped into some sort of pop culture craziness, a part of me relishes her story being told so openly.

"Mom?" Molly asks again, "Are you ready to go?"

I look around at them, my lovely makeshift family. "I think so."

GERALD

The producers have decided to film my parts outside the manor so that I can show them where I was when Archie was murdered. I lead them down the front steps and around the side of the manor, stopping under the stone balcony.

The crew begins to set up. Even though the sun is shining, they must first arrange key light and fill lights. I grow fidgety just waiting and recommend an angle that uses the side of the manor wall as a point of reference.

"Please just sit here so we can finish setting up," a woman says, directing me to a folding chair. I look toward the lawn, where the edge of the tent would have been visible. There will likely never be a tent here again. It doesn't make me sad, it's just a fact. A puff of white vapor floats from around the corner of the manor. My body tenses with recognition.

"Excuse me," I say, pulling myself up out of the chair and starting toward the corner of the manor. "I just have to—"

"Please stay," the interviewer says, leaning forward and putting a hand on my wrist. "I think we are just about ready." I jerk my arm away from her, still distracted by the plume of smoke. The corner is less than six feet from me. I could be there and back in only twenty seconds, which is really no time at all. I will tell them this, appeal to their common sense.

"Are we ready?" she calls out to the crew, her voice sharp.

"Almost," someone behind me says.

"Where's Graham?"

"I'm coming, jeez." I recognize his voice before I even see the tall man striding around the corner, putting something small and silver into his pocket. He's shaved his beard, but there is no question who he is. I am excellent at identifying faces. He takes his place at the camera behind the interviewer, giving me a perfect view of him.

Before I can tell anyone else what I'm witnessing, the interviewer begins to speak. "Welcome to Grafton Manor, the setting for one of the most fascinating sets of murders in recent history."

He must have been the one with Melanie that night I fell from the balcony. I replay their conversation in my head.

"Gerald?" The interviewer is saying my name, leaning forward. She must have asked me a question, but I don't have time for it right now.

"It was him!" I stand, my folding chair tipping back as I do.

"What do you mean, Gerald?"

I step forward, shaking my finger at him. "This man sabotaged me! He destroyed my bake! He opened Pradyumna's refrigerator! He switched Peter's salt and sugar!"

"Are you getting this?" I hear one of the producers whisper.

"You better believe it," someone whispers back.

The camera operator looks at me. He seems surprised that I should level such an accusation against him.

"What do you have to say for yourself?" I demand.

"Are you serious?" He looks to the crew for help, but the interviewer folds her arms in front of her chest.

"I'd like to hear it, actually. You are the only crew member here from that season."

He rolls his eyes.

"Fine. But I'm telling you, we were not trying to hurt anyone. It was just for the ratings. The show had gotten too boring," he says. "It was Melanie who wanted it done. We were ordered to do it."

"Really? You sabotaged innocent *Bake Week* contestants? Do you know how seriously people took the integrity of that show?"

"Yeah. Are you some kind of monster?"

"Oh, come *on*, it's not like I murdered someone." He throws his hands up in disgust.

"Oh, poor form, Graham." There are groans around me from the crew.

"I don't need this shit," he says, turning to leave.

I find myself growing calmer as the crew and producers become more agitated. A sense of peace washes through me.

"Make sure we add that to the documentary."

"Oh, definitely."

"What a scumbag."

Someone picks my chair up. And I find myself sitting again, relaxed now.

Across from me, the interviewer has resumed her former stance and is leaning forward to ask me a question.

"Now where were we? I think you were going to tell us how you climbed up a drainpipe."

"Yes, well, it's really just a matter of physics," I say, smiling.

HANNAH

I am wired up with a small mic that clips to the collar of my dress. I sit down in a plush armchair, one of two facing each other between two groupings of cameras and mics. The lights are hot on my face, but I am used to it now. I take a deep breath to ease my nerves. The interviewer sits across from me. She is a pretty brunette wearing a stylish designer suit. I have the same one at my apartment, so I know how expensive it is. She's absolutely salivating to talk to me but tries to hide it by crossing her legs and leaning back in her chair casually. She gets the signal to start.

"I'm going to just jump right in. What happened that night, Hannah?" she asks. My heart jerks in my chest, but I maintain my composure.

I smile, falling into a rehearsed pose, resting my palms in my lap. I glance down at my hands. My nails are long and red, unbitten. I've been working on it. I've been working on a lot of things. I'm different. My mother noticed it right away when I returned. "There is something about you," she'd said, circling me like a shark, trying to get to the bottom of it. She was the one who helped me pack up my life for New York. She knew I needed to move on from Eden Lake. She never even brought up Ben when she drove me to collect my things. I appreciated that. "I'll come visit you in New York," she'd said when she dropped me off at the airport. "My little TV star!" She hasn't yet.

The news about Archie's death blew up before we even left Grafton. By the time we reentered society, the four of us were already mini celebrities, and Betsy was already a villain. The calls and emails for interviews came in for weeks. You'd better believe I said yes to each and every one. As soon as my TV appearances began, I started to film myself baking and upload the clips to my YouTube channel. Within the first week, I had half a million subscribers.

The smile freezes on my face. There are still creepers, of course. People with their own YouTube channels and blogs dedicated to conspiracy theories. They love to speculate about what happened at Grafton. Some say it wasn't Betsy at all. That the timeline doesn't make sense. Some even think that *I* did it. I try not to let them bother me, but I can't help it, my knees get weak and my palms go clammy every single time.

"What do you remember most about that night?" The interviewer is leaning forward in her chair. People love a good murder mystery.

"The rain. I've never seen so much rain," I tell her. "And then the power went out. We were just stumbling around Grafton in the dark. It was terrifying . . ."

I don't tell her how I remember Archie's face when I opened the door. The big white smile that didn't quite cover a flash of irritation. It was odd, I thought, him being annoyed by me showing up less than twenty-four hours after I'd slept with him and he'd promised me the world. I'd brushed my confusion aside. It must be just frustration related to the show, I'd figured. He and Betsy *had* seemed off during the day. I pushed past him into his room.

"I broke up with Ben," I'd told Archie proudly, leaning back on his bed in my tall black boots, trying to look at him seductively so that he'd come join me there. But he didn't. He paced instead. "Who?"

He didn't recognize the name, even though I'd told him about Ben at least three times.

"Ben? My boyfriend? I called him and told him I met someone." Archie finally looked at me then. Whenever I start to feel guilty or question myself, I try to remember that look. Pure and instant derision. Like I was the stupidest person who has ever lived.

"Why would you do that?" he'd said very slowly.

"So you and I would be free to do whatever we want, to be together." I'd shrunken into myself as I'd said it, realizing the mistake. The utter miscalculation.

His mouth opened and closed in shock. Then this look of amusement came across his face. "You honestly thought that," he sputtered, his finger flipping madly between the two of us. "That we? Oh, Hannah, there's definitely been a misunderstanding." He is laughing now, a dry, humorless chuckle.

"I'll scream," I said, my humiliation calcifying into white-hot anger. His smirk vanished. "I'll tell everyone everything about you. About how you seduced a helpless young contestant." I batted my eyelashes, showing him how easily I could turn it on when needed.

"You wouldn't." He was suddenly on top of me, pressing a palm against my mouth.

"You will not," he'd whispered. His eyes were small and ugly. How had I ever thought they were beautiful? A hand went to the top my arm. Squeezed hard. He was hurting me. I couldn't breathe, and I started to panic. Everything I'd wanted for myself, I felt it disintegrating. The door had opened then, and Stella stumbled in.

Beautiful Stella trying to save me from myself, or whatever she thought she was doing. Her mouth opened in horror when she saw us there.

The interviewer crosses her legs. "And then you heard a scream?" I sit up taller, trying to outdo her with my confidence.

"Yes. It was Betsy Martin. We rushed down to the staircase, and she was there crouched in the foyer. She said she'd just found Archie outside. We didn't realize then that she'd been, you know, the one to do it. Now we all know, of course, but she really convinced us it was an accident."

Behind the interviewer, Stella nods, smiling at me encouragingly. She was the one who'd convinced me to do the interview. "It will be cathartic," she'd said. "Plus, think of all the eyeballs." I'm no longer jealous of Stella. It's hard to be envious of people when you know all the things they've gone through. She's more like a big sister to me now. I don't know how I would have navigated New York when I first got there if she hadn't taken me under her wing, let me stay with her. We've saved each other in a way.

"So you saw Archie . . . dead?" the interviewer asks.

I look down at my lap, making sure the cameras catch me struggling, showing them that remembering the scene is causing me great distress.

"I'm sorry, Hannah. I know this must be difficult for you."

"It was. I will never unsee it."

And that's not a lie.

He'd leapt off me when Stella came in, trying to save his reputation, to pretend that nothing had happened.

"I don't know what she's doing here." He'd chuckled and turned as though he were about to say something. Sweat was beaded on his brow.

"Oh, spare me your bullshit," Stella said, stepping farther into the room. "I know exactly what's going on."

Archie's face dropped as he looked from me to Stella. I could see the confusion in his eyes, his desperate attempt to calculate what he should do to save himself.

"You think you can just take whatever you want, don't you?" Stella continued, her eyes flashing. "That you can destroy whatever life you choose. That you get to decide."

Archie shrank back as Stella spoke, and I watched his power over me evaporate like a balloon deflating. I no longer loved Archie; I hated him.

"You bitch," Archie growled. He lunged at Stella, catching her in the ribs and pushing her toward the back of the room, where the window still swung wide open was letting in torrents of rain.

I picked up a heavy ceramic vase off the mantel and swung it at him, hitting him hard above his left eye. He looked so surprised when he dabbed his face and his hand came back covered in blood. His eyes were so angry, so spiteful. All I'd ever done was admire him, love him, even. He'd betrayed me. He blinked, regaining his composure. Then lunged at Stella again, gripping her shoulders in his hands. I ran to them, prying his fingers from Stella's arms, using all my strength to pull him off her. Together we drove him back, holding our ground. His balance was off and he staggered to the side, his knees buckling slightly as he struggled to stand. It didn't take much to push him out the window. Stella was the one who gave him the final shove. He tipped right over the side, his shoe catching on the edge of the balcony before he disappeared.

"There are some who still don't believe Betsy killed Archie," the interviewer says, pulling in closer to me, as though I might have some bombshell to drop.

"Well, if you have any other information, please share with me first," I say primly.

Beyond her, Stella smiles at me and winks.

The truth is, Stella is completely over her blackouts now. She hasn't had one since Grafton. Something about that night and remembering, really looking at what happened to her with that horrible guy at her old job. It cured her.

At first, we were prepared to admit what we'd done, to say it was done in self-defense. But then all that past business about Lottie's mom came to light. And Betsy was just acting so crazed. She was already implicated in one murder, having confessed to killing Lottie's mother. So why not tack on another as well? After all, we weren't even allowed in the East Wing, so who'd have known? Melanie told everyone how she'd heard Betsy and Archie fighting. I just let people assume it was what happened. I didn't even have to cover it up. It was a piece of cake. *Haha.*

PRADYUMNA

We sit around the fireplace in the library. All six of us are back. "Wine?" Lottie says, holding up a bottle.

"None for me, thanks." I sit back in my chair.

After the police came and carted Betsy away, effectively putting an end to season ten of *Bake Week*, we were all a bit shell-shocked. We gathered our things and were taken to a local motel for the night in the back of several police cars. The police questioned us all afternoon. I told them what I knew, about Lottie and me searching for clues about her mother and how Betsy had admitted killing Agnes in a jealous rage as a child. She probably wouldn't have had any jail time—she was only a minor at the time—were it not for Archie's death. That part is still a bit murky to me. Do I think that Betsy killed him? I don't know.

I look across the room at Hannah and Stella. They are leaning into each other on the sofa. It's funny how they've bonded. I remember watching them together during *Bake Week*. They did not take to each other at first; they almost seemed repelled by each other. It doesn't necessarily mean anything, of course. People bond when they share a trauma, and we all lived through a trauma that night. But I do remember those legs sticking out the side of Archie's bed that morning. And I know that when we gathered in the kitchen later, Stella's hair was wet. The discrepancies were enough to make me always wonder.

But I am not in the blaming business. As I've said before, as someone with slippery morals myself, I'm not going to be the one to judge. And Archie was a bit of a twat. Did he deserve to die for it? Probably not. But people get all sorts of things they don't deserve. Take me and my millions. I certainly didn't deserve to make that kind of money from an app that is no longer even available. (Turns out alerting people to available spaces was making people overly aggressive and caused a fistfight on more than one occasion.)

I've been trying to reframe how I look at my wealth. The way I see it, it's a tool for me to help people. Right now, I'm using it to fix up Grafton. We've hired Peter to do some repairs, which means that he is here too. Of course, we have him bring his partner Frederick and their little girl. That's the way we are here. The more the merrier, or something like that. I'm happy to have them here. Peter has turned into a true friend. Lottie asked me once if I'm worried that I'll be sad when the work is done and he leaves. I thought, but did not say, that the nice thing about giant manor homes like Grafton is that the work is never really done. Besides, once we add the bakery building out front and resuscitate the old gardens, it will be a destination that will need a lot of upkeep.

It's funny how things have changed for me. Before I came to *Bake Week*, I'd been depressed. I'm not afraid of calling it that now. I was looking for solace in activities and drinking. It was because there was just me, I think. I look across the room at Lottie. She is sitting in the wingback chair, her feet clad in a pair of fuzzy slippers. She looks like she has always lived here. Sometimes it's hard for me to even remember the way Grafton was before, when Betsy was here and we were all strangers. Who'd have known when I applied for *Bake Week* on a lark that I'd be changing the course of my life for the better? These people mean more to me than winning any competition ever could. Lottie catches my eye and smiles. They always tell you that you have to be enough for yourself before you can heal, and I respectfully disagree. I, by myself, was not enough. I think you need others to even be able to see yourself fully. The best way to find the value in yourself is by being good to someone else. There, you find your purpose, and that is the sweetest thing I have ever tasted.

Epilogue

BETSY

The biggest surprise of it all, by far, has been how well she's adapted to her entire life falling apart. It isn't as though she enjoys being in prison. She is repulsed by the food, and no one in their right mind wouldn't be disturbed by a sudden and complete lack of personal freedom. But there is something about it that she has been able to appreciate. She would never say it out loud but Betsy can't recall a time when she has been less worried. There are some days when she just reads a book all afternoon. She can't remember the last time she did that. There are moments when she finds herself thinking about Grafton—she can't help it of course. But the realization will hit her all at once, a mix of horror and relief: her main secret has already been exposed. After so many years of imagining the worst happening, it was a relief in a way to have had it finally happen. The big secret that destroyed her family exposed for all to see. She has a pang of regret, as she often does, that it didn't happen sooner when her parents were still alive. It would have been better if her mother had allowed Betsy to take the blame for what she did. Then maybe her father wouldn't have vanished slowly and painfully. Perhaps some healing could have occurred before it was too late.

There is a scraping of metal as a warden opens the grate on her cell door. "You have a visitor."

She'd nearly forgotten her weekly meeting with Francis. She'd lost track of time since she'd been here. She stands up and combs her hair out with her fingers, runs her hands across her jumpsuit to try to smooth it out. Her clothes are what she misses most of all. If she could just have her cashmere sweaters here, she could almost be comfortable. *Almost.* Despite how well she'd adapted to prison life, Betsy still wants to leave. This is just a chapter in her story, it is no long-term place for someone like her.

Betsy follows the guard down the corridor. He waves his badge at a keypad that unlocks the door in front of them with an angry buzz.

She sees Francis from across the visitors' room. His back is to her. His bald spot seems to have grown even larger in the time she's been here, threatening to take over his entire head. She walks up to the table and sinks into a molded plastic chair across from him. "Francis."

He smiles pityingly when he sees her. "How have you been? Are you feeling okay?"

"How do you think I'm doing?" Betsy snaps. She leans in, watching him intently, wanting to shake him down for information. "Have you spoken to the producers? Listen, I've been thinking, and I know there is a real chance for us to develop something when I get out of here."

Francis clears his throat. "It may not be so simple."

"I don't see why," Betsy says. "Martha Stewart went to prison, and look at her comeback. If anything, people like her more than they did before."

"Martha Stewart didn't murder two people," Francis counters.

"One person, Francis," Betsy interrupts him. "I murdered *one* person. And I was twelve years old."

"I don't suspect that is the line your defense will go for." Francis leans back, crossing his arms.

"If you're not going to be a help, I don't know why you even visit me here. I could be sitting in my cell reading right now." She makes as if to stand and watches Francis's face fall.

"Betsy, wait. I've been talking to your lawyers. There is something there, you're right. *If* they can prove you *didn't* kill Archie."

Betsy perks up, interested.

"There's a statute of limitations on most crimes. Unfortunately for us, murder is not one of them. However, seeing as you were a minor at the time of Agnes Bunting's death, your lawyers and I were discussing a possible appeal to the judge, suggesting based on the crime and the amount of time that has passed that it would only be fair that you be tried as a child and not as an adult."

"And what will that do for me?"

"Well, given how long ago the crime was and how few people are left to testify, you'd be more likely to serve one or two years at most. Children usually have far reduced sentences."

The idea of facing Lottie in court and having her stand there accusing her makes Betsy squirm with anger. It was disgusting how she had used Betsy's departure to swoop in and take over. When she sees Lottie, she will remind her that no matter what, Betsy still has claim to half of Grafton when she gets out of here, half of her father's estate. She thinks of what she'd like to do with the money when she emerges: a nice apartment somewhere near the water. A new television show, one that clears her name.

"And how long until we can get a court date?"

"We're working on it. Now, this would all depend on proving that you did not kill Archie."

"That should be easy enough. I was nowhere near him. I hadn't even seen him the evening he was murdered."

"Well, technically you were the only other person in the East Wing."

"Goodbye, Francis." Betsy picks herself up and makes her way to the door.

"Just wait. We'll make a plan," Francis calls after her. She doesn't turn around, just waves back at him, tilting her hand back and forth like the queen of England. She shuffles through the common room, stopping to look at a newspaper. "Right Hand of Disgraced Baking Show Host Called Out for Rigging Competition in Documentary." Betsy picks up the paper, unfolding it to reveal a photo of Melanie. The photographers have caught her leaving her apartment. She looks undone, her hair wild, her clothes baggy. Betsy never had time to exact her revenge on Melanie, but reading through the article it would seem that Gerald has done the job for her. She always did like Gerald. At least some good has come of that terrible documentary; Melanie and that vile cameraman will never work in television again. Betsy smiles smugly as the door buzzes, locking her inside.

ACKNOWLEDGMENTS

Mostly, I need to thank my mother, for all of the time she spent with me on the phone patiently going over the plot in excruciating detail and for her countless brilliant insights. I wouldn't have had the confidence to pursue writing a novel without her. Or most other things for that matter.

I'm fortunate to have such competent and inspiring women in my corner. Lindsay Sagnette is fully to thank for turning this into a real book. It has been a dream come true working with her. Because of her and the Atria team I have felt so supported through this process.

Thank you to Alexandra Machinist for seeing the potential in this book the way you hope and pray someone will while you're in the fog of writing it. I couldn't ask for a better agent. They just don't exist.

Thanks to Jade Hui for keeping everything together and to Falon Kirby, Maudee Genao, and Morgan Hoit for getting it in front of people.

Thank you to James Iacobelli for the brilliant and gorgeous cover. Better than I ever could have imagined! Chef's kiss!

I am forever grateful to Danny Yanez for his introductions and friendship.

A humongous thank you to my husband, Tim, who never wavered in his belief in me or this book, even though I'd never done something like this before. Your encouragement and excitement for my endeavors mean the world to me. Love you.

ABOUT THE AUTHOR

Jessa Maxwell lives in Jamestown, Rhode Island, with her husband, two cats, and three-legged dog. *The Golden Spoon* is her first novel.